REME First edition.
SCIENCE

A Romantic Comedy

SUSANNAH NIX

Haver Street Press

This book is a work of fiction. Names, characters, places, incidents, tirades, opinions, exaggerations, prevarications, and dubious facts either are the products of the author's inscrutable imagination or are used fictitiously. Any resemblance to actual events or persons—living, dead, or otherwise—is entirely coincidental.

REMEDIAL ROCKET SCIENCE. Copyright © 2017 by Susannah Nix

FIRST EDITION: July 2017

ISBN: 978-0-9990948-0-8

Printed in the United States of America

Haver Street Press | 448 W. 19th St., Suite 407 | Houston, TX 77008

Edited by Monica Black, www.wordnerdedits.com

Ebook & Print Cover Design by www.ebooklaunch.com

For Dave,
my best friend

Chapter One

BOSTON, THREE YEARS AGO

*M*elody Gage checked her phone for the tenth time in five minutes.

Nothing.

Sighing, she reached for her pint glass and took a swig. The condensation felt nice and cool against her palm. It was warm inside the bar, and she was still wearing her leather jacket, which she couldn't take off because there was a hole in her shirt, right at the seam running across her shoulder blades. Besides, taking off her jacket would have been like admitting she was staying more than another few minutes—which she wasn't.

She couldn't believe she'd actually dressed up for tonight. She'd worn her favorite leather jacket, even though the weather was too warm for it. It was the nicest thing she owned, despite the fact that it had come from a thrift shop. She'd even exchanged her usual Doc Martens for a pair of cute ballet flats. And for what? A no-show.

Melody felt someone jostle her arm as they slid onto the barstool beside her. She looked up hopefully, but it wasn't Victor.

The guy who wasn't her date leaned toward her, grinning. "How you doing tonight?"

He was young, college-age like her, and like a lot of the other patrons at the Cask 'n Flagon, he was sporting a Red Sox cap. He was also wearing a T-shirt for a fraternity "Pimps & Prostitutes" party, which earned him a few demerits. He wasn't bad looking, though. In fact, she might even be tempted to call him attractive.

Too bad she was waiting for someone...who was fifteen minutes late. Not exactly a promising start to a first date.

Melody offered her new seat mate a polite, but guarded smile. "I'm doing okay."

"You're really fine, you know that?" he said, leaning in closer.

Gross. She had always despised that word in that context. *Fine.* Had a man ever described a woman as "fine" without sounding like a sleazebag? Also, his breath smelled like garlic. No thank you.

"Thanks, but I'm waiting for someone." She stared down at her phone again. Still no text.

"You know, I'm not usually into chicks with short hair," her companion said, gesturing at her brunette pixie cut, "but I might be willing to make an exception for you."

Ugh. That was what she got for venturing outside her comfort zone. She probably should have known tonight was going to be a bust when Victor had a) picked a sports bar near Fenway for their date, and b) suggested they meet instead of coming together. She'd only agreed because she'd been desperate to break out of her routine. Desperate to do something—anything—other than spend another Saturday night studying in her dorm room or working in the computer lab.

And look what it had gotten her.

"I bet you know you're fine," the wannabe pick-up artist said, undeterred by Melody's unwelcoming body language. "You probably have guys telling you that all the time, right?"

WHERE ARE YOU??? Melody texted Victor, mashing her thumbs against the screen of her phone.

She didn't even like Victor all that much. They were chemistry lab partners, but the only sparks between them were the ones they used to light the Bunsen burner. He was nice enough, but a little dull.

The biggest thing he had going for him was the fact that he'd actually asked her out, which was more than anyone else had done lately. He was the only guy who'd shown any interest in her all year. As her roommate had helpfully reminded her, Melody hadn't been so much as kissed since that guy with the butt chin during orientation week—and he hadn't remembered her the next day when he'd sobered up.

Not that she'd been putting herself out there. Almost all her time had been divided between studying and working to pay the portion of her tuition not covered by scholarships. MIT was *hard,* in a way school had never been for her before. Her whole life, she'd always been at the top of her class. But everyone else at MIT had been at the top of their classes, too. She'd had to work twice as hard just to stay in the middle of the pack. Melody didn't like the middle of the pack. She wanted to be at the top again. Or at least close to the top. And if that meant missing out on a few parties, so be it. No big loss.

Only...now that her freshman year was almost over, it had occurred to her that everyone else had been going out, meeting new people, sleeping around, falling in love, breaking up, and falling in love again while she'd been buried in her books. They'd been having *experiences.* If Melody wasn't careful, she'd be heading out into the world with a bachelor's degree and the social maturity of a high school student in three years. She figured she ought to devote some effort to leveling up her life skills along with her academic skills.

Which was how she had ended up in this godforsaken bar, being negged by a frat boy who reeked of Axe body spray and desperation.

Her new friend leaned in even closer, pressing his shoulder right up against hers, and blew another cloud of garlic breath in her face. "What's a girl like you doing here all by herself, anyway?"

"I'm waiting for someone," Melody repeated through gritted teeth. She craned her neck, scanning the crowd milling by the door on the off-chance Victor had shown up.

"A girl like you shouldn't be all alone. How about I keep you company until your friend gets here?"

"How about no?"

"What are you drinking? Lemme buy you another one."

"I don't want another—"

"One more of whatever she's having," the creep shouted to the bartender, ignoring her. It was like talking to a brick wall.

"Don't bother," Melody told the bartender. "I'm not staying."

Seriously, screw Victor. She was not waiting around one second longer.

"Hey, where you going?" Creepy Guy protested, making a grab for her arm as she slid off the barstool.

Melody twisted out of his grasp, spinning around to make her escape—and crashed face-first into a male chest. Startled, she looked up into a pair of dazzling blue eyes belonging to a *very* tall, very *cute* guy. "Whoa," she blurted.

"I'm so sorry I'm late, babe!" The cute guy beamed a dimpled smile at her and squeezed her arm like he knew her.

Melody stared at him, open-mouthed. She was positive she'd never laid eyes on him before in her life. *What was happening right now?*

When he stooped to kiss her cheek, she was so stunned, she couldn't move. Only, instead of actually kissing her, his lips hovered near her ear, and he whispered, "Play along if you want to get away from this guy."

Oh. *Hell yes,* she would play along if it got Creepy Guy off her back.

She threw her arms around Cute Guy's neck and hugged him with exaggerated enthusiasm. Wow, his back was muscly. And he smelled fantastic, like a really expensive redwood forest. She may have hugged him a smidge longer than necessary, just to get an extra sniff in.

"Where have you been, Boo Bear?" she demanded in her best bubbly girlfriend voice.

He tilted his head, his eyes crinkling in amusement as his mouth curved into a smirk. "Well, *Schmoopy Pants*, I guess I got mixed up about where we were supposed to meet."

"Oh, you big silly, it's a good thing you're so pretty." She let out a tinkly fake laugh and punched him playfully in the arm. Then she wrapped her hands around his biceps—his *very firm* biceps—and dragged him off toward the hostess stand.

As they were retreating, Cute Guy shot a pointed, don't-mess-with-my-girl glare at Creepy Guy, who was already backing away with his hands up in the universal sign for *hey, man, sorry, I didn't mean anything by it*. Figured. The jerk hadn't been willing to take *her* no for an answer, but the second another guy staked his claim—like she was a piece of property—he threw up the white flag and fled the scene. Asshole.

Not that she wasn't grateful for the intervention. She was. But it was also possible she'd just leapt out of Jabba the Hut's barge and into the sarlacc pit. So, as soon as they were out of sight of the creep at the bar, Melody let go and took a big step back, putting a few feet of distance between them.

Her benevolent savior shoved his hands into the pockets of his madras shorts, sidestepping a party of four as the hostess led them to their table. He was wearing boat shoes and a polo shirt with the collar popped, like he'd stepped out a Ralph Lauren ad. "Are you okay?" His brow scrunched in concern as his eyes dropped to her arm. "That guy didn't hurt you when he grabbed you, did he?" He had unusually kind eyes for someone who dressed like a prep school douche.

"No, I'm fine." Melody clenched her hands into fists, resisting the urge to rub her forearm where the creep had touched her. "Thanks for the assist, though."

"Do you need a ride home?" As if he'd just realized how that sounded, he added, "I mean, I can call you a cab if you want."

She shook her head. She was a girl with a hole in her shirt and a thrift-store jacket—no way could she afford cab fare on her work study salary. "Thanks, but I'm good." She'd get herself home on the T—the same way she got there.

"All right," he said. "If you're sure."

"I'm sure."

He nodded and sauntered off toward the back of the restaurant, without even hitting on her or expecting anything in return for his good deed. Huh. Apparently, chivalry wasn't dead after all.

Melody's phone buzzed in her hand. It was a text from Victor.

Sorry got hung up and can't make it.

Great. Wonderful. Perfect.

"Hey!" she called out, hurrying after the Cute Guy. "Wait."

He turned around, eyebrows raised. His sandy hair flopped across his forehead, and he reached up to push it back, smiling at her. He had cute dimples when he smiled. She'd always been a sucker for dimples. They were her kryptonite.

Melody took a deep breath, ignoring the hamsters running nervous laps in her stomach. All she had to do was talk to him. She could do that. It wasn't like it was rocket science or anything.

No, it's way worse. Rocket science, she could handle. Talking to cute guys, on the other hand—*that* was intimidating. Especially heavenly-smelling, well-muscled paragons of kindhearted chivalry.

Flo Rida blared from the bar's speakers as a group of people in Sox jerseys pushed through the space between Melody and the cute dimples, trying to get to the bar. She elbowed her way past them, giving dirty looks as good as she got, until she was standing right in front of him.

"What's your name?" At five-foot-six, Melody was hardly what you'd call short, but he was tall enough she had to tip her head back to look at him when they were this close.

"Jeremy."

"Well, Jeremy, I think I owe you a drink."

He shook his head, and his hair flopped onto his forehead again. "You don't owe me anything." He paused, running his hand through his hair. "But if you're propositioning me of your own free will..." There was that smirk again. How dare that kind of sass be so sexy? A smirk like that had no right to make her feel so swoony, but it did. It really, really did.

"Let's not get carried away," she said, unable to control the smile on her face. "I'm offering to buy you a drink. That's all."

He did that head tilt thing again, which she was starting to love. Then there was the matter of his eyes, which were outrageously blue, now that she was looking at them up close. Cerulean blue, like that *X-Files* episode about the guy who hypnotized people.

"You didn't tell me your name," Jeremy said, gazing at her with his preposterously blue eyes.

"Melody," she said, trying to pretend like this was totally normal for her, like she went around offering to buy drinks for cute guys with hot smirks and adorable floppy hair all the time.

He grinned. "In that case, I accept your offer, Melody."

Chapter Two

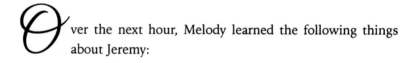ver the next hour, Melody learned the following things about Jeremy:

1. He was from Los Angeles.
2. He'd just flunked out of Syracuse, which was the *second* college he'd flunked out of in four years (the first was Brown).
3. Instead of telling his parents he'd flunked out (again) he'd decided to drive to Boston for the weekend to hang with one of his buddies who went to BU.
4. He was rich. Like, super rich, apparently.
5. He and Melody had *absolutely nothing* in common.

"OKAY, how about the last movie you saw?" Jeremy asked, reaching for his bottle of Shock Top.

They were sitting at a table in the far back corner of the Cask 'n Flagon, playing one of those get-to-know-you games where you take turns asking each other questions.

"*Princess Mononoke*," Melody said as a cheer rang out from the direction of the bar. Something exciting must have happened in the Red Sox game on all the TVs. She wasn't facing any of them, so she couldn't tell what, but there'd been a lot more cheering than booing, so she assumed Boston was winning.

Jeremy's eyes flicked to the screen behind her head, then immediately back to her. "Never heard of it."

The question game had been her bright idea, but she already regretted it. It had only served to highlight how very much they were *not* each other's type.

"It's an animated film from Japan."

Jeremy made a face. "Like anime?"

"Yeah, but it's amazing. Trust me."

He looked skeptical. "If you say so. What was the last movie you saw in a theater?"

"Still *Princess Mononoke*—it was a Miyazaki film festival." Melody reached for the pint she'd bought with her fake ID. She'd been nursing it for over an hour, so it was lukewarm and going flat —kind of like her whole night. "Last TV show you watched?"

"Does *Monday Night Football* count?"

"No, scripted television only."

He reached up and pushed his hair off his forehead while he thought about it. It flopped right back down again as soon as he let go of it. The guy needed a haircut badly. "What's that one about the nerds with the hot neighbor?"

Melody winced. "*The Big Bang Theory?*"

"Yeah, that's it."

Of course it was. The show that made people like her into punchlines, like her very existence as a human who was good at math and liked sci-fi was a hilarious joke. The show that promoted "awkward nerd boy meets hot girl" clichés while clinging to the stereotype that comic book superheroes were the exclusive domain of hardcore male geeks instead of, like, a mainstream pop culture sensation.

"The last book you read for fun?" she asked, changing the subject even though it wasn't her turn.

He shook his head. "I honestly can't remember. I don't really read for fun."

Of course he didn't. And given his academic record, he probably didn't read for school either.

His eyebrows jerked up. "Wow, you're totally judging me right now, aren't you?"

"I'm not!" Melody protested, her cheeks growing hot with embarrassment.

Jeremy laughed, his eyes crinkling with amusement. "You're a terrible liar, you know that?"

"In my defense, I do actually know that," she said, unable to resist smiling back at him.

"So, why MIT?" Jeremy asked after they'd exhausted most of pop culture and moved on to autobiographical topics. "Why not Harvard or some other smarty-pants school?"

Melody took a sip of her beer. They were on their second round, this time courtesy of Jeremy's black AmEx card. "It's the best for what I want to study."

"What's that?"

"Computer science." Her fingers traced a lopsided heart carved into the surface of the table. Next to it was a vaguely demonic-looking smiley face. "Why'd you choose Brown originally?"

Jeremy shrugged. "I didn't. It's where my dad went. He got me in." He was trying to sound casual, but the way his fingers tightened around his beer bottle spoke otherwise.

"You didn't want to go there?"

"To be honest, I was never that interested in college in the first place." He shrugged again. "I didn't much care where I went."

Leaning back in her chair, she rested her forearms on the table and cradled her pint glass. "What are you going to do now?"

"I don't know. My dad will probably give me a job at his company."

Melody couldn't help sounding sour. "Must be nice to have everything handed to you without ever having to work for it."

Jeremy made a noncommittal noise. "Yeah, I guess." He reached for his beer and took a big swallow. His fingernails were all bitten down to the quick, and she wondered what someone with his cushy life could possibly have to be stressed about.

"What, like it's not?"

He shifted in his seat, rubbing his palms on his thighs. "Look, I know I'm lucky, okay? I'm not trying to act like it's a hardship to have money. It's just...no one's ever bothered to ask me what I actually want to do. I'm just expected to follow whatever path my parents lay out for me. Makes it kind of hard to get too excited about it, that's all."

"So, what do you want to do?" Melody asked, since apparently no one ever had.

Shaking his head, he stared down at the table. "I don't even know. How's that for pathetic? I have no fucking clue what I want, which is sort of the whole problem, I guess." He looked up, and a tingle ran down her spine when his eyes found hers. He had this way of looking at you like you were the only one in the room. "Do you know what you want to do?"

She'd known since she was ten, when she got her first computer, an old Compaq Presario—a hand-me-down from one of her mom's friends. "I want to be a software developer."

"Why that?"

"Because I'm good with computers. Because I love puzzles and losing myself in code. Because it pays well, and it's a field with a lot of job growth, so I won't have to struggle to get by like my mom always did."

"What'd your mom do for a living?"

"What didn't she do? Cashier, waitress, esthetician, retail.

She's always hopping from job to job, chasing the next big break—which never seems to materialize."

Jeremy nodded, as if he understood what it was like living with that kind of financial insecurity, even though he couldn't possibly. "What about your dad?"

"I never knew him. He took off when he found out my mom was pregnant."

"That sucks."

It was Melody's turn to shrug. "It's easy not to miss someone who was never there in the first place."

Jeremy leaned forward, his eyebrows drawing together. "Don't you ever wonder about him? Or how your life might have been different if he'd stuck around?"

"Not really." The cut-and-run routine didn't exactly speak to stellar parenting skills. Whoever he was, she figured she was better off without him. Child support might have been nice, though.

"Sorry if I'm being too nosy."

"It's fine," she said, waving her hand. It shouldn't have been, but it was.

She'd avoided talking about her background since she came to Boston. Most of the students at MIT came from more affluent households with better educated parents, and she didn't want to stand out as the poor kid whose single mom hadn't even finished high school. But she didn't mind talking to Jeremy about it, despite their difference in pedigrees. Maybe because she knew she was never going to see him again, so she didn't have to care what he thought of her.

He tilted his head and smiled that dazzling smile again. "And here you are, putting yourself through MIT, doing exactly what you want to do with your life."

It was hard to look directly at him when he was smiling at her like that. Casting her eyes downward, she concentrated on rubbing the condensation off her glass with her thumb. "I guess, yeah."

He reached across the table and touched her on the arm. His fingers were soft and warm on her skin. "It's impressive," he said. "You're impressive."

Guys this rich and good looking weren't supposed to be this *nice*. She didn't know what to do with it. She'd never been good at taking compliments anyway. Her instinct was always to argue, which was a habit she'd been trying to break to improve her adulting skills. But that just left her with the urge to hide her head under a blanket and pretend it hadn't happened.

"I don't think I've ever been good at anything in my life," he said, sounding wistful. "You're lucky."

How crazy was that? A guy with a million-dollar trust fund thought *she* was the lucky one. She would have laughed out loud, except he seemed completely earnest, like he really wanted her to believe him.

The strange thing was, she did.

MELODY HAD no idea where the time had gone. How had it gotten to be midnight already? Somehow, she and Jeremy had been talking for hours. She was surprised how much she'd been enjoying herself—and how much she actually liked him.

Which was insane. Jeremy was *so* not her type. They had nothing in common. Like, seriously, nothing. But he was easy to talk to. He made her feel like he really cared about whatever she was saying. Like she was the most interesting person he'd ever met.

It was possible Melody was a bit smitten. Okay, sure, on the surface, he was exactly the sort of pretty, spoiled rich boy she usually despised. But she couldn't help feeling like there was more to him than that, like there were hidden depths under the boyish charm.

Maybe that was just wishful thinking on her part. Or a byproduct of the three beers she'd had. Or the way her knees went weak whenever he smiled at her…

Whatever. He was cute. She would 100 percent sleep with him if he asked. Which he hadn't, even though she'd been making her best heart-eyes at him for the last hour.

Seriously, was she not doing this flirting thing right? He wouldn't still be here if he wasn't interested in her, would he? Should she come right out and tell him she wanted to sleep with him? Or would that freak him out? What did she need to do to close this deal? Because she was ready to bag him up and take him home.

The best part was it didn't matter that they had nothing in common. He was only in town for the weekend, so there were no issues of compatibility. No question of commitment. No awkward encounters on campus for the next three years. It could just be one night of hot sex with a cute guy, then they never had to see each other again. Win-win.

Jeremy drained the last of his beer and gestured to her almost-empty glass. "You want another?"

"I think I've had enough," she said, shaking her head.

He looked at her for a long moment, long enough for her to feel self-conscious.

"What?"

"I'm trying to figure out how drunk you are."

"I'm not drunk, I just don't want another beer."

When he smiled, she could have sworn his eyes actually *twinkled*. "In that case, do you want to get out of here?"

Another tingle ran down her spine. "Okay."

Chapter Three

*a*s they stepped out of the bar, Jeremy reached for her hand like it was the most natural thing in the world.

This is it, Melody thought, squeezing his fingers between hers. *I did it.*

She felt proud of herself. Gleeful, even.

That must have been what made her stop on the sidewalk in front of the Cask 'n Flagon, hook her hand around Jeremy's neck, and drag his mouth down to hers. Which was *so* not her. She was not that girl, but there she was, being *that* girl.

She didn't have any explanation for it other than the fact that she'd spent the last couple hours screwing up her courage to put the moves on him, and now that he was hers for the taking, she didn't want to wait any longer. She wanted to make sure he knew she was all in. Because she was. *All in.*

After a brief moment of surprise, Jeremy kissed her back with enthusiasm. His lips were warm and delicious. And soft. Like pillows, with just a hint of prickle around them from his stubble. If Melody weren't careful, she could melt right into them.

"Sorry," she mumbled when they came up for air. She wasn't

actually sorry, not even a little. "I guess that was kind of forward, wasn't it?"

His mouth curled into *that* smirk again—the one that made her feel so swoony. "I hope there's a lot more where that came from." His voice was low and breathy, and the sound of it made her toes curl in anticipation.

They were already standing close, but he moved even closer, pressing his chest against hers as he held onto her waist. His hair had fallen across his forehead, and she reached up to push it back for him. He had a perfect nose. Perfect teeth. And deep crinkles around his eyes from smiling, like he smiled all the time. God, he was gorgeous.

His hands came up to either side of her face and slid into her hair. His breath was warm on her cheeks, and she couldn't help rising onto her tiptoes, like a sunflower straining toward the sun.

He smiled a slow, warm smile, like he was looking at something beautiful, then kissed her again, so deeply, she could feel it all the way down to the soles of her feet.

She'd thought their last kiss was good, but this one was something else altogether. Melody had never been kissed like this before. Not by the guy with the butt chin during freshman orientation, or either of the boyfriends she'd had in high school. They were all rank amateurs compared to Jeremy. He was in the big leagues. By far the best she'd ever encountered in her not-so-extensive experience. She could go on kissing him forever, basically. He was that good.

When his lips moved away from hers, she let out an involuntary whine of protest—which quickly dissolved into a contented sigh as he mouthed a trail of kisses along her jaw and down her neck. Her hands roamed over his shoulders, then his arms, then his hips. She couldn't get enough of touching him. She pressed her thigh between his legs and was rewarded with a low growl, which was just—*wow*. She'd actually made a guy growl. That was a new milestone for her scrapbook.

Melody couldn't believe she was doing this. Here, on the side-walk. Outside a bar. She despised people who made out in public. She'd always thought they were gross. Now, she was one of them, and she had absolutely no regrets. Zero.

"My car," Jeremy panted against her collarbone. "That way." He waved vaguely down the street.

"Right." As much fun as they were having here, they could be having so much more somewhere less public. "Come on." She grabbed his hand and pulled him down the sidewalk.

They walked hand in hand to a parking garage a few blocks away, and he held open the passenger door of a shiny new Mercedes sports coupe. The interior was all leather, and it smelled like luxury...and french fries.

As soon as he climbed in behind the wheel, Jeremy twisted in his seat, reaching for her. His fingers stroked her cheek before curling around the back of her neck to pull her toward him.

She had to lean over the console to reach his lips, and although the kissing part was terrific—obviously—it was also awkward. They were too far apart, and there was too much stuff between them. Even when she tucked one leg up underneath her and turned toward him, she couldn't get close enough. He must have felt the same, because he kept shifting in his seat, jockeying for a better position as his tongue explored her mouth.

The loud blast of the horn startled them apart when his elbow accidentally bumped against it, and they both dissolved into laughter. "Oops," he said, smiling against her forehead.

Melody pulled back to look at him. "Your place?"

He grimaced, brushing her hair off her forehead. "I'm crashing on my friend Drew's couch this weekend."

"Right," she said. "My dorm room it is." Thank god her room-mate went home to Worcester almost every weekend to see her boyfriend.

Jeremy leaned in for another kiss, but she pushed him away.

"Nuh-uh, mister, let's get this car started. Come on, mush, mush."

He gave her a look—like he couldn't believe she'd just said that to him, but also like he wanted to tear her clothes off—and it almost melted her resolve. But then she thought about all the other cars parked around them, and how someone might walk by at any second, and how much she did not want to be seen having sex in a parking garage. She gave his shoulder another shove, and he sighed and twisted around to start the car.

"All right, all right," he said, rolling his eyes. "I'm mushing, sheesh."

THEY HAD to park about a mile from her residence hall, of course. Then there was the awkward business of signing him in at the front desk, but eventually they made it up to the privacy of her dorm room.

Jeremy stepped in for a kiss almost before she got the door closed. As their mouths crashed together, she shrugged out of her jacket and let it fall to the floor behind her, which she probably shouldn't have done, but she was way too busy kissing a cute guy to care.

His hands wrapped around her hips, then he lifted and carried her over to the bed. He laid her down on the narrow mattress and stretched out alongside her, propped up on one elbow. His other hand rested on her stomach, his fingers splayed wide and curled slightly into her.

He nudged his nose against her cheek, and she turned toward him, capturing his lips with hers. Their tongues slid together, eager and searching. He leaned into her, the warm weight of his body pressing down on hers, and his hand slipped under her shirt.

Goose bumps shivered over Melody's skin as his fingertips trailed over her waist, her stomach, her ribcage. Then his hand moved higher, finding her breast and cupping it in his large palm.

Her pulse pounded in her ears, and her chest felt tight, like she couldn't get enough air.

She wanted this. She was certain of that. But something had changed.

It didn't feel like it had outside the bar. Before, she'd felt weightless and carefree, like she was in a dream. Now, here, in the harsh fluorescent light of her dorm room, lying on her creaky twin bed with Jeremy's hand on her breast, it didn't feel like a dream anymore.

It felt real.

They were alone in her room. It was actually happening. And she'd gone and made the fatal mistake of *thinking* about it, which was inevitably when everything started to go wrong.

She'd been doing so well up until now, too. She'd been so dazzled by Jeremy's blue eyes and dimpled smile, it had been easy not to think about anything else.

Like how a guy this hot and rich probably had girls throwing themselves at him everywhere he went—not nerdy bookworms like her, but the sort of girls who routinely threw themselves at hot men and consequently had a lot more experience than she did.

Which had sort of been the whole point of coming out tonight. To do something new. With someone new. And Jeremy was so much hotter than Victor. Only, now that she actually had him in her room, she was terrified she wouldn't know what to do with him. That she wouldn't measure up.

He must have sensed something was wrong because he stopped kissing her, which was so, so unfortunate. She let out a sigh of frustration.

"You okay?" he asked, frowning.

"Yep! Great!" she chirped with a brightness she didn't feel. Her brain needed to *shut up*. This guy was gorgeous, and more importantly, he actually seemed nice. She wanted more than anything to be able to relax and enjoy this instead of being sabotaged by her stupid brain.

His frown deepened, and he rolled off her, which—*argh*—was not how this was supposed to go. "You're not—you're not a virgin, are you?"

"No! God! Definitely not. I've totally done this before."

He exhaled in relief. "Okay, good."

"Once," she mumbled at the ceiling—not something she'd planned on admitting. It just slipped out.

His face softened, and he laid his hand on her arm, squeezing gently. "Hey, we don't have to do anything you don't want to do. If you're not comfortable—"

"No!" she protested. "I'm comfortable. Super comfortable! The comfortablest. I want this. I want you. I'm just…a little nervous, I guess."

He gave her an encouraging smile. "You don't have to be nervous with me."

Melody snorted. "Yeah, you say that, but you strike me as a guy with pretty extensive experience in this department. Me…not so much. I'm just afraid I'll be a disappointment is all." Which was exactly the kind of over-sharing she should probably be trying to avoid.

Weirdly, though, he didn't seem to mind. "Melody," he said, gazing at her with an intensity that made her stomach do cart-wheels, "you're not going to disappoint me, no matter what happens or doesn't happen tonight. Okay?"

She let out a shaky, high-pitched laugh. "Yeah, that just shows how little you know me. I happen to be an expert at making an idiot of myself."

He smiled again—and oh god, he really did have a great smile. "This is not going to be one of those times."

"How do you know? You don't even know me. If you did, you'd know I'm crazy good at embarrassing myself. I'm sure I can find a way to do this wrong if I set my mind to it."

He shook his head, still smiling. "You're thinking about it like it's a driving test or something, like you're going to be graded on your performance."

"Well, yeah," she said, giving him her best *duh* look. "I mean, aren't I?"

"No!" He laughed. "I'm not going to grade you. It's supposed to be fun. The whole point is to relax and do whatever comes naturally. Live in the moment." He reached up and tapped her forehead. "Stop thinking so hard, MIT."

"Yeeeaaah, see, that's kind of the whole problem. Not thinking isn't exactly my strong suit. My brain's pretty much always going at, like, a million miles an hour, and—"

He shut her up by kissing her, and she sagged against him. "You're thinking again," he murmured against her lips.

She exhaled a breath that came out as a sort of moan, and he kissed her again, longer and deeper. *Screw it,* she decided. So what if she was nervous? She was with a boy who was *cute* and *nice*—a combination that didn't occur often in nature. She was going to make the most of it.

Right. Damn. Now.

"Too many clothes," she groaned as her hands worked their way under his shirt.

He sat up and yanked his shirt over his head, then quickly shucked off his shorts, leaving him impressively, magnificently naked except for a pair of gray Calvin Klein boxer briefs. Melody took a deep breath and followed suit, pulling off her top and shimmying out of her black skinny jeans. Thank god she'd had the foresight to shave her legs and put on her best lace bra and panties, even though it had totally seemed like wishful thinking at the time.

His gaze was hungry and intense as it roved over her body. "You're beautiful," he said, and she felt herself blush. But before she had time to feel too self-conscious, he was leaning in to kiss her again.

Melody rose to meet him halfway, closed her eyes, and let herself live in the moment.

AFTERWARD, they lay wrapped up together on her tiny bed, and for once in her life, Melody felt perfectly relaxed and content. She wished she could bottle this feeling and carry it around with her all the time.

"You doing okay?" Jeremy asked, pressing a kiss to the top of her head.

"Mmmm," she sighed into his chest. "Never better."

"Good."

"So, did I do all right?" she asked, unable to help herself. Because he'd definitely seemed to enjoy it, but she needed to know for sure. For science.

He made a noise of amused exasperation. "What did I tell you? It's not a test. You weren't being graded."

"Yeah, okay," she said with an impatient huff, "but if you had to give me a grade, what would it be?"

Jeremy's chest vibrated with laughter. "You're a crazy person, you know that?"

"So I've been told. But seriously, if you were grading on a curve—"

"Definitely an A."

She lifted her eyes to his. "Really?"

"Really." His cheeks dimpled. "A-plus, even."

"Yes!" she said, pumping her fist in the air.

He rolled his eyes and shook his head at her.

Melody laid her head on his chest again. If she held perfectly still, she could feel his heartbeat thumping against her cheek.

She wondered how much longer he was going to stay. Guys didn't usually spend the night after a hookup, did they? But it didn't seem like he was in any hurry to leave. Maybe he was as tired as she was. And he was so warm and comfy. She wouldn't mind if he wanted to stay a little longer.

She nestled against him and let her eyes drift closed.

IT WAS BARELY light when Melody woke, pulled out of sleep by the sound of Jeremy fumbling around for his clothes. When she opened her eyes, he was bent over, retrieving his clothes from the floor, and she let herself enjoy the view for a second before sitting up. "Never would have pegged you as an early riser."

He turned around and smiled at her. "I'm not, but as of five minutes ago, my car's on an expired meter, and my dad threatened to disown me if I got any more parking tickets." He pulled on his shorts and reached for his shirt, which hung over the back of her desk chair.

"It's too bad you're leaving today."

He tugged his shirt down and came over to the bed, perching on the edge beside her. "Look, Melody—"

"Don't make promises," she said. "Last night was perfect. Please don't ruin it with lies."

He nodded and reached up to run the pad of his thumb over her cheekbone. "Drew's about to graduate, and I don't know when I'll be coming back to Boston—or if I'll be coming back at all."

"It's fine. Really." It was. Not that she didn't like him, but she had her own life to get back to, and he didn't exactly fit into it.

"But if I do...can I call you?" They'd exchanged numbers last night at the bar, but she wasn't naive enough to think she was ever likely to hear from him again.

Biting her lip, she nodded. "But no promises."

"You know, if you're ever in LA—"

"Yeah, right."

He gave her that head tilt—the one that had made her fall for him in the first place. "If you're ever in LA," he said, "you can call me—if you want to. And if I'm free, maybe we can get together. Fair?"

"Fair."

He kissed her one last time, slowly, like he was savoring it. "Take care of yourself, MIT."

Then he was gone. Out of her life forever.

She snuggled back under the covers and fell asleep with visions of his dimples and his dumb, floppy hair in her head, not quite ready to forget about him yet.

Chapter Four

*S*ix weeks from the end of her senior year, Melody was pacing around her cramped studio apartment like a restless zoo cat.

It was a lousy apartment for pacing: just a rectangle with a tiny kitchen at one end, a bed at the other, and barely enough room in between for a broken-down couch—courtesy of the former tenants —and a rickety IKEA bistro table that doubled as desk. The situation was further aggravated by Melody's congenital messiness. Navigating around all the books, random computer parts, laundry baskets, and shoes littering the limited floor space made it impossible to work up to a satisfying stride.

After a few minutes, she gave up and sank down onto the couch.

Her travel was officially booked for her interview in Los Angeles next week. There was no good reason for putting this off anymore. If she was going to do it, she needed to do it now or admit she was chickening out.

She could chicken out. There was no shame in it. She didn't have to do this unless she actually wanted to.

Her thumb hovered over the number in her contacts—a

number she'd never once called or gotten a call from in the three years it had been stored there, all but forgotten.

A lot could happen in three years. A lot *had* happened.

This is a stupid idea.

Or was it? She chewed on her lip, debating with herself.

What was the worst that could happen? He could say no. Which would be uncomfortable, admittedly, but only for about five seconds, then she never had to talk to him again. It was a survivable humiliation.

There was also a decent chance he wouldn't remember her—which, again, would be awkward, but not, like, end-of-the-world awkward. He would either remember her or he wouldn't. If he didn't, she'd just apologize, delete his name from her phone, and move on with her life. No big loss.

He had told her to call him if she were ever in Los Angeles. Granted, it was the morning after a one-night stand, so there was a pretty good chance he hadn't meant it. Only…it kind of felt like he had? Maybe she was too gullible, or maybe he was better at lying than most guys, but she'd gotten the impression he was hoping she'd call.

Yeah, who was she kidding? She was probably just gullible.

On the other hand, he was literally the only person she knew in LA, and if she was maybe, possibly going to move there, connecting with someone in town could be helpful.

She was trying to start her life over, after all. New beginnings and all that. She needed to open herself up to the possibility of new relationships. That was what her therapist had said. Make some new friends. Put herself out in the world again. *Move on.*

This could be a first step.

Screw it. She hit dial before she could change her mind.

Jeremy answered on the second ring. "Melody?"

Okay, so he still had her number saved on his phone, which was a good sign. But he'd also said her name like a question, which sounded like either he didn't remember who she was, or he couldn't believe she was calling him—that wasn't so great.

"Jeremy. Hey...um, I don't know if you remember me, but—"

"I remember. MIT girl."

"Yeah," she said, exhaling. "That's me."

"Wow, it's been forever."

"Yeah, it has. I know this is probably super weird, but you said if I was ever in Los Angeles I should call and—"

"You're in LA?" It was impossible to tell from his inflection whether he was happy or horrified, but it was definitely one or the other.

"Not yet," she explained, hoping she didn't sound like some crazy stalker popping up out of his past, "but I have a job interview there next Friday, and I don't know anyone else in town, so I was thinking, if you're free, maybe we could meet for coffee or something, and you could help me decide if it's someplace I'd like to live."

Wait, did that make it sound like she was expecting him to entice her with sex? It totally sounded like she was fishing for sex, didn't it?

"I mean, you could answer some questions," she added before he could say anything, "about, you know, the cost of living, the best parts of town to live in, that sort of thing. I could also just Google it. No pressure."

"Coffee sounds great." She wasn't 100 percent sure, but it sounded like he might be smiling. "Where's your interview?"

"Glendale?"

"Perfect, that's near where I work. Neither of us will have to fight traffic."

"I should be done around four, they said."

"How about we meet at five? There's a Coffee Bean & Tea Leaf on Brand."

"That sounds great. I'll see you next Friday."

After she disconnected the call, a goofy grin spread over her face. Her heart was thumping in her chest and she felt giddy with relief. Which was ridiculous. It wasn't like it was a big deal or anything. She wasn't expecting to hook up with him again. All she wanted was a little friendly advice. He wasn't even her type, from what little she could remember of him.

It was totally whatever. Casual. Totally casual.

THE JOB INTERVIEW ended up going long, which was hopefully a good sign, but it meant Melody was running late to meet Jeremy. Fortunately, the coffee shop was within walking distance of her interview. Unfortunately, it was a ten-minute walk in high-heels and a black blazer with the California sun beating down on her back.

Sweaty, panting, and limping a little, she pushed through the door of the Coffee Bean & Tea Leaf and scanned the faces scattered around the small cafe. She *thought* she remembered Jeremy well enough to recognize him, but people could change a lot in three years.

Melody was certainly proof of that—the Emma Watson-inspired pixie cut from her freshman year had grown out into longish brown waves, she'd started wearing glasses, and her interview power suit and four-inch heels were a far cry from the jeans and leather jacket she'd been wearing when they met. And those were just the physical changes. Underneath it all, she was a very different person than the one he'd known in Boston. That adventurous, plucky girl who'd picked up a handsome stranger in a bar was a distant memory.

She recognized Jeremy immediately, sitting alone at a table by the window and staring at his phone. His hair was a lot shorter, and he was dressed in a business suit instead of the frat boy aesthetic he'd been sporting when they first met, but it was unquestionably him.

Her memory certainly hadn't exaggerated how good looking he

was. If anything, he was even more gorgeous now. Which didn't seem like it should be possible, but there he was, basically looking like a Greek god in a suit and tie.

This is fine. Nothing to freak out about. It was only her first date in almost a year—not that it was a date-date. She wasn't trying to date him; she was just renewing an acquaintance. Networking.

Breathe. Try not to think about how gorgeous he is.

Melody wound through the scattered tables and chairs, clutching the strap of her bag tight enough to make her fingers tingle as she approached him. "Jeremy?"

He looked up, and his mouth opened in surprise. "Melody? Is that you? Whoa."

"Yeah, I guess I look a little different," she said, touching her hair.

He stood and greeted her with a light kiss on the cheek. "I like it." His smile hadn't gotten any less dazzling, that was for sure. Or his eyes any less blue. "It's a good look on you."

She felt herself flush and ducked her head, hoping he wouldn't notice. "Sorry I'm late. They kept me longer than I expected."

"That's okay. I haven't ordered yet. What can I get you?"

"Non-fat vanilla latte?"

"Coming right up." He gave her a flirty wink that only made more blood rush to her cheeks before heading to the counter to place his order.

While Jeremy got their drinks, Melody slipped into the ladies' room to freshen up. The reflection in the mirror confirmed the trek over had left her red-faced and shiny, and her lipstick was all but non-existent. She did the best she could to blot the sweat from her face and pits with paper towels before touching up her makeup. Once she'd made herself more presentable, she took a few deeps breaths to steady her nerves, and went out to face her very platonic coffee date with her superhumanly hot hookup from three years ago.

Jeremy was already waiting at the table with their drinks, and he stood when she approached, waiting for her to sit before taking his own seat again. He was gorgeous *and* he still had good manners. She'd almost forgotten men like that existed.

"Thanks for the coffee," she said, reaching for the cup he slid toward her. It was too hot to drink, so she took off the lid and blew across the top.

Jeremy smiled and shook his head slightly. "I can't believe it's really you."

A nervous laugh bubbled out of her throat. "In the flesh," she said, trying to sound cool and nonchalant and not totally flustered. Her babble reflex was trying to kick in, so she took a sip of her coffee to head it off at the pass.

Shit! Ow! Still too hot. She swallowed the scalding liquid, trying not to let on that she'd just cauterized her tongue. So much for cool and nonchalant.

"You know what's really funny?" Jeremy said. "I was just thinking about you not too long ago."

Melody forgot all about her burned tongue. "Really?"

"Yeah, I thought I saw you at O'Hare a few weeks ago."

"I've never flown through O'Hare."

"She looked like you used to look, you know, with the short hair. Anyway, it got me wondering what you were up to these days and how you were doing." He grinned and leaned back in his chair. "And now here you are. Crazy, huh?"

"Totally," she agreed, lowering her eyes to the table. That smile of his was straight up unfair. It was like a solar eclipse: mesmerizing, but dangerous to stare at directly.

"So, how'd your interview go?"

She moved her hands to her lap so he couldn't see how fidgety they were. "Pretty well, I think. They seemed to like me, and I think I managed to avoid making an ass of myself, so fingers crossed, I guess."

"You were a freshman, right? You graduate this year?"

She nodded, impressed he remembered that much about her.

"In just a few more weeks, which means it's job market time—hence the interview."

"Good for you."

His hair looked a lot better short. It was spiky and attractively tousled on top, but on the sides, it was tapered and smooth, like velvet. It made her want to run her fingers through it to see if it felt as good as it looked.

Melody cleared her throat and reached for her coffee again. "What about you? Did you ever go back to school?"

His smile twisted into something wry. "Yeah, believe it or not, I finally stopped running from my responsibilities and buckled down. I'm almost like a real grown-up now." He gestured to his suit. "Got a business degree and a job and everything."

"That's great—I mean, assuming you're happy with it." He didn't seem all that happy about it.

He shrugged. "It's not as bad as I thought it'd be. Sometimes I still miss the old days when I could party all the time, but mostly I'm glad I'm not that guy anymore." The edge in his voice made it sound like he was trying to convince himself as much as her. He shifted in his chair, straightening his spine and rolling his shoulders back. "So, what kind of job are you interviewing for?"

"Corporate IT."

"Just like you wanted." Wow, he really did remember her.

"Yeah." She felt herself flush again. "It's just entry level, but there's a lot of room for growth."

"What company?"

"Sauer Hewson Aerospace."

He burst out laughing. "You're kidding."

"What?"

He shook his head in amusement. "We never exchanged last names, did we? You really don't know."

"Know what?" she asked, starting to feel annoyed that she wasn't in on the joke. "What's your last name got to do with it?"

"My last name is Sauer," he said with a smirk. "My mother is the CEO."

Melody's mouth fell open. "Your mother is Angelica Sauer? Are you kidding me? You have to be kidding."

He reached into the breast pocket of his jacket and produced a Sauer Hewson security badge with his picture on it and the name Jeremy Sauer.

"Oh my god!" She clapped her hand over her mouth. "I can't believe it. I had no idea. I never would have...if I'd known—I mean, I totally wasn't trying to—"

Jeremy laughed again as he tucked his badge away. "It's okay, Melody. I know you didn't know."

What were the odds that some random guy she'd hooked up with three years ago would turn out to be the heir apparent to the company she'd just interviewed with? It was unreal.

"Wait," she said, "if your mother is Angelica Sauer, that means your father..." she trailed off as Jeremy's expression darkened.

"Yeah," he said, jaw clenching.

She'd done a lot of research on Sauer Hewson to prep for her interview, and one of the things she'd learned was Angelica Sauer had taken over as CEO after her husband, company founder William Sauer, died of pancreatic cancer. "Oh, Jeremy, I'm so sorry."

He lowered his eyes. "Thank you."

Something else occurred to her. "That was almost three years ago, right? Wouldn't that make it around the time we, um...you know...met?"

He nodded grimly. "Dad was diagnosed the week after I got back from Boston. The doctors gave him three to six months—he only lasted two."

Melody reached across the table for his hand. "I'm so sorry. It must have been awful."

"It's funny," he said, looking down at their hands, "I think about that weekend in Boston a lot. It was sort of my last hurrah.

The last time I can remember when my life was still carefree. After that..." he pressed his lips together and shook his head, "well, I guess I grew up pretty fast after that."

"I can't even imagine," she said, even though she could. She knew all too well how tragedy could change you—how you weren't the same person when you came out on the other side. She'd lost someone of her own last year, and she still carried the scars to prove it. Not a parent, like Jeremy had lost, but someone she'd loved. Someone she'd thought she couldn't live without.

Jeremy gave her a tight smile she interpreted to mean he'd rather be talking about anything else right now—and she knew that feeling, too. Oh, how she knew it.

She let go of his hand and picked up her coffee. "Tell me about your job," she said, forcing brightness into her voice. "What's your role in the family business, Mr. Sauer?"

He gave her a grateful look and started talking about work. He was in something called the Challenger Program, where management trainees did eighteen-month rotations shadowing different executives and learning about the business. At the moment, he was working under the CFO, but he'd done his stint with the CIO last year, so he knew a lot of people in IT, including the hiring manager Melody had interviewed with.

They talked about some of the big projects the company was working on, then moved on to the pros and cons of living in Los Angeles.

Pro: it was sunny and seventy-eight degrees practically year-round.

Con: the traffic was apocalyptic and there were no decent public transportation options.

The longer they talked, the more convinced Melody became that she wanted this job. A lot. She'd interviewed with another company outside Seattle, but it was smaller and the starting salary wasn't great compared to the cost of living. Also? It was only sunny seventy-one days out of the year in Seattle, which was outrageous. If there was one thing Melody had learned from her four years in Boston, it was that she was susceptible to seasonal affective disorder. Seattle did not seem like a great fit. Los Angeles, on the other hand, seemed just about perfect.

It wasn't only the city she was enamored with, either. Jeremy was as easy to talk to as he had been three years ago. It was like picking back up with an old friend, right where you'd left off. She felt oddly comfortable with him—and more like her old self than she'd felt in a long time.

Before she knew it, two hours had passed and Jeremy was glancing at his phone. "Shit, is that the time already?"

"Do you have plans?" she asked and immediately felt like an idiot. "Of course you do. What am I saying? It's Friday night. I'm sorry. I didn't mean to keep you so long."

"It's fine," he said, getting to his feet. "I've still got time to make my dinner reservation if I leave now." Then, almost apologetically, he added, "I'm meeting my girlfriend."

"Oh," Melody said, feeling thrown. "Right. Of course."

She was being ridiculous and needed to stop it right this second. It was fine that he had a girlfriend. It didn't matter to her one bit. And it wasn't at all odd that he hadn't mentioned her until then. Not odd at all. Except...it kind of was, wasn't it?

She didn't say anything as she gathered her purse and carried her empty coffee cup to the trash. Jeremy held the door for her, and they stepped out onto the sidewalk to make their goodbyes.

It was hard to know what to say in a situation like this, where you weren't exactly friends, but you weren't strangers either. Melody had no idea *what* they were, or if she was ever going to see him again. All she knew was everything felt awkward now.

"When are you flying back to Boston?" he asked.

"Tomorrow morning."

He responded with a nod, followed by a pregnant pause. "Can I drop you somewhere?"

She shook her head and hooked her thumb over her shoulder. "I've got a rental car."

"Right. Well, I guess this is goodbye for now." Another pause. "It was good seeing you again, Melody."

"You too." *There is no reason to feel weird.* All she'd done was catch up with an old acquaintance and possibly make a useful business connection in the process. It was perfectly harmless and innocent, and exactly what she'd wanted out of this meeting. "Thank you for the coffee. And for making the time to see me."

He bent down to kiss her cheek again. It was brief and perfunctory, like something he did with all his female acquaintances, not just the ones he'd slept with. "You'll call and let me know if you get the job, won't you?"

"Sure," she said, not at all sure whether she actually would or not.

Jeremy gifted her with another smile before he strode off. She watched him walk away, feeling conflicted and a little embarrassed.

She was glad she'd worked up the courage to see him, but she'd let herself get carried away in the moment, and that had been a mistake. Nice as it was to know she was still capable of feeling that way, it was just as well that Jeremy had a girlfriend. The absolute last thing Melody wanted was to get romantically involved with anyone right now.

She wasn't ready for something like that yet. Not after what had happened to Kieran, her last boyfriend—ex-boyfriend? Former boyfriend? Late boyfriend? Yuck. That made it sound like he was tardy instead of...

Anyway, it was a relief to know Jeremy was off limits. That way, there wouldn't be any temptation or misunderstanding—on anyone's part.

Everything was good. Everything was great. Couldn't be better.

Chapter Five

Two weeks after her interview, Sauer Hewson made Melody a job offer—a seriously excellent job offer, much better than the one from the company in Seattle.

It was her dream job. The money wasn't just good, it was life changing. As soon as she got off the phone with the recruiter, she spent a good five minutes dancing around her apartment, celebrating.

Only after the initial bubble of excitement had worn off did it occur to her that she might not have gotten the job on her own merits.

She hadn't planned on calling Jeremy, despite what she'd told him, but now she grabbed her phone and scrolled through her contacts, needing to make sure he wasn't behind this.

"Hey!" he said when he answered. "I was hoping to hear from you. Any word on the job yet?"

"I got it." She was still a little out of breath from the spontaneous dance party. "Sauer Hewson just made me an offer. A great offer, actually. Almost too good to be true."

"That's terrific! Congratulations! Have you decided if you're going to take it?"

She bit her lip. "Did you have anything to do with it? Tell me the truth."

"Me? No, of course not."

She didn't say anything. She couldn't tell whether he was lying or not. Not over the phone, anyway.

"Melody, I swear to you, I did not intervene. I haven't talked to a single person at the company about you. You earned that job all on your own."

She exhaled, feeling ridiculous for jumping to such an insane conclusion. Why on earth would she think he'd do something like that for her? What interest could Jeremy Sauer possibly have in whether she worked at his family's company or not?

"I'm sorry," she said. "I didn't really think you'd do anything like that, but I had to make sure."

"It's fine, I get it. I thought about it, to be honest, but figured you didn't need my help. And I was right. So, are you going to accept?"

"I already did. I start next month."

MELODY TOOK a few days off from preparing for her undergraduate thesis presentation to fly out to Los Angeles and go apartment hunting.

Jeremy had very kindly offered to help her find a place, and she had very kindly thanked him and told him she could manage on her own. She was starting a new chapter in her life, and she didn't want to be dependent on Jeremy Sauer or anyone else.

Not that she was above engaging professional assistance—the Sauer Hewson offer had come with a relocation package, including a real estate agent to assist with her apartment search, and she planned to take full advantage of it.

The agent's name was Santiago, and he looked like a movie star. Melody spent a whole day being chauffeured around Los Angeles in Santiago's pristine black Mercedes convertible. Leaning back in the plush leather seats with the top down and her sunglasses on, she felt a little like a movie star herself.

They looked at nearly a dozen different places in her price range before she signed a lease on a modern two-bedroom twenty minutes from her new job. While the leasing agent made copies of the paperwork, Melody texted pictures of her new apartment, with all its shiny new appliances, to her mom.

OH MY GOD IT'S GOOOOORGEOUS, her mom texted back, followed by a whole screen of exclamation points and heart-eyes emojis.

It wasn't the swankiest place by LA standards, but it was far nicer than anywhere Melody had ever lived. Growing up, she and her mom had moved from one shabby apartment and dumpy rental house to another, trying to stay ahead of the creditors. On one particularly memorable occasion, they'd had to pack up their meager belongings and slip out in the middle of the night to avoid a forcible eviction.

But with her new job, a nice apartment—one with a whole extra bedroom, a courtyard tub, working heat, and carpet that didn't smell like cat pee or stick to the soles of your feet—was easily within Melody's means. It was hard to believe this was all really happening.

She didn't know how to live any way other than paycheck to paycheck. Money had always been a persistent, oppressive worry hovering under the surface of everything she did. But now? Now she could afford to pay rent on this outrageously nice apartment, lease a car, buy groceries, make her student loan payments, and *still* have money left over to put into savings every week. It was madness.

To celebrate, Melody took herself out to dinner at a fancy restaurant near the beach in Santa Monica, and splurged on a bottle of champagne and the lobster thermidor. She didn't actually know what lobster thermidor was, but it sounded like something rich people ate, and she wanted to feel rich and fancy—lobster thermidor and champagne fancy.

Sipping her champagne, she gazed out the picture window at the Santa Monica Pier as the sun sank toward the Pacific Ocean. The lobster thermidor was fine, but hardly seemed worth the exorbitant price tag. In retrospect, she probably would have been better off with the tenderloin. Lesson learned. For dessert, she had a slice of chocolate mousse cake so rich, she could only finish a few bites of it.

The champagne had left her feeling muzzy, so after she paid the check, she went for a walk along the beach to clear her head. The sky against the palm tree silhouettes was yellow-amber, like a Polaroid photo filter, and she felt more alive than she had in a long time, but also strangely unreal, like she'd stepped into someone else's life.

Crossing her arms against the ocean breeze, she stared out at the dark, crashing waves and tried to believe this was exactly the fresh start she needed.

Everything was going to be better now.

It had to be.

AFTER ROCKING HER THESIS PRESENTATION, Melody told MIT to mail her diploma to her new address in Los Angeles, then crammed the entirety of her life into a few cardboard boxes, flipped the bird to Boston, and moved to the opposite side of the country.

The first thing she did when she got to LA was lease an electric blue MINI Cooper—the first new car she'd ever owned. So long, public transportation! No more unidentified fluids, or jockeying for space with drunks, manspreaders, and people who thought their backpacks deserved their owns seats! Hello, fighting her way through rush-hour traffic and competing for parking spaces with the other six million LA drivers!

Melody had never had so much money to spend all at once before, and it was tempting to go a little crazy. Fortunately—or sadly, depending on your perspective—she was far too sensible to actually do anything that irresponsible. She let herself spend half her signing bonus on a work wardrobe and some furniture for her apartment, and the other half went into savings. She bought a brand new couch and mattress—on clearance, of course—but after that, she scoured discount shops and thrift stores.

It was too hard to let go of a lifetime habit of penny-pinching. The memories of how much even a small unexpected expense cropping up could hurt for weeks, or even months, were too ingrained to be shaken off at the sight of one fat check. Every dollar Melody spent involved a certain amount of rocking back and forth trying to convince herself it was okay, she could afford it, she was still being responsible.

She was half afraid this was all going to turn out to be some sort of mistake or cruel trick. That Sauer Hewson would call, ask for their check back, and tell her there'd been a mix-up and this had all been meant for someone else. Not her. Surely. How could this be her life?

The night before she was supposed to start her new job, Melody lay in her new bed in her new apartment, staring at the unfamiliar ceiling. She still wasn't used to the sounds of this strange new city at night. She wasn't used to the traffic noise outside, or the rumble of the ice-maker in her freezer, or the muffled voices and thumps of her new neighbors.

Her brand new sheets were scratchy, and her skin felt irritated and hyper-sensitive. It was possible she was allergic to the laundry detergent she'd bought. Or maybe it was the air in LA. The smog here was supposed to be the worst in the country. What if she was allergic to the whole city?

What if her new coworkers didn't like her? What if her boss didn't like her? What if she wasn't any good and they realized they'd made a mistake?

Melody rolled over and reached for her phone to check the time. 1:18 a.m. If she fell asleep right now, she'd get almost five hours of sleep.

Or she could pull up Google Maps and double-check the route she was planning to take to work in the morning. Just one more time. Just to make sure she remembered it. Just in case.

Instead, she got up and went into the bathroom for a Xanax. Then she got back in bed and pulled the covers up under her chin.

She'd get used to it here; she just needed to give it time. Everything would be fine.

AFTER ALL THAT WORRYING, the new job turned out to be a cinch. A little too much of a cinch, really. She'd been worried she wouldn't be able to live up to expectations, but they didn't seem to *have* any expectations of her.

For her first assignment, they put her to work re-imaging servers, which any monkey with an MIS could have done. She was vastly overqualified for it, but she supposed she had to put in her time at the bottom and prove herself before she could move on to bigger and better things. She understood this, rationally, but it didn't stop her from being bored out of her wits.

At least her new boss was nice enough, even if he seemed in over his head. When she tried to explain how she'd hand-built the new image for one of the servers because the old one was using the wrong drivers, she got the sense he only understood about half of what she was saying. But he was content to let her do things her way, so long as everything got done and he came out smelling like a rose to his boss.

Her coworkers were harder to get a read on. As the lowest person on the totem pole, Melody was stuck at the only available workstation, which happened to be off by itself in what was essentially a glorified closet outside one of the server rooms. It didn't afford her much opportunity to interact with anyone else in her department, and on the rare occasions she did, they seemed a bit standoffish. She couldn't tell if they were actively unfriendly, worried she posed a threat to their jobs, or simply disinterested.

Whatever. It was a good job, and she was grateful to have it. Things were good. Things were fine.

AT THE END of Melody's first week, Jeremy showed up at her office.

"Hey," he said, lounging against the open doorway. "A little bird told me you started this week."

She tilted her head to the side. "A little bird? Really?"

"Okay, it was your boss." He flashed that movie star smile of his—the one that had made her weak in the knees the first time they met. "I may have called and asked him when you were starting. I hope you don't mind."

"No, it's fine. I'm sorry, I meant to call you when I got to town, but everything's been kind of crazy." Which was a lie. Things had been crazy, but not calling him had been completely intentional.

Aside from the fact that pursuing a friendship with an ex-flame who had a girlfriend felt like a wicked bad idea, Melody had Googled Jeremy and what she'd found was...enlightening. The DUIs, trashed hotel rooms, and incidences of public intoxication caught on camera seemed to have petered out in the last three years at least, but he still made semi-regular appearances on some local society pages and gossip sites. There were more than a few paparazzi photos of the handsome young Mr. Sauer, heir to a billion-dollar aerospace empire, arriving and departing from high-profile hot spots around town with various beautiful women on his arm—some of them recognizable actresses and models.

Oh, there was also the matter of him being named one of the country's "50 Sexiest Bachelors" by *Town & Country* magazine last year—which was a real thing that had actually happened.

So, yeah. Even if Jeremy hadn't had a girlfriend, he would still be so far out of Melody's league, he might as well be in the next solar system. Which was perfectly fine, because she was absolutely, positively not looking to hook up with him again—no matter how hot he was.

"How are you settling in?" He cast his eyes around her dreary little workspace. "I see they put you in the gold star accommodations."

"It's not so bad," she said with a shrug. "At least I have my own office."

"Making new friends?"

Melody forced a smile. "Yep. Everyone's been great." Not strictly true, but not *not* true, either.

"I was thinking I could take you to lunch to celebrate the end of your first week. If you're free, that is."

She couldn't have been freer. The formatting software practically ran itself, and there wasn't anything for her to do but wait until it finished, which wouldn't be for hours. Also, she was starving. And a bit lonely. She'd barely talked to anyone since she'd arrived in Los Angeles, aside from her mom during their weekly phone calls. On the other hand...

"You don't think your girlfriend would mind?"

His eyebrows lifted. "Would she mind if I had lunch with a coworker? Probably not."

"We're not just coworkers, though, are we? I mean, that's not how we met."

The corner of his mouth dimpled into that charming smirk of his. "No, it's not."

Melody refused to be charmed. "Did you tell her about me? After we met for coffee, I mean?"

The smirk faded into something more sincere. "I told her about you *before* we met for coffee. I don't go around asking women out behind my girlfriend's back. Lacey knows all about you."

"Really?" she said, trying to decide whether he was telling the truth.

"Really. So, can I take you to lunch?"

"I'd like that," she replied with a smile. What the hell, right? She had to eat. And the thought of having yet another sad ham and cheese sandwich alone at her desk was too depressing to contemplate.

The restaurant was around the corner, and the hostess recognized Jeremy on sight, addressing him as "Mr. Sauer" and asking if he'd like his usual table, which turned out to be in a quiet corner in the back, away from prying eyes.

It didn't escape Melody's notice how effortlessly he flirted with the hostess, flashing his billion-dollar smile and touching her on the arm. She remembered him doing the same with her the night they first met, and it was so clearly an act, she felt a little ashamed at the memory.

"Wow," she said as soon as the hostess retreated.

He looked up from his menu. "What?"

"Nothing." She shook her head. "It's just—you really know how to lay on the charm, don't you?"

His shoulders lifted in a careless shrug. "Making connections is a big part of my job. It's second nature at this point."

"Mmmhmm," she said, not bothering to hide her skepticism. "I'll bet you've always been like that, though. You were probably charming phone numbers out of girls on the playground in kindergarten."

The smirk made another appearance. "Maybe."

"That's exactly how you acted with me when we met." She scrunched up her nose. "I can't believe I fell for it."

"I'm glad you did." That smile of his was like a superpower. Even though she knew he must use it on everyone he wanted to impress, she couldn't help getting a little breathless when it was directed at her.

Melody raised her menu to hide the color rushing to her

cheeks. "What's good here?" she asked, changing the subject. "Since you obviously come here a lot."

Jeremy recommended the steak, but she decided to stick with soup and a salad. He ordered the fifty-dollar prime rib and a twenty-five-dollar scotch—just in case she needed another reminder of how different his world was from hers.

When he asked about her first week on the job, she gave him benign, nonspecific answers. She was hyperconscious of the fact that he was the CEO's son, and the last thing she wanted to do was complain about her new job to someone in management. But then he asked about her new apartment, and Melody found herself getting excited as she told him all about it, and about her new furniture and car.

Jeremy had had money all his life, so she didn't expect him to understand what it meant for her to be able to afford all these nice things for herself—but strangely, he seemed to. Or maybe he was just good at pretending to understand. Whatever. She'd take it. He was the only person she knew here, and it was nice to have someone to talk to.

They ended up taking a two-hour lunch, which she probably should have felt bad about, seeing as it was her first week and all, but it wasn't like anyone at work was going to miss her or even notice she was gone.

"I'll write you a note," Jeremy teased as they walked out of the restaurant.

It was a gorgeous day, just like every day in Los Angeles. Melody was still getting used to the fact that she didn't have to check the weather forecast before she left the house. That and the lack of humidity, which was doing amazing things for her hair.

Jeremy ambled along at a leisurely pace, but his legs were so long, Melody had to hustle to keep up. He started telling her about a contract they were bidding on with NASA, to build a winged spacecraft to resupply the International Space Station. It was a fourteen-billion-dollar contract, but Jeremy seemed more excited about the tech than the money.

"See, SpaceX and Orbital's cargo craft both return to Earth by splashing down in the ocean," he was saying as they stepped into the lobby back at the office. "Which is a pain in the ass to recover. But ours is going to glide back to Earth and land on a runway." He made a motion with his hand to illustrate.

"Like the space shuttle," Melody said.

"Exactly!" he said, grinning. "It means scientists will be able to access the results of ISS experiments within just a few hours of reentry. It's game changing." He was dangerously cute when he got excited about science.

"Do you think we'll get the contract?"

He shrugged. "Who knows? Government stuff is unpredictable." He cocked his head toward the coffee cart. "I'm gonna grab some coffee before I head up. You want any?"

She shook her head. "I better get back upstairs and check on my format. Thank you for lunch. It was fun."

"We should go out to dinner sometime."

Melody froze. "What?" He had a girlfriend, what was he doing asking her to dinner?

"You, me, and Lacey."

Right. With Lacey. His girlfriend. That made much more sense.

"What do you say?" he asked.

"Sure," Melody said. "That sounds fun."

He was already walking away. "I'll call you," he said over his shoulder. "We'll pick a date."

Chapter Six

The last thing Melody expected was for Jeremy to follow through on his dinner invitation. She assumed it was just one of those things people said to be polite, like *let's do lunch* or *we'll get together soon*. And Jeremy Sauer struck her as the kind of guy who routinely made promises he had no intention of keeping.

So, she was surprised when he texted her the following week to firm up plans for dinner.

They agreed to meet on Saturday night at a restaurant in the Arts District. A quick internet search told her it was one of the hottest new restaurants in the city and the typical wait for a reservation was six weeks—unless you were Jeremy Sauer, apparently.

She decided to treat herself to a new outfit for the occasion. She was worried about fitting in at a super-trendy LA restaurant and didn't think any of the sensible slacks and button-down shirts she'd bought for work were up to the job. Also, her fashion expertise was limited to deciding what color Converse to wear with which novelty T-shirt, so she needed help.

"Oh *my god*, are you serious?" the saleswoman at Nordstrom said when Melody told her where she was going. "That place is impossible to get into. Come on." She took her firmly by the arm and lead her over to a rack of dresses. "I'm going to find you the perfect thing. You're gonna be a stunner."

Melody seriously doubted that, but she was encouraged by the saleswoman's enthusiasm. Her name was Jasmine, and her outfit was cute and stylish without being overly trendy, which gave Melody hope she wouldn't steer her wrong.

"What kind of dinner is it?" Jasmine asked, flipping through the rack with the efficiency of a casino dealer. "Is it like a date, or a girls' night out, or what?"

"Um..." Melody chewed on the inside of her cheek. What kind of dinner was it? She wasn't entirely sure how to describe it. "I guess it's like a work dinner?" she said, figuring it was better to play it safe. "Like a work dinner with friends, let's say."

"So, nothing too slutty, right?"

"Definitely nothing slutty." The last thing she wanted was to look like she was trying to throw herself at Jeremy, especially *in front of his girlfriend.*

Jasmine pulled out a dress and stared at it, pursing her lips and twisting them to the side. "What night of the week?"

"Saturday."

"Okay, good." She hung the dress on the end of a nearby rack and went back to flipping through the hangers. "Since no one's going straight from work, it gives you a little more freedom to play around with your style."

See? Melody never would have thought of that. Thank god she had Jasmine.

By the time Jasmine was done searching through the racks, there were five different dresses for Melody to try on. The first one didn't fit. The second was way too low cut—like so low cut, it looked like her bosoms were in danger of heaving their way to freedom. The third one Melody vetoed as ugly—the pattern reminded her of her grandmother's hideous couch. The fourth and fifth were both pretty great, though.

Jasmine was pushing hard for the fifth: a stretchy, color-block dress she insisted made Melody's ass look spectacular. Melody wasn't sure she wanted her ass to look that spectacular, so she ended up going with the fourth: a simple black dress with a narrow skirt and tastefully plunging neckline.

It seemed like the more versatile of the two—easy to dress up or down—and therefore, the more sensible investment. Even though she knew black was boring, Melody liked the way the dress made her feel—like an adult instead of a kid playing dress-up.

"Girl, you look *goood*," Jasmine said as Melody spun in front of the mirror. "You're gonna fit right in."

God, she hoped so.

Despite some low-key feelings of dread about meeting Jeremy's girlfriend and the potential awkwardness that might entail, she was jazzed about the dinner. It was her first time going out in LA with other people.

Maybe she and Jeremy's girlfriend would hit it off. Maybe they'd even end up being friends. It was hard to imagine she could have much in common with the girlfriend of someone like Jeremy Sauer, but it was worth a shot.

As hard as Melody had been trying to pretend like everything was going great, the loneliness was starting to get to her. She still hadn't gotten to know any of her coworkers, and her neighbors were like ghosts she could hear but only caught rare glimpses of. From Friday afternoon to Monday morning, she barely talked to a single living soul, except maybe the check-out clerk at the grocery store or the pizza delivery guy. She'd started giving serious thought to getting a cat—even though she was allergic—just so she'd have someone to talk to besides herself.

She really needed to make a friend. Things were getting dire.

MELODY GOT to the restaurant ten minutes early, because she was so worried about the traffic, she ended up overcompensating.

She didn't want to seem anxious and uncool—even if she definitely *was* anxious and uncool—so she parked a few blocks away, sat in her car, and waited until she was a good two minutes late before driving up to the valet stand.

After all that, she was still the first one there, but at least she wasn't early. A glamorous hostess with a tight ballerina bun and a judgy expression showed Melody to an empty table, and another ten minutes passed before Jeremy finally showed up with a gorgeous Latina woman in a curve-hugging pink dress.

"I hope you haven't been waiting long," Jeremy said.

"Nope, just got here," Melody lied. For some reason, she seemed to lie a lot around Jeremy. Little white ones. Reflexive lies. She wasn't sure why. Nerves, maybe.

He introduced his girlfriend, Lacey Lopez, who offered Melody a tight smile and a perfunctory, "Hey." She was exactly as beautiful as Melody had feared a woman dating Jeremy Sauer would be. Big brown eyes, silky black hair, glowing skin, and an ass that could give Serena Williams a run for her money. Between Lacey and the hostess, Melody was already feeling like the nerdy, plain Jane outsider. Things were off to a super start.

"Our fourth texted that he's running late," Jeremy said.

"Shocking." Lacey rolled her eyes as she reached for the cocktail menu.

"Fourth?" Melody asked, her smile frozen in place.

"Yeah, I invited my buddy Drew to join us. I hope it's okay."

She forced herself to unclench her teeth before she ground them into tiny stress nubs. "Sure," she lied again. It was just a surprise blind date. No big deal, right? Who wouldn't be okay with that?

"Don't worry, I'm not trying to set you two up," Jeremy said. "Four's just a better number for dinner than three, and you both went to school in Boston, so I figured you'd hit it off."

"Drew's hung up on my sister anyway," Lacey volunteered, snagging a tiny biscuit from the bread basket.

The look Jeremy cut her in response made it seem like there was more to that story, but it was quickly replaced by a smile as the waiter arrived to take their drink orders.

They made strained small talk over cocktails. Jeremy and Melody did, anyway. Lacey barely spoke at all. Jeremy tried to draw her into the conversation a few times, but she remained persistently disinterested in anything other than her vodka martini and the bread basket. Surprisingly, the frowning looks he kept throwing her way didn't seem to do much to warm her up.

Melody couldn't tell whether Lacey was unhappy because of her—and her history with Jeremy—or if this was how Lacey always was. Maybe both. Either way, it was uncomfortable. They hadn't even ordered, and Melody was already itching for this dinner to be over.

When Drew showed up a full thirty minutes later, Melody almost wept in relief. Jeremy was so right about four being a better number. Maybe he'd known going in Lacey would be antisocial, but if so, why bother setting this up in the first place?

Jeremy's friend Drew Fulton was polished and handsome, just like Jeremy, but with brown eyes and thick, dark hair. He leaned over to give Lacey a peck on the cheek, which she tolerated with neither objection nor enthusiasm, and flagged down a passing waiter to order a drink before regarding Melody with a lopsided grin. "It's nice to meet you, finally," he said with a wink.

Melody had no idea how to take that. Did that mean Jeremy had told Drew about her? *What* had he told him about her? She stared down at her hands, which were twisted in her lap.

"Drew works in the movie business," Jeremy said. Despite his insistence that this wasn't a setup, it sounded like he was trying to sell Melody on Drew. Maybe it was just second nature to him— a part of that whole making connections thing he'd mentioned at lunch.

She offered Drew a polite smile. "Oh yeah? What do you do?"

"Development," he said, flipping through the menu. "Mostly,

it's reading a lot of scripts, identifying the ones that are right for the studio, then shepherding them into production. Or trying to, anyway."

Melody was a pop culture junkie, so she knew what development was, but she nodded like this was completely new information to her. Then hated herself for playing dumb to flatter a guy's ego.

"Don't forget the part where you're constantly wined and dined by agents," Jeremy said. "It's a real hardship."

"Well, you know me," Drew said, flashing his lopsided grin. "Always with my nose to the grindstone."

The waiter came by to drop off Drew's drink and take their dinner orders—thank god. Melody was starving, and Lacey had cleaned out most of the bread basket.

"How'd you break into film development?" Melody asked Drew when the waiter left.

"My dad got me the gig. He's the president of the studio."

Right. Of course. More nepotism—the one trend that never went out of style among the rich and powerful.

Drew leaned back, swirling the ice around in his scotch. "I've got this great script I've been trying like hell to push through. It's an action thriller about this ex-marine SWAT rescue specialist who has to save his daughter when she gets kidnapped by a Mexican drug cartel."

"Wow," Melody said, nodding with phony enthusiasm, like a vapid pliable idiot with no opinions of her own. "That sounds great." Or, you know, like the exact same crappy action movie Hollywood had already made a hundred times. It would probably make gobs of money, though, which was why they kept churning them out.

"It's gonna be huge if we can get the right actor. We were *this* close to signing The Rock before he went with another project."

"That's too bad." It was the first sincere thing she'd said all night. She liked The Rock; she might almost be willing to see it if he were in it.

"Now we're in talks with Ben Stiller. It's looking pretty good so far. We'll see."

"I'm sorry, did you say Ben Stiller?" Melody couldn't quite manage to hide her disbelief. "As an ex-marine?"

Drew nodded, looking pleased with himself. "It's unexpected, right? No one would have pegged Liam Neeson as an action hero either, before the *Taken* movies."

No one except everybody who'd seen him in *Rob Roy*, or *Darkman*, or *The Phantom Menace*, but okay. Sure. Melody clamped down on her tongue and reached for her wine glass.

"Casting against type gives us an edge in the marketing. Now we just have to find our female lead. I'm thinking someone like Victoria Justice or Kate Upton."

"As the daughter?" Melody had assumed the daughter would be a teenager.

"No, the love interest. The daughter's barely in the movie. We'll probably cast an unknown to save money."

Melody barely managed to suppress an eye-roll. Of course they'd cast a love interest half the age of the male lead. This was exactly why she didn't go to movies unless they were based on a comic book or novel she liked.

"What happened to Ashley Decker?" Jeremy asked. "I thought you were trying to woo her."

Drew shook his head. "She's out—rehab. And not just drug rehab, either—that we could work around. Psychiatric." He lowered his voice on the last word, like saying it too loud might bring bad luck. It was the same way Melody's mother always said words like *cancer* or *divorce*—as if they were something you could catch from speaking them at full volume.

"Too bad," Jeremy said, shaking his head. "She was hot."

"Yeah, her dad and her manager were basically pawning her out around town to the highest bidder. Really messed her up."

"That's horrible," Melody said.

Drew shrugged. "You wouldn't even believe how common that sort of thing is. I could name a dozen others just like her. Disney Channel stars, pop singers, that cute kid who won the Oscar three years ago. This town chews people up and spits them out."

He said it like it was something that happened on its own, as if it had nothing to do with him or the people he worked with every day, and the things they tolerated and even encouraged in their quest to make money.

After the waiter dropped off their entrees, Melody changed the subject by asking Drew about his college days at BU. They got to reminiscing about Boston and eventually wound up in a debate over the relative merits of Dodger Stadium versus Fenway—which was patently ridiculous, there was no comparison with Fenway—but it kept the conversation going until the waiter came back to clear away their plates.

Which was when Lacey, who hadn't uttered a word for almost fifteen full minutes, turned to Melody and said, "Wait, how do you know Jeremy again?"

"I *told* you," Jeremy said, shooting Lacey a pointed look, "we met when I was visiting Drew in Boston a few years ago."

"Yeah, he picked her up at a bar and totally bailed on me," Drew said. "Dick move, by the way, bro."

Jeremy looked uncomfortable, but Lacey just nodded. "Ah, so *you're* one of the girls he cheated on my sister with." She raised her glass to Melody in a mock salute. "Welcome to the club."

Wait—what?

"Lacey," Jeremy said through clenched teeth.

"I'm sorry," Melody said slowly, turning to look at Jeremy. "*What?*"

She had no idea what Lacey was talking about, or what her sister had to do with anything, but Melody was not a cheater. Or a cheatee. She didn't do that kind of thing. Ever.

"Jeremy dated my sister, Charlotte, all through college," Lacey said with a careless shrug. "And while they were together, he sometimes slept with other girls." Her whole body was one big shrug. Her tone, her posture—everything about her expressed her indifference to the bomb she'd dropped.

Drew snorted into his drink. "Sometimes."

Melody stared at Lacey, trying to process all this new information. Jeremy used to date Lacey's *sister*? While he was away at college? Like, when he and Melody met? When they—*oh god.*

"It's not a big deal," Lacey said. "He cheated on her with me, too." This was just another thing she was apathetic about. She'd slept with her sister's boyfriend, but so what? Why would that be a big deal?

"Oh," Melody said, feeling numb. "Wow." She reached for her wineglass with a shaking hand and gulped down the last of her zinfandel.

"It was a long time ago," Jeremy said, like that somehow made it okay. Like it didn't matter that he was someone who'd habitually cheated on his girlfriend. That he'd cheated on her with Melody.

She was the other woman. He'd made her into the other woman and she hadn't even known.

Jeremy was still talking, trying to explain himself—trying to make excuses. "You have to understand, Charlotte and I were having some problems at the time—"

"Understatement of the year," Drew muttered.

"*Drew.* You're not really helping."

"I wasn't aware I was supposed to be," Drew replied with no trace of amusement.

Lacey pushed back her chair. "I'm going to the ladies' room."

Melody was frozen in place, paralyzed by complete and utter mortification. This whole night had been a disaster. She didn't belong in this world with these people. They were all awful. It had been a mistake to think she could be friends with them. She should have known better.

"Look, I'm sorry," Jeremy said. She felt his eyes on her, but refused to look at him. "I probably should have told you about Charlotte before now—"

"She didn't know?" Drew's voice dripped with disdain. "Nice, Jeremy."

"*Jesus Christ, Drew.*"

Melody got to her feet. "I think I feel a migraine coming on." Something inside her had finally snapped, and she couldn't stand to be there another second. "Thank you for dinner, and please say goodnight to Lacey for me." Grabbing her bag, she fled before anyone could say anything to stop her.

She made it all the way to the valet stand before Jeremy caught up with her. "Melody, wait. I'm sorry. I didn't mean for it to go this way."

She handed her ticket to one of the valets and rounded on Jeremy. "How did you mean for it to go, exactly?"

He threw his hands in the air. "I don't know, better than this. I just wanted you to meet some of my friends. I thought it would be fun. Obviously, I was wrong."

"Obviously," she repeated in a tone so bitter, it burned the back of her throat. "Why didn't you tell me you had a girlfriend back when we first met?"

Sighing, he pressed his lips together. "If I'd told you, you probably wouldn't have slept with me, and I really wanted you to sleep with me. I was kind of a shit-heel back then, in case that wasn't clear."

"But why didn't you tell me before now? How could you let me find out like this?" She was trying so hard not to cry. She hated crying when she was angry. She didn't want to cry in front of him. In front of all these people.

"I don't know. It's not exactly an easy thing to slip into conversation. I guess I was ashamed." He shoved his hands into his pockets, deflating a little. "Maybe I was afraid you'd look at me the way you're looking at me right now."

"I can't believe you," she said, unmoved by his kicked puppy face. "You looked me right in the eye and told me you don't go around asking women out behind your girlfriend's back."

"I don't."

She crossed her arms, glaring at him. "But you used to—all the time, apparently."

He ducked his head in guilt. "I told you I'm not that guy anymore."

"So you keep saying."

"Because it's the truth. Look, I'm sorry I deceived you, Melody, and I'm sorry I cheated on Charlotte. I'm not proud of my past. If I could go back and change it, I would, but I can't."

He seemed sincere, but then he would, wouldn't he? That was probably a big part of his job, too: looking people in the eye and selling whatever story he needed them to believe. He probably didn't even have to work hard at it. He was probably a natural born liar.

"This was such a mistake," she muttered, shaking her head. "What am I even doing here?"

"I thought we could be friends," Jeremy said. "We still can be."

He wasn't the person she'd thought he was when she met him three years ago. He was a liar and a cheat, and the more time she spent with him, the more he made her into a liar and a cheat, too.

The valet pulled up with her MINI Cooper and jumped out to hold the door for her.

"I'm sorry," Melody said, backing away from Jeremy. "You're not the kind of person I want to be friends with."

She handed the valet his tip, got into her car, and drove away without looking back.

Chapter Seven

---

*M*elody spent all day Sunday dreading the inevitable call from Jeremy to offer some pathetic attempt at an apology, but it never came. Then she spent all day at work on Monday expecting him to show up at her desk to try to talk to her in person, but he didn't.

Instead, Lacey called her on Wednesday. Which was...weird.

"So, there's this yoga class I go to sometimes on Saturday mornings," Lacey said, like they'd all had a perfectly nice time last weekend and were totally friends now. "I was wondering if you wanted to come with me."

"Yoga?" Melody didn't think Lacey even liked her. Why would she invite her to a yoga class out of the blue? Could she be planning some kind of *Carrie*-type prank? Were there going to be buckets of pig's blood waiting for her at the yoga studio?

"I don't know if you're into yoga or not," Lacey said, "but I've got a free guest pass if you want to try it out. Or not. Whatever."

Melody chewed on her bottom lip. "Why are you asking me? Did Jeremy put you up to this?"

"No," Lacey said. "And I wouldn't have done it if he had, believe me."

"Okaaay," Melody said, not sure what to believe.

Lacey sighed. "Look, I feel bad about the other night, all right? There's some stuff going on with me and Jeremy, and with Jeremy and Drew, that has nothing to do with you. We shouldn't have dragged you into it like that. I could tell from your face you had no idea Jeremy was with my sister back when you—you know. Anyway, I thought you already knew about all that stuff. I honestly didn't mean to ambush you."

"It's fine," Melody said stiffly. "Like he said, it was a long time ago."

"Yeah, well, he told me you were new in town and didn't know anybody. A bunch of the women at yoga usually go out for coffee after class, so I thought it might be a way for you to meet some new people. It's cool if you're not interested, though."

"No, I'm interested," Melody said. It did sound like a way to make some friends, and it was always possible Lacey was actually being nice and not secretly plotting her public humiliation. "It sounds great, actually. Thank you."

"Cool." Lacey gave her the name and address of the yoga studio, and told her to meet her there five minutes before class so she could sign her in.

What the heck? Melody thought. *How hard can it be to get pig's blood out of yoga pants, anyway?*

"YOU'VE DONE YOGA BEFORE, RIGHT?" Lacey asked as Melody walked up to the yoga studio. In her cute patterned sports bra and matching capri tights, Lacey looked just like a Lululemon model. She even had the abs of a Lululemon model. Yay.

"Yep," Melody said, trying not to feel self-conscious about her T-shirt and plain black yoga pants from Old Navy. "Totally done yoga before."

Doing yoga in her living room along with DVDs counted, right? At least she had her own yoga mat, and knew her downward-facing dog from her triangle pose. Okay, so sometimes she got the warrior poses mixed up, but she figured she knew enough to fake her way through it.

"Have you been doing this class long?" Melody asked as she followed Lacey inside.

"Almost a year." She bent over a clipboard sitting on the desk inside the door and reached for a pen. "Tessa's an amazing instructor. You're gonna love her. She's gotten my mayurasana at least fifteen degrees higher."

"Cool." Melody nodded like she knew what that meant. "I only fall down on tree pose like half the time now."

"You're adorable," Lacey said, smiling at her.

"Um...so, is this like a beginner class or intermediate?" Melody asked, eyeing the other women coming in. They all looked more or less like Lacey: abs of steel, Wonder Woman thighs, butts to die for. Melody was starting to worry she might be in for something worse than pig's blood.

Lacey laughed. "Come on, I'll introduce you to Tessa."

IT WASN'T a beginner or an intermediate class, Melody quickly discovered. It was an *advanced* yoga class. Like, super-advanced. Superhuman, maybe. She refused to believe it was possible to contort yourself into those ridiculous positions without the benefit of actual superpowers.

Melody struggled her way through the warm-up, more or less managing to keep up, but once they moved on to the real practice, she was done for and ended up alternating between downward-facing dog and child's pose for most of the class. Meanwhile, on the next mat over, Lacey moved smoothly and flawlessly through one gravity-defying pose after another like some sort of magical forest elf.

"Wow," Melody said, stooping to roll up her mat when it was finally over. "That was some class."

Lacey mopped the sweat from her face and grinned. "I hope you didn't feel too left behind. You did really well for your first time."

"Oh sure, I corpse-posed like a boss there at the end."

Lacey laughed. "Hey, you hung in there longer than I did my first time."

"Seriously?"

"Seriously." Lacey slung a sweaty arm around Melody's shoulders and steered her toward the door. "Coffee's my treat."

THE COFFEE PART was pretty great. All the women with the Wonder Woman thighs were super welcoming and supportive of Melody's novice efforts. But the biggest surprise was Lacey, who turned out to be friendly, sociable, and genuinely nice—so basically a completely different person from the one Melody met last weekend.

She remembered Lacey saying there was some stuff going on with her and Jeremy, and she wondered if they'd had a fight that night, or if Lacey was always like that when she was around him. Not that it mattered. Melody was done with Jeremy Sauer.

She wouldn't mind being friends with his girlfriend, though. She and Lacey had a lot more in common than Melody had expected. Lacey didn't come from money like Jeremy and Drew— her father was a cop and her mother taught English at Los Angeles City College.

At the moment, Lacey was a bartender, and she'd worked part time to put herself through UCLA, so she was no stranger to minimum wage. She and Melody had a good time bonding over their shittiest shitty jobs.

"Definitely pizza delivery," Lacey said. "After a while, the smell made me want to die. And I could never get it out of my car. I had to sell that thing—that's how bad it was. To this day, I still can't touch the stuff."

Melody could top that easily. "You know those poor bastards dressed up like the Statue of Liberty who stand around on street corners during tax season?"

Lacey's eyes went wide. "You didn't."

Melody nodded. "During high school. And everyone I went to school with would honk at me whenever they drove by, which they did a *lot* because the tax place was on a busy street near our school."

"Oh my god, that's the worst," Lacey said, laughing.

"It totally was."

"But hey, now you've got a big fancy corporate job."

"I wouldn't exactly call it big or fancy. My desk is literally in a closet. And my mom has no understanding of what I do for a living. Every time I try to explain it, she just tunes out and then changes the subject—usually to how disappointed she is I'm not married yet."

Lacey huffed out a humorless laugh. "Can't win, I guess. My mom's terrified I'm gonna marry Jeremy and turn into some lazy socialite. Not that my parents are wild about me bartending, either. They'd rather see me in law school, like my perfect sister." She looked down at her hands as she twisted an engraved silver ring on her index finger. Her fingers were long and slender, but the nails were all bitten down to the quick, just like Jeremy's.

"But do you like what you do?" Melody asked. "That's all that matters."

"It's okay. The tips are pretty great where I am now, but it's not the sort of thing you grow up dreaming about doing, you know?"

"I did," Melody said.

Lacey snorted. "Sure."

"I'm serious. My mom worked as a cocktail waitress to put herself through cosmetology school. I remember watching her hustle drinks and thinking the bartenders had it made. They had a special skill, you know? They weren't just carrying around stuff other people made. For, like, two whole years when I was a kid, I totally wanted to be a bartender when I grew up. Until I got into computers."

"That's sweet." Lacey smiled, then shook her head, looking wistful. "I don't know, I keep thinking one day I'll figure out what I want to do with my life. But I'm still waiting for inspiration to strike."

"Don't listen to her," Tessa, the yoga instructor said, coming over to join them. She squeezed in beside Lacey and gave her a one-armed hug.

Tessa was lithe, tan, and relentlessly positive, in that way the best fitness instructors tended to be. Her blonde hair was braided loosely down her back with a few wavy tendrils falling around her face—the perfect beachy waves, just like all the hair products and beauty magazines promised but never delivered.

"She knows exactly what she wants to do," Tessa said, giving Lacey an affectionate shake. "She's just afraid to do it."

"What do you want to do?" Melody asked.

Lacey shook her head at Tessa, blushing. "Stop."

"She wants to go to the police academy like her father," Tessa told Melody.

Melody was impressed. The physical requirements alone sounded terrifying, not to mention the whole carrying a gun and going after criminals of it all.

"Yeah, and there's no way my dad will ever let that happen," Lacey said bitterly. "Every time I mention it, he looks like he's going to have a stroke."

"You shouldn't let that stop you," Melody said. "If it's really what you want, you can't let anyone else talk you out of it."

"That's exactly what I keep telling her," Tessa said, beaming at Melody. "You did great today, by the way. You've got a lot of potential."

"I don't know about that." Melody ducked her head shyly. "But thanks. I really enjoyed the class."

"You're coming back next week, right?" Lacey asked.

"Yeah," Melody said, smiling. "I definitely am."

Chapter Eight

*L*ife in LA started to settle into a routine, and Saturday yoga became a part of that routine.

After only a few weeks, Melody was already making some real, albeit incremental, progress. Tessa was an excellent teacher. She had a soothing, encouraging manner that made you believe you could do anything simply because she believed in you. She was one of those people who'd probably be calm and reassuring even in the middle of the zombie apocalypse. She'd be the character on *The Walking Dead* swinging a machete with the grace of a ballet dancer while doling out inspirational advice.

Lacey only made it to Saturday yoga about half the time, but she always came to coffee afterward when she did show up. Sometimes she'd be super chatty and friendly, and other days, she seemed moody and withdrawn. Melody couldn't help wondering if it had anything to do with Jeremy, but she was afraid to ask since Lacey almost never talked about him.

Melody hadn't seen hide nor hair of Jeremy since the night of that disastrous dinner—which was fortuitous, considering they worked in the same building. Sauer Hewson was a big company, though, and it wasn't like they moved in the same circles. He was way up on one of the executive levels, and Melody was down in the bowels of the IT department. They might as well be a world apart.

She still hadn't managed to make any friends at work. It was a lot harder making friends in the real world than it had been in college. In college, you could make friends without even trying. There was a never-ending supply of people your own age you ran into all the time—in class, the residence hall, study lounges, computer labs, dining areas—and everyone always seemed open to making new friends.

The people she worked with now didn't seem particularly interested in being friends. They already had friends, apparently. Or they had families. Not that they were unfriendly. They were friendly-ish, they just weren't friends.

The women at yoga were friendlier, but they hadn't crossed over to being friends, either. Melody wasn't actually sure how you were supposed to cross that barrier in the real world. She chatted with the yoga ladies at coffee every week, but no one ever suggested doing anything else. There were no invitations to get together for dinner or go to a movie sometime. Everyone just drank their coffee, then went their separate ways until the next yoga class.

But things were fine. Work was fine. Los Angeles was fine. Her life was fine.

Things were so fine, the days blurred together. There was no changing of the seasons in Los Angeles, not like Boston, or even Florida, where she'd grown up. In Florida, there was a rainy season, a temperate season, and a hotter-than-the-seventh-circle-of-hell season. In LA, the weather always seemed more or less exactly the same, which made it easy to lose track of the days. Somehow, June came and went without Melody really noticing. She woke up one morning and it was July first, the one-year anniversary of Kieran's death.

She tried to pretend she was fine. It was just a number. A

meaningless, arbitrary anniversary, like President's Day or National Pancake Day—only, you know, horrible. Nothing was any different than it had been the day before. It couldn't possibly hurt any more than it had on any other day.

Only...it did. It hurt a lot more.

She almost called in sick, but the thought of sitting around her apartment alone all day was more daunting than sitting around at work trying to pretend there was nothing wrong. At least at work she'd have something to distract her.

So Melody went into the office and tried not to think about it. She'd finished re-imaging the servers and been assigned to a hardware audit, which meant going from office to office checking the serial numbers on all the computer equipment and making sure people had what they were supposed to have. It was more busywork, but at least it got her out of her dreary office and forced her to interact with other humans. She didn't enjoy making small talk with strangers, but it kept her from thinking about Kieran and the hell she'd gone through on this date a year ago.

She worked straight through lunch and on past five o'clock. Unable to bear the thought of going home to her empty apartment, she kept working until the whole building had emptied out. Until she'd done all her work for the rest of the week, and some of next week, too—anything to keep busy.

Sometime after eight, it belatedly occurred to her that she hadn't eaten all day. She didn't feel hungry, but knew she should probably try to eat something. There was nothing in her apartment but depressing frozen dinners, so she thought she'd treat herself and stop somewhere on the way home. Maybe sushi.

The sushi in LA was amazing. You could go to any random hole-in-the-wall sushi place in some desperate-looking strip center and the sushi would be a thousand times better than anywhere back home.

Sushi would definitely cheer her up. She couldn't believe she'd actually given it up, along with pretty much everything delicious in life, for eight whole months because Kieran had decided to go vegan—

Then she was thinking about Kieran and blinking back tears. Because Kieran was dead. It had been a whole year, and Kieran was still dead, and it was still her fault.

Melody grabbed her purse and ran out of the office, praying she didn't run into anyone on the way. Fortunately, it was late enough that the only person she saw was the security guard in the lobby, who barely looked up from his sudoku as she hurried past.

She made it all the way to the relative privacy of her car and managed to get in and lock the doors before falling completely apart.

After Kieran died, Melody had cried herself to sleep every night for an entire month until she'd run out of tears. It still hurt as much as ever, but she hadn't cried once since. Not even while watching the *Fringe* series finale, or the "Doomsday" episode of *Doctor Who*, or any of the things that usually made her reach for the Kleenex. It was like her tear glands had given up the ghost and retired from the crying business altogether.

But, now, a whole year's worth of tears came all at once, like her body had been saving them up for one truly tremendous breakdown. Melody crossed her arms over the steering wheel, hunched forward in the driver's seat, and sobbed uncontrollably.

She had no idea how long she'd been at it when a tap on the passenger-side window startled her.

Jerking upright, she saw Jeremy frowning at her through the window. Of course. Of all the people who could have happened by, it *had* to be him.

"Are you okay?" he shouted through the glass.

"Do I look okay?" she shouted back, swiping at her face.

"Not really."

She dug around in her glovebox for a pack of tissues. "Please go away."

"Melody, there's no way I'm leaving you alone in a parking

garage crying." He tried the door handle, but it was locked. "Will you please let me in so we can talk?"

Why did he have to show up now, of all times? Why couldn't he have kept walking instead of trying to be all chivalrous?

"I don't want to talk to you," she said, and blew her nose.

"Fair enough. But if I have to keep shouting at you through the glass, security's going to notice and it won't just be me standing here trying to talk to you."

Melody grudgingly hit the unlock button, and Jeremy folded himself into the passenger seat. "What happened?" he asked, twisting to face her. The top of his head nearly reached the ceiling of her little MINI Cooper.

"Nothing."

"That's clearly a lie."

She blew her nose again, choosing to remain silent.

"Do you want to talk about it?"

"No." She folded her arms and stared straight ahead. What she wanted was for him to get out of her car and leave her alone.

"Do you want me to drive you home?"

"I can drive myself home as soon as you get out of my car," she said through clenched teeth.

She saw him shake his head out the corner of her eye. "You shouldn't drive when you're this upset. If you want to go home, I'll drive you—or I'll put you in a cab if you'd rather, but you're not driving." He waited. "Do you want to go home?"

She blew out a long breath and leaned back against the head-rest. "Not really."

"Did something happen at the office?"

She swiveled her head to glare at him. "I told you I don't want to talk about it. If you can't respect that, you can just get out."

"Fine," he said, putting up his hands in a pacifying gesture. "I won't ask you any more questions."

"Good."

"Except one—"

"Jeremy—"

"It's not what you think."

Melody sighed loudly. "What?"

"Do you like ice cream?"

She blinked. "What?"

"Ice cream," he repeated, absolutely serious. "Do you like it?"

"Of course I like ice cream. Who doesn't like ice cream? What does that—"

"Get out and trade seats with me," he said. "I'm taking you for ice cream."

"What? No. Why?"

"Whenever my sister or I were upset, our dad would take us out for ice cream, and it always made us feel better."

Melody lifted her glasses and rubbed her eyes. "You honestly think ice cream is going to fix my problems?"

"No, but it will make you feel better." Jeremy tilted his head, a smile curling at the corner of his mouth. "You know it will. Come on, get out so I can drive. I know this great place that's only five minutes away."

The thing was, now that he'd put the thought in her head, ice cream sounded pretty great. "Can you drive a stick?" she asked him doubtfully.

His expression turned disgruntled. "I'm offended you would even ask me that."

"Sorry," she said, opening the door and getting out. "Not everyone learned to drive in Maseratis and Lamborghinis, Mr. Playboy Billionaire."

Jeremy came around and got behind the wheel while Melody sank into the passenger seat and fastened her seatbelt.

"For your information, I learned to drive in a nineteen eighty-nine Ford pickup," he said, starting the engine.

She raised her eyebrows. "Really?"

He put the car into reverse, eased his foot off the clutch, and smoothly backed out of the parking space. "It was the gardener's truck," he admitted, shifting into first. "I may have sort of stolen it and gone joyriding."

"I knew it," Melody said, smiling despite herself. "Spoiled brat."

Jeremy grinned and let out the clutch.

"Do you want to try some of my rocky road?" Jeremy offered. "It's really good."

"No thanks." Melody wasn't a fan of nuts. And she was thoroughly enjoying her cookie dough ice cream with hot fudge sauce.

They were the only customers, and the place had technically closed five minutes ago, but after the enormous tip Jeremy gave the guy behind the counter, he didn't seem to mind them hanging around.

"Look, Melody," Jeremy said, frowning, "I'm not trying to pry, but if something happened to you at work, I really wish you'd tell me. Or at least tell human resources."

"It doesn't have anything to do with work."

"Okay." He went back to eating his ice cream and didn't ask any more questions, just like he promised. The only sound was the heavy thrum of the freezers and the occasional buzz of a fluorescent bulb loose in its fixture.

Melody stabbed at a congealing chunk of hot fudge with her spoon. "It's today's date," she said, feeling like she owed him some kind of explanation. "Something—" She grimaced with the effort of getting the words out. "Someone died. A year ago today."

Jeremy nodded. He didn't ask who, just waited to see if she wanted to tell him anything else.

She didn't. She hadn't even wanted to tell him that much. She hated talking about it. She hated anyone even knowing about it.

"The first couple years after my dad died," he said when it was clear she wasn't going to volunteer any more details, "it was hard whenever the anniversary rolled around. For all of us. My sister—"

He stopped and pressed his lips together. "She got into some trouble. Always around that time of year."

"I'm fine," Melody insisted, which she realized was a ridiculous thing to say to someone who had found her bawling her eyes out.

"It gets easier," Jeremy said without bothering to contradict her. "It doesn't go away, but you learn how to live with it. It just becomes another part of you. Like scar tissue."

She blew out an unsteady breath. "I don't want it to be a part of me." Her voice wavered a little, and she winced, hating how weak she sounded.

"I know," he said gently. "But it'll always be there. That's what's so hard. You have to figure out how to live with what's left behind."

Melody nodded. "When you come out of the storm, you won't be the same person who walked in."

"Exactly. I like that."

"It's from a book. *Kafka on the Shore*."

"I'll have to check it out." He pulled out his phone. "K-A-F-K-A?"

"Yeah, it's by Haruki Murakami. It's one of my favorite books."

He nodded, smiling to himself as he typed. "Then I'll definitely check it out."

She swallowed a big chunk of cookie dough. "It's about running away."

He looked up at her. "Is that why you moved out here? Were you running away?"

She shrugged, stirring her melting ice cream around with her spoon. "Kind of. Maybe. Probably." She thought about it. "Mostly, I just wanted a fresh start. But I guess that's sort of the same thing."

"Did it work?"

"No. Wherever you go, you always take yourself with you."

The look he gave her was soft and sympathetic. "That's not necessarily a bad thing, you know."

It was difficult to reconcile this side of him with the other things she knew about him. She genuinely liked this Jeremy—the one who was a good listener, and who took her for ice cream because she was sad. The Jeremy who was kind and compassionate and genuine. This was who she remembered spending the night with in Boston three years ago. It was who she'd hoped to get to know again when she moved to Los Angeles.

He pushed his empty cup away. "I tried running away from everything after my dad died," he said without looking at her. "Took his favorite car out of the garage and went on a bender. I thought I could drink the pain away. Instead, I ended up totaling the car and giving myself a concussion." His mouth twisted at the memory. "I was lucky that's all the damage I did. It was stupid and selfish, and it didn't even help."

"It was my boyfriend," Melody found herself saying, so softly, it was almost a whisper. "The person who died was my boyfriend." She had to brace herself to get the next words out. "He killed himself."

Jeremy cringed. "Jesus..." He looked at her helplessly. What else could he say to something that awful? It was the ultimate conversation stopper.

She let out a breath that was half laugh and half sob. "I don't know why I told you that. I never talk about Kieran. With anyone. For some reason, I keep wanting to trust you even though you haven't given me any reason to." She tucked a stray wisp of hair behind her ear and shook her head.

"I have a trustworthy face," Jeremy said, flashing his charming smile—the one he used on hostesses and girls in bars.

Melody frowned and looked away. She detested that slick playboy act of his.

"Sorry," he said, dropping the smile. "You *can* trust me, Melody. But I understand if you don't."

The guy working at the shop was off in the back somewhere, whistling a tune she couldn't make out. *We should go,* she thought. *He's waiting for us to leave so he can lock up. I should tell Jeremy to drive me back to the garage so he can get his car.*

"It was my fault Kieran killed himself," she said instead.

Jeremy shook his head. "I don't believe that."

"You don't even know what happened. If you knew the whole story..." She shuddered.

"It doesn't matter. Whatever you think you did, there's no way it was your fault."

"We had a fight. I found out he'd been selling prescription drugs on campus and threatened to break up with him if he didn't stop. He stormed out, then a few days later, they found him. He'd taken a whole bottle of tranquilizers."

She never should have let him leave that night. She should have followed him. At the very least, she should have checked on him instead of leaving him on his own for days. She knew he was bipolar; she just hadn't realized how serious it was. She hadn't ever thought he was a suicide risk. He'd been on medication to manage it, and most of the time, it worked pretty well. It had kept him more or less level—until suddenly it hadn't.

Jeremy laid his hand over hers. "It wasn't your fault."

She blew out a shaky breath. "That's not what his mother told me."

"That was her grief talking. It wasn't fair of her to put that on you."

Melody jerked her hand away from his and dried her face with a napkin. She didn't deserve absolution, and she certainly didn't want it from him.

"Anyway," she said, sniffling, "now you know what an awful person I actually am. And a total hypocrite, too, judging you for cheating on your girlfriend. Bet you never killed anyone, huh?"

He winced. "Melody—"

"It's fine," she said, waving her hand. "I mean, it's not fine, clearly. It's awful. But I'll get through it."

Jeremy smiled at her—not the smug grin he used for flirting, but a softer, more sincere smile. "I know you will."

"We should probably go," she said, pushing her chair back and standing up. It was too hard to look at him when he was being this nice to her.

Jeremy chucked his ice cream cup in the trash, then drove her back to the Sauer Hewson garage. Before he got into his own car, he gave her a hug.

It was the first hug she'd had in months. Even though it was brief and sort of awkward, it felt good in a way she was afraid to let herself think about too much.

Chapter Nine

*A*fter the Night of Embarrassing Crying and Ice Cream, Melody was even more apprehensive about running into Jeremy at work. She was afraid things would be weird between them—or weirder, she supposed. It wasn't like they weren't plenty weird before.

Just her luck, it happened only a few days later.

"Afternoon," Jeremy said, coming up behind her as she waited for the elevator in the lobby.

Melody started at the sound of his voice, but schooled her expression before turning to greet him. "Afternoon, Mr. Sauer!" she chirped with more enthusiasm than necessary. Great. She sounded like a deranged talking Barbie. Way to be cool.

If he thought she was acting weird, he didn't show it. He simply offered a benign smile, like everything was perfectly normal between them—like he hadn't watched her cry into a scoop of cookie dough ice cream the other night. Amazingly, he didn't look at her like she was broken or sad or deserving of his pity, and she was so grateful for that.

She wanted to tell him how grateful she was, but that would

mean acknowledging the other night had happened in the first place, which she preferred to avoid at all costs.

The elevator doors opened, and he gestured for her to precede him.

"What floor?" she asked as she punched in the number for hers.

"Twenty."

Of course. The executive level.

They passed the short ride to the fifth floor in silence. But it wasn't uncomfortable. It was more...companionable. Normal. Just two coworkers, riding the elevator together. It wasn't weird at all...weirdly.

"Enjoy the rest of your day," Jeremy said when the doors opened.

"You too." Melody exited the elevator. Just before the doors closed, she snuck a look back at him. He lifted his hand, smiling as the elevator slid shut.

That hadn't been so bad after all. She'd survived with her dignity mostly intact. Letting out a relieved breath, Melody headed to her office with a lighter step than usual.

LACEY DIDN'T SHOW up at yoga that week, but the following Saturday when she did, Melody couldn't help but wonder if Jeremy had said anything to her. He must have, right? Lacey was his girlfriend. He probably told her everything.

Lacey didn't say anything about it when she greeted Melody before class, though, and she didn't seem to treat her any differently. At coffee afterward, Melody was fidgety, waiting for her to bring it up, but Lacey just talked about work and the contemporary dance company she and Tessa had gone to see during the week.

Maybe Jeremy hadn't told her after all? Or maybe he'd asked her not to say anything?

Melody couldn't decide whether she should raise the subject with Lacey herself. She didn't want it to seem like she was keeping it from her, or that she was spending time with Jeremy behind Lacey's back. The problem was, she couldn't figure out how to bring it up. *"Oh, by the way, your boyfriend found me blubbering in my car over my dead ex and took me out for ice cream,"* didn't exactly slip into casual conversation.

But the biggest thing holding Melody back was that she really, *really* didn't want to talk about Kieran anymore. If she brought it up to Lacey, they'd have to talk about it.

"You okay?" Lacey asked Melody as they were walking out.

"Why?" Melody braced herself.

Lacey tossed her empty coffee cup in the trash and pushed the door open with her hip. "I dunno. You seem distracted."

"I'm fine," Melody said, squeezing her to-go cup as she followed her outside.

"All right." Lacey shrugged and dug in her bag for her keys. "I'll see you next week," she said, waving as she headed for her car.

Apparently, they weren't talking about it.

Over the next few weeks, Melody bumped into Jeremy a handful more times at work, and he was always pleasant and professional, and didn't treat her any differently than anyone else. By then, Melody's coworkers had begun to notice the CEO's son knew her by name, and a few had responded by acting friendlier toward her, while others had grown even colder than before. She honestly had more respect for the ones who were chillier—at least they weren't pretending to kiss her ass.

"Good morning," Melody said, getting in line behind Jeremy at the coffee cart in the lobby.

"Good morning," he replied, directing a smile her way before giving the barista his order: a soy cinnamon latte, just like he'd ordered the last two times she'd seen him at the coffee cart.

"It's funny," Melody mused while he was waiting for his latte, "the first couple months I worked here, I never saw you at all, but now I seem to run into you all the time."

He reached across her to stuff a few bills in the tip jar and lowered his voice. "That's because I was avoiding you."

The admission took her by surprise. "You were?"

He glanced around to make sure no one else was close enough to overhear. "You made it pretty clear you didn't want anything to do with me, and the last thing I wanted was to make you uncomfortable at work. So, whenever I saw you around the building, I just...went somewhere else."

Melody winced at the memory of how harshly she'd spoken to him outside the restaurant. "I feel bad. You shouldn't have had to do that."

"It did cut my latte habit back," he said, patting his stomach as though it had ever been anything other than washboard flat. "Which wasn't necessarily a bad thing."

She rolled her eyes. "Well, I'm glad you're not doing it anymore. It's much easier this way, isn't it?"

"Definitely."

"Oh, how was Passenger?" At yoga on Saturday, Lacey had mentioned they had tickets to see them play at the Wiltern.

"What?" His face scrunched in confusion.

"The concert? Lacey said you guys were going to see them last night?"

"Oh, right. Yeah." His expression had gone flat. "We didn't end up going. Well, I didn't."

"Why not?"

He shrugged and lowered his eyes. "I had to work. She took one of her friends instead."

"Work on a Sunday night? Wow. Must have been something important."

He blew out a puff of air that might have been a laugh. "Yeah."

It seemed like there was more going on, but he clearly didn't want to talk about it, so Melody dropped it. Maybe they'd had another fight. Whatever. It wasn't any of her business.

The barista dropped off Jeremy's latte. "Here you are, Mr. Sauer."

"Thank you," he said, flashing his killer smile as he picked up his order. He gave Melody a nod. "I'll see you later," he said, hurrying off.

IT WAS eleven o'clock on a Wednesday night, and Melody was curled up around her laptop, watching Netflix in bed. It was what she did most nights to fall asleep. Cueing up one of her favorite shows lulled her brain into stillness as she listened to the dialogue she knew by heart and watched the characters as familiar as old friends.

After a few episodes, the judgmental dialogue box popped up, inquiring if she was still watching. *Mind your own business, Netflix,* she thought as she reached out from beneath the covers and tapped the trackpad to dismiss it. As the next episode started up, she burrowed deeper into her pillow and tucked her favorite fuzzy blanket under her chin.

The thing they didn't tell you about LA was that it could get *cold* at night, even in the summer. Not Boston cold, but colder than Melody's thin Florida blood had expected to encounter in sunny Southern California. She'd grown up in a swamp, but Los Angeles was a desert, and deserts got cold at night. As soon as the sun went down, the temperature went down with it. It was a different kind of cold than she was used to—different than the damp, frigid winters in Boston. Something about the dryness and contrast to the glaring daytime sunlight left her with chills she couldn't shake, like a fever or sunburn—hence the pile of blankets on her bed in July.

Melody's phone vibrated on the nightstand, startling her out of her *Parks and Recreation* episode. She paused the playback on her computer and stretched out a reluctant hand for the phone, expecting to see her mom's name on the screen.

It wasn't her mom. It was Jeremy.

"I'm sorry to call so late," he said when she answered. "I hope I didn't wake you."

"Nope," she said. "What's up?"

"I'm in trouble. I need your help."

She sat up, kicking off her blankets. "What's wrong?"

"It's my laptop. I did something really stupid to it and I've got this big presentation tomorrow morning and Geoffrey's counting on me and I don't know what I'm going to do." He was speaking so fast, the words all came out in a rush that was hard to follow.

"Wait, slow down. What's wrong with your laptop?"

"I spilled a latte on it, and now I can't get it to boot up, and my presentation is on there."

"Okaaay. But you have it backed up, right?"

"No...which I realize now was stupid."

"Pretty stupid, yeah."

"Melody!" There was an edge of panic in his voice.

"Well, it is!" she said, because seriously? People who didn't back up their work deserved what they got.

"I need your help. Please tell me there's a way to salvage that presentation."

"Yeah, no problem." It was probably a super simple fix, if you knew what you were doing. Which she totally did.

"Really?"

"Pffft, yeah. Do you have an extra laptop? One you can use tomorrow for the presentation?"

"I can get one."

"Okay, bring it and your broken one over to my place—I'll text you the address."

He blew out a long breath. "Thank you. You're a lifesaver."

A half hour later, Jeremy showed up on her doorstep clutching both laptops like they were the tablets of the covenant brought down from Mount Sinai. "I really appreciate you doing this," he said, gray-faced.

He was still in his work clothes, his tie loosened and hair rumpled like he'd been dragging his hands through it repeatedly, yet somehow, it managed to make him look even more like a *GQ* model than usual, which was really unfair. Melody couldn't help feeling underdressed and slovenly standing next to him in her threadbare hoodie and yoga pants—even though this was her apartment and *she* was the one doing *him* a favor in the middle of the night.

"This way." She led him through the living room and into the spare bedroom she'd set up as an office. "Give me the dead one."

Without a word, he handed her one of the laptops. The keyboard was good and sticky, smelled faintly of cinnamon, and— yep, nothing happened when she tried the power button.

Jeremy watched her, rubbing his palms on his thighs like a kid in the principal's office.

"Not to fear," she said, digging around in her desk for a screwdriver.

She removed the battery, opened the laptop case, and popped out the old hard drive, which fortunately looked to have survived The Great Latte Incident unscathed. It took a few minutes of digging through all the boxes of computer equipment she had stacked in the corner to find the right disk enclosure for Jeremy's hard drive, but eventually, she put her hands on the one she needed.

"You've practically got a whole IT department of your own in here," he said with a raised eyebrow.

"I like to tinker in my free time. Kind of a hobby." It used to be, anyway. Back in college, she'd made extra money by building computers out of refurbished parts and selling them to her fellow students, but she hadn't touched any of this stuff since she'd moved.

"Lucky for me, I guess."

She smiled at him as she slotted the hard drive into the external case and attached the connector pins. "Go ahead and boot up that other laptop."

By the time it was up and running, she was ready with the external hard drive, which she plugged into the USB. "There you go," she said when the file list showed up onscreen.

"Is it there?" Leaning over the desk, he reached for the trackpad and double-clicked on a file name. "Oh thank god," he breathed when a PowerPoint presentation opened up.

"You can just copy all your old files over to the new laptop and you'll be good as gold."

Jeremy beamed the full force of his thousand-watt smile at her. "You're amazing."

She felt her cheeks warm. "It's no big deal."

"I thought for sure I'd lost all of my work. I can't believe you got it back."

"It was nothing. Easy as one, ten, eleven."

He stared at her, uncomprehending.

"It's a binary joke. See, it's funny if you know that one, two, three in binary is—" She stopped and shook her head. "You know what? Never mind, it's not that funny if you have to explain it."

The way he was gazing at her, with a weird sort-of smile on his face, made her feel self-conscious. Which made her babble reflex kick into a higher gear.

"You know what they say," she blurted out before she could stop herself, "there are only ten kinds of people in the world: those who know binary and those who don't." She laughed nervously. "I've got like a whole stable of binary jokes. They really killed in the Comp Sci department. Hexadecimal jokes, too, like—"

"Thank you," Jeremy interrupted before she could keep going. Then he hugged her.

"You're...welcome?" she said into his shoulder. This wasn't one of those fleeting hugs like their hug in the parking garage had been. This time, Jeremy's arms tightened around her, and he sort of sagged against her and just...hung out like that for a while.

On the one hand, it felt nice—like, *really* nice. It was the most action she'd gotten since Kieran—yeah, *so* not going there. Suffice it to say, it had been a long time since anyone other than her mom had held her like this, and Jeremy was an exceptional hugger... which was a problem. Standing there in his arms made her think about the last time he'd held her in his arms, three years ago, which was not something she should be thinking about right now. Because—and this was the other thing—he had a girlfriend. A girlfriend Melody was friends with. Hugging your friend's boyfriend for a weirdly long time when you were alone together in your apartment late at night was a *very bad thing*.

Just before she worked up the courage to pull away, Jeremy let go and dropped into the chair in front of the computer. "This is great," he said, reaching for the trackpad again.

"Uh huh." Melody adjusted her glasses. "So, uh—what's so all-fired important about this presentation anyway?"

He frowned at the screen as he dragged his files over from the external drive to the laptop. "Geoffrey Horvath, the CFO—he's giving his quarterly presentation to the board tomorrow morning and asked me to prepare the financial benchmarking analysis. It's a lot of responsibility because it's a huge portion of the presentation—which...evidently, I should not have been trusted with."

"Hey." She touched his shoulder, and he looked up without meeting her eyes. "You did just fine. Everything's going to be okay."

He gave her a half-hearted nod and turned back to the computer screen.

She realized her hand was still on his shoulder and shoved it behind her back. "You'll see. Mr. Horvath is going to rock that presentation tomorrow because of you."

Jeremy pressed his lips together and shook his head. "Believe it or not, my career to date has not exactly been marked by success."

"Come on, it can't be that bad."

He shook his head again, his eyes still fixed on the screen. "I've been a screw-up for so much of my life, I don't think I know how to be anything else. I've been trying to do better, to do what my father would have wanted, but I don't know what I'm doing half the time, and it feels like everyone's just waiting for me to fuck up again."

"That's not true," Melody said. He looked so defeated—and so vulnerable. It wasn't something she ever would have expected from him.

His tongue skimmed over his bottom lip. "Trust me," he said, still dragging files over from one hard drive to the other. "Corporate politics is pretty much kill or be killed. Most of the people at Sauer Hewson would be perfectly happy to step over my corpse if they thought it would help them get ahead. Even my mother—" He broke off, shaking his head again, and Melody's heart constricted at the look on his face. "She says she wants me to succeed, but it feels like all she sees are my mistakes.

"Geoffrey's the only one—" He hesitated, blowing out a breath. "Sometimes it feels like Geoffrey's the only one who actually believes in me. He was my dad's best friend and he's been great these last few years, looking out for my mom, my sister, and me. He's sticking his neck out to champion me at the company and I just—I really don't want to let him down."

"You won't." Melody hated seeing him like this. He'd worked so hard and didn't deserve to feel like a failure over one dumb accident. "Look, you got the presentation done, and I'll bet it's killer. And okay, there was a small incident with a hot beverage, and you and I are going to have a serious talk at some point about backing up your work to the cloud, but you knew exactly who to call to fix it, and now everything's going to be fine."

"I don't know how to thank you," he said, running a tired hand through his hair.

The urge to smooth his hair down was almost overpowering,

86

SUSANNAH NIX

but she managed to resist it. Barely. "How about you just knock 'em dead tomorrow?" She pointed a stern finger at him. "Then come see me downstairs, because I am serious about backing up your work, buster. I'm going to set you up with automatic backups so you never have to worry about something like this again."

He mustered a faint smile for her. "It's a deal."

THE NEXT AFTERNOON, Jeremy showed up at Melody's office with a coffee and a laptop. "Nonfat vanilla latte," he said, setting the coffee cup on her desk. "With extra sugar."

"For me?" she asked, impressed he'd remembered her coffee order.

"For you. To say thank you."

"Well, anyone who brings me coffee is always very welcome." She reached for the cup and popped the lid off. "How'd your presentation go?"

"It went okay, I think." His shrug was modest, but he looked pleased with himself. "Geoffrey didn't seem to have any complaints, at least."

"That's great!"

He beamed at her. "And I owe it all to you."

"Well, not all of it," she said, feeling herself flush. "You did the presentation. I just retrieved it for you. So you only owe, like, five percent of it to me."

His cheek dimpled. "Five percent? That's really all the credit you want to claim?"

"Maybe seven," she conceded.

He smiled a little wider, and his eyes did that twinkling thing, like he was a live-action Disney prince or something. "How about we call it an even ten?"

"I'll take it."

"You mentioned something about setting me with up with

automatic backups?" he said, holding up his laptop. "Do you have time now?"

"Sure. Slide on in here." Melody scooted over to make room for him.

He shifted a stack of binders off the spare chair in the corner and dragged it over to the desk while she got to work.

When the installation was done, she walked him through the basics: how to get to his backed-up files, how to check to make sure it was running properly, and how to keep it up to date. He listened intently to everything she said, his mouth slightly turned down and forehead creased in concentration.

At one point, he reached for the trackpad and his fingers brushed against hers. She pulled her hand away, but then, a minute later, he leaned in for a better look at the screen and pressed his chest against her arm. He was close enough she could smell his cologne, or aftershave, or whatever it was he wore. It was subtle but heady, and it made her feel dizzy.

Her office was always a chilly sixty-eight degrees because of the servers in the next room, but it felt precariously warm with Jeremy's excellent-smelling body pressed so close to hers.

"So, that's pretty much it." Melody scooched her chair away, putting some distance between them. "Think you've got it now?"

"Yeah, I think so." He got to his feet and collected his laptop. "And if I don't, I know where to come for help."

She nodded, twisting a strand of hair around her finger. "Your friendly neighborhood IT department: always here to help."

His hand landed warmly on her shoulder. "Thanks again, Melody."

She swallowed and nodded again. "Anytime."

He withdrew his hand. "I guess I'll see you around?" he said, making it sound like a question.

"Yep. I guess you will."

Chapter Ten

$\mathcal{T}$he annual Sauer Hewson company picnic was apparently a very big deal. Melody wasn't a super-fan of picnics, given her aversion to insects, sunburn, group activities, and portable toilets. But her boss had made it clear the fun was mandatory, so there she was in Agoura Hills, sweating through the same lime green Sauer Hewson T-shirt as the other eight hundred employees wandering around in the August heat.

August in LA? Not so temperate. All of California had been hit by a heatwave, and it was a brutal ninety-eight degrees on this particular Saturday afternoon. At least it was a dry heat, and not the dense, muggy heat she'd grown up with in Florida. If you stayed in the shade, it wasn't that bad—except it was hard to stay in the shade at a stupid picnic.

The event mostly seemed to be geared toward kids, which was probably nice if you had kids—or were one. But since neither of those conditions applied to her, there wasn't a whole lot to actually do. The petting zoo was fun for about five minutes, until she started to feel weird about being the only adult not accompanied by a child. There was a band playing on a stage set up at one end of the park, but when she wandered over to check it out, they were playing a reggae cover of Metallica's "Enter Sandman" that was just—*no*. So much no.

Which left the interdepartmental softball, volleyball, and flag football games going on over at the playing fields. Melody hadn't signed up for any of the IT department teams because she wasn't a team sports kind of girl, but she figured she'd go and spectate for a while—not that she was particularly interested in watching the accounting department play sand volleyball against the facilities department, but at least it was somewhere to sit.

It was strange to think this was her life now. That she was actually a person who attended mandatory company picnics and wore logo-ed company event T-shirts. A faceless cog in the capitalist machine, chained to her desk forty hours a week, worrying about her 360 review and 401k.

God, what would Kieran think of her now? Nothing good, that was for sure.

Kieran had been a pathological do-gooder, a molecular biology major convinced he'd been put on the earth to make it a better place by curing cancer, saving the whales, going to pro-choice rallies, or whatever else happened to be his cause *du jour*.

Not that he wasn't sincere about it. He just didn't have much of an attention span. He'd get passionate about a cause and put all his energy into it for a while, only to lose interest a few months later and move on to something else that inspired him. It wasn't his fault, really; it was just a symptom of his bipolar disorder.

When he was up, he had this infectious enthusiasm for life that drew people to him like a tractor beam. He loved everything and everyone around him with a fierceness that made you want to love them, too. For a born-and-bred pessimist like Melody, it was a whole new way of experiencing the world. He'd opened her eyes to so much joy—from little things like wildflowers growing up through the cracks in asphalt to big things like a grassroots political movement happening halfway around the world—and she'd worshipped him for it. Even if she'd maybe secretly believed, deep down, his idealism was a little naive. A lifetime of cynicism didn't go away overnight, after all—not even when you were in love.

Kieran would have hated that she'd gone to work for Sauer Hewson. He would have told her she was wasting her intellect, selling out her talent for money. He would have hated this stupid company picnic, and he really would have hated this ugly T-shirt that had probably been made by oppressed children in some sweatshop somewhere.

"Melody!"

She spun around at the sound of her name, narrowly avoiding a collision with a roaming pack of sticky children, and spied Lacey running toward her. She was wearing a floral tank top and cut-off denim shorts that showed off her perfectly toned legs—the only person there who'd eschewed the vile green T-shirt.

"Oh thank god." Lacey thew her arms around her like an old friend. "Finally, someone I know."

"I didn't know you'd be here," Melody said, relieved to have found a friendly face.

"I came with Jeremy. But of course he's gone off to schmooze with work people and left me on my own. So I've just been wandering around, bored out of my mind."

"Yeah, me too."

"Well, now we've got each other, so we can be bored together." Lacey hooked her arm through Melody's. "Let's go get us some drinks!"

Lacey dragged her over to a concession stand and ordered two large iced lemonades.

"The problem with family-friendly events is there's never any alcohol," she said, thrusting the cups at Melody to hold. "Which is why I always bring my own." She pulled a flask out of her patchwork bag and tipped a generous quantity of clear liquid into each of their cups.

Melody took an experimental sip. It tasted like vodka. A lot of vodka. It was delicious.

"I'm so glad I ran into you," she told Lacey happily.

Lacey sucked on her straw and smirked. "Stick me with me, kid. I'll look out for you."

IT WAS possible Melody was slightly drunk. Possibly more than slightly. On the other hand, she was finally enjoying herself at this stupid picnic.

She was on her second cup of vodka lemonade. So far, she and Lacey had had their palms read, gotten their faces painted— butterfly wings for Lacey and a glittery pink unicorn for Melody— and bribed an attendant to let them jump in the bouncy house with the kids. Melody had vetoed the rock climbing wall, but agreed to go on the bumper cars, the giant slide, and something called Sally the Sea Serpent, which turned out to be an enormous inflatable maze that took them twenty minutes to stumble their way out of.

Then there was an announcement about the start of the executive games, and Lacey dragged her off toward the playing fields. "Believe me, you do not want to miss this," Lacey said. "They make the company officers play all these stupid field day games."

It sounded pretty entertaining, so Melody followed as she pushed her way to the front of the gathering crowd.

"Look, there's Jeremy," Lacey said, pointing.

Sure enough, Jeremy was in the middle of the field with a bunch of other executives, getting ready to play tug-of-war. Melody didn't know enough of the faces to understand how the teams were divided up, but she recognized the CIO on the team opposite Jeremy.

Once the contest started, the crowd got into it, shouting and cheering on the competitors, and Lacey and Melody joined in, both rooting for Jeremy's team. It was back-and-forth for a while, but Jeremy's side finally managed to drag the flag across the marker, and the spectators went crazy as the opposing team was pulled into the dirt. Melody whooped and hollered, both because she was a little—maybe a lot—drunk, and because it was pretty damn satisfying to see her boss's boss fall flat on his face.

After that, there was a sack race, where she got to see the CIO fall face-first in the dirt yet again, then they started setting up for the three-legged race.

"Who's Jeremy partnered with?" Melody asked when she saw him teaming up with a pretty teenage girl.

"That's his sister, Hannah. Oh, wow, their mother's actually going to join in."

Angelica Sauer had a reputation around the office for being humorless and terrifying. Today, she was smiling and laughing as she crouched beside a man Melody recognized as the CFO, Geoffrey Horvath, tying their legs together for the race.

When the race started, Jeremy and his sister shot forward like a perfectly synchronized unit and left all their competitors in the dust to take an easy first place. Melody suspected they'd perfected their three-legged-race technique at a lot of Sauer Hewson company picnics over the years. Meanwhile, Mrs. Sauer and Mr. Horvath lurched along far behind the pack, laughing as they made their ungainly way across the finish line.

The next event was the water balloon toss, and Jeremy teamed up with his mother while his sister partnered with Mr. Horvath. Melody could tell Jeremy was being careful to toss his mother the balloon gently, so he didn't ruin her tasteful, and probably very expensive, blow-out. When the balloon broke, it was in his hands, drenching the front of his shirt.

Poor Mr. Horvath wasn't so lucky. Hannah pelted the balloon at him and laughed as it burst all over his legs on their second toss. He seemed pretty good-natured about it though, smiling as he shook the water out of his slacks.

After that, the games seemed to be over, and the crowd started to break up. Lacey waved her arm to catch Jeremy's attention, and he made his way over to them.

"There you are," he said, picking Lacey up in a big bear hug and swinging her around. "I missed you."

It was the first time Melody had seen them together since that awful dinner. They looked a lot happier today. Like one of those couples in the stock photos that came with picture frames: beautiful, glowing, and perfect.

"Ew, you're all wet!" Lacey said, laughing as she pushed him away.

He kissed the tip of her nose. "I like your butterfly wings. It looks like a superhero mask."

"Melody got a unicorn," Lacey said.

"Hey, Melody." Jeremy smiled at her. "Are you having a good time?"

"Yup." Melody raised her lemonade cup. "Thanks to Lacey."

Jeremy snatched Lacey's cup out of her hand. "Uh oh, what do we have here?" He sucked on the straw and coughed out a laugh. "Wow! No wonder you two look so happy."

"Hey, that's mine! Don't drink it all!" Lacey said, grabbing for the cup.

"Mmmm, I think I better confiscate this for your own good."

Lacey lunged at him, sparking a game of keep-away. Jeremy had the size advantage, but Lacey was spry, limber, and kind of ruthless, going straight for his ticklish spots.

"Hello, Lacey, dear," Angelica Sauer said coolly, coming up behind them, and just like that, all the fun was sucked out of the moment.

Lacey's posture went rigid, and she let go of Jeremy like he was on fire. "Hello, Angelica."

Mrs. Sauer leaned in to kiss Lacey's cheek in a manner that seemed less like an affectionate greeting than a mafia don delivering the kiss of death. Then she focused her formidable gaze on Melody and arched an elegant eyebrow. "Aren't you going to introduce me to your friend?"

Jeremy passed Lacey her drink and stepped forward to make

the introduction. "Mom, this is Melody Gage. She works in the IT department."

"Lovely to meet you, Melody." Mrs. Sauer flashed a patrician smile as she extended her hand.

"The pleasure's mine, Mrs. Sauer," Melody said, desperately hoping she didn't sound as tipsy as she felt, and wow—ouch—Angelica Sauer had a grip like an Olympic weightlifter.

"Did you happen to see where your sister went?" Mrs. Sauer asked, turning to address Jeremy.

He shrugged. "She said she was going to meet up with some friends."

Angelica Sauer's fingers curled at the base of her throat. "I see."

"She'll be fine, Mom."

His mother gave him a tight smile. "I'm sure you're right."

Jeremy frowned. "Do you want me to go find her?"

"No, darling, you should enjoy the rest of your day." His mother patted his arm. "Oh, look, there's Edgar Harmon. I should go say hello. Excuse me," she murmured, and nodded at Lacey and Melody before moving away.

Melody felt an unexpected rush of affection for her own mom, who, for all her many flaws, was like a basket of fluffy kittens compared to Jeremy's mother. She couldn't imagine what it must have been like to grow up with Angelica Sauer for a mother.

"You want to go look for Hannah, don't you?" Lacey asked Jeremy.

He sighed. "Maybe."

"We'll come with you," Lacey said, squeezing his arm. "Right, Melody?"

"Sure." Melody shrugged. It wasn't like she had anything better to do.

————

FINDING a single teenage girl amongst eight hundred people all wearing the same T-shirt was easier said than done. The three of them wandered around for almost an hour before they found Hannah Sauer getting a henna tattoo.

Hannah—or Shorty, as her brother adorably called her—rolled her eyes like only a sixteen-year-old could when she saw them. "Did Mom send you after me?" she asked with a beleaguered sigh. She had Jeremy's golden brown hair and piercing blue eyes, and her mother's natural frown.

"No," Jeremy told her, which was not technically a lie. He seemed relieved to have found her, and Melody remembered him saying his sister had gotten into some trouble after their father died.

"What do you think?" Hannah showed off the intricate design on her hand. "Don't you love it?"

"Very cool," Lacey said.

"Mom's gonna be thrilled." Jeremy sighed. "Tell me that's not permanent."

"It fades in a few days," Hannah said with another eye-roll. "Just wait, though. The second I turn eighteen, I'm getting a real tattoo and Mom can suck it." She gave Melody a wary once-over. "Who are you?"

"Hannah, this is Lacey's friend, Melody," Jeremy said.

"Hi." Melody smiled like she wasn't the least bit bothered by Jeremy describing her as Lacey's friend instead of his. Why should she be bothered? It wasn't like it wasn't true. And she couldn't exactly blame him for not wanting to explain to his little sister how they'd really met.

"Hey," Hannah mumbled, having already lost interest in Melody.

"What happened to the friends you were meeting?" Jeremy asked.

"They were boring."

Jeremy looked like he wanted to question her further, but

before he had a chance, Lacey cut in. "We were going to get something to eat. Wanna come?"

Hannah shrugged. "Sure, why not?" She said it like the prospect was almost as much fun as getting her braces tightened.

They made their way over to the food tent and loaded their paper plates with ribs and brisket. Jeremy found an empty picnic table, and they slid onto the wooden benches and stuffed their faces while arguing about their favorite kinds of barbecue and the virtues of a vinegary sauce versus a sweet sauce—except Hannah, who pushed her food around on her plate and barely said a word.

"Everything okay?" Jeremy asked her eventually, wiping his hands with a wet nap.

"Yeah."

"Shorty," he said in a gentle voice, "what happened with your friends?"

"It's nothing." She stared at her plate. "They wanted to get high, and when I told them I didn't, they took off."

"Hey." He gave her shoulder an affectionate jostle. "I'm proud of you."

"Whatever," she muttered, though it was obvious she was pleased.

"Who wants ice cream?" Jeremy said, tossing his napkin into the trash.

"Me!" Lacey and Hannah cheered in unison.

Jeremy's eyes found Melody's. "What about you?" he asked, smiling like they were sharing a secret. "Do you like ice cream?"

Melody smiled back at him. "Who doesn't like ice cream?"

BY THE TIME they were done with their ice cream, it was getting dark, so they headed back over to the playing fields to stake out a spot to watch the fireworks. Jeremy sweet-talked a spare blanket off an executive assistant, and the four of them kicked off their shoes and crowded onto the blanket together, lying on their backs and gazing up at the darkening sky.

"Star light, star bright, first star I see tonight," Hannah said, pointing at the brightest pinpoint of light overhead.

"Make a wish," Jeremy told her.

"That's Venus," Melody corrected before she could stop herself. "But it's called the Evening Star," she added apologetically, "so it probably still works for wishes."

"Do you know any other stars or constellations?" Hannah asked, showing an interest in Melody for the first time.

"Um…" Melody scanned the sky for something recognizable. "See that group of stars over there? That's Sagittarius. It's supposed to look like a centaur holding a longbow."

"Looks more like a blob to me," Hannah said, scrunching up her nose.

"That's because the rest of the stars in the constellation are too faint to be visible. Some people call it the teapot because that's kind of what the central stars look like. On a really clear night, away from the city lights, you can see the Milky Way coming off the spout like a puff of steam."

"Where'd you learn all that stuff?" Hannah asked Melody.

"School," Jeremy answered for her. "Melody studied hard in high school, so she could go to MIT for college."

"Gee, big brother, thanks for the subtle life lesson," Hannah said sarcastically, shoving him with her elbow.

Melody reached up to brush a wisp of hair off her face, and her fingers grazed the paint on her cheek. "Oh my god!" she said in horror.

"What's wrong?" Jeremy asked.

"I had a sparkly unicorn painted on my face when I met your mother!" She'd totally forgotten the stupid thing was there.

Jeremy, Hannah, and Lacey all dissolved into laughter.

"It's not funny," Melody said, burying her face in her hands. "The CEO thinks I'm an idiot now."

"Don't worry about it," Jeremy said. "You look adorable. She's not gonna hold it against you."

"Yeah, she'll be too busy holding the fact that you're friends with me against you," Lacey offered helpfully.

"Terrific," Melody muttered.

"Hey, fireworks," Hannah said as bright lights shattered the sky overhead.

They fell silent as the explosions rumbled through their chests. Dazzling bursts of color splashed across the sky, and the smell of gunpowder filled the air, drifting past in clouds of bluish smoke.

It occurred to Melody, as she lay there on the grass beside Lacey with fireworks painting the night sky above, that it had been a perfect day.

This was exactly what she'd been hoping for when she moved here—to feel like she was part of something again. To have friends to share it with.

For the first time in a long while, she was happy.

Chapter Eleven

"Mom," Melody groaned into the phone. "Do not give me an OK Cupid membership for my birthday. I told you, I'm not interested in online dating."

Melody's mother had seriously ratcheted up the nagging about her about her love life lately. She was convinced that, at the advanced age of twenty-two, Melody was in imminent danger of turning into a dried up old maid.

"Have you gone on even one date since you moved out there?"

"Well..." Technically, she could say yes, if she counted her disastrous dinner with Jeremy, Lacey, and Drew. But then her mom would demand more details, and that would be opening a whole can of worms she wasn't willing to invite her mother into. "I've been busy."

"I just don't want you to be lonely, honey."

"I'm not lonely." *Most of the time.* "I've got friends." Lacey counted as a friend, right? Even if they didn't really hang out or talk regularly. They were sort of friends.

"You're all the way out there in a new city all by yourself. I worry."

"I'm doing fine, Mom."

Her mother let out a melodramatic sigh. "It's been over a year since you lost you-know-who, baby."

Melody's mother never said Kieran's name. She knew Melody didn't like to talk about him, but she couldn't seem to refrain from bringing him up, so instead, she just avoided using his name —like he was Voldemort.

"We're not having this conversation," Melody said through clenched teeth.

"I'm just saying, it's time to get back on the horse. If you wait too long, you might forget how."

"I haven't forgotten how."

Or had she? She kept telling herself she didn't *want* to get involved with anyone yet. That she wasn't ready. But maybe that was just an excuse. Maybe she didn't know how to let herself love anymore. Maybe she wasn't even capable of it. Like when you stopped using your legs and the muscles atrophied. Maybe her heart had atrophied.

"I know you, Melody," her mom said. "You want to shut yourself off from the world and hide when things get tough, but you'll never find happiness that way. You have to put yourself out there. Join a book club or something."

"I go to yoga every week."

"There are no men in yoga classes."

Fortunately, the doorbell rang, offering Melody an escape from the conversation. "Mom, I have to go. My pizza's here." She made a hurried goodbye as she went to answer the door.

"Jeremy!" she said, stepping back in surprise. "You're not my pizza."

He was soaked to the skin. The heatwave had broken and it was actually raining tonight—for the first time since Melody had lived in Los Angeles—and he didn't have a jacket or an umbrella with him. Water dripped down his face and his expression was so stony, it took her a moment to realize how red his eyes were—like he'd been crying.

"Did you know?" he growled before she could ask what was wrong.

"What?" she asked, taken aback.

"About Lacey and Tessa."

She blinked at him, bewildered. "What about Lacey and Tessa?"

The anger drained out of him, and he deflated before her eyes. "Lacey broke up with me," he said in a shaky voice. "For Tessa."

For a second, Melody was too stunned to say anything. It didn't make any sense—except the longer she thought about it, the more it kind of did. She remembered all the times she'd seen Lacey and Tessa together, and how close they'd always seemed. How affectionate. How happy. And how Lacey never talked about Jeremy. Like, at all.

Which was when Melody realized it made perfect sense, and she was an idiot for not seeing it sooner.

"Come inside," she said, holding the door open wider. When Jeremy didn't move, she took him by the arm and tugged him over the threshold. "You're drenched."

"Sorry," he mumbled as he dripped on her living room floor.

"Take off your shoes. I'll get you a towel."

When she came back with an armful of towels, he was still standing in the exact same spot, but his shoes were sitting beside the door. "Here," she said, thrusting one of the towels at him. She laid another out on the floor and pushed it around with her toe, mopping up the puddle at his feet.

He rubbed the towel she'd given him over his head, making his hair stand up all spiky on top, then wiped his feet on the towel on the floor.

"Sit down," she said, gesturing to the couch.

"I'll get your couch all wet."

She draped another towel over the cushions and patted it with her hand. "Sit."

Without a word, he lowered himself onto the towel. It was

heartbreaking to see him sitting there barefoot in his sodden clothes, clutching a towel around his shoulders like a security blanket. He looked like he was still in shock; he must have come straight over after Lacey delivered the news.

Melody sat down next to him. "Tell me what happened."

He bent his head and rubbed his eyes with the heels of his hands. "She said she's not in love with me. She said she's in love with her fucking yoga instructor." He let out a bitter laugh. "I mean, what a goddamn cliché. It sounds like the plot of a bad movie, doesn't it?"

"I'm sorry." Melody started to lay a consoling hand on his back, but chickened out at the last second and dropped it onto the couch instead.

"I can't even believe it. My girlfriend is a lesbian."

"Bisexual."

Jeremy gave her a blank look.

"Lesbians don't usually date men. Lacey's probably bisexual."

"She's been cheating on me," he said miserably, ducking his head between his hands again. "For *months.*"

It was hard to feel *too* sorry for him, considering his track record in that department. But he'd said he'd changed, so maybe he had been faithful to Lacey. Either way, it was obvious he hadn't seen this coming.

"It must have been hard for her to tell you the truth," Melody said. Lacey was her friend, and she couldn't help thinking about how unhappy she must have been all this time, hiding who she was.

"I didn't take it very well." Jeremy squeezed his eyes shut. "I said some stuff I probably shouldn't have."

Melody bit her lip. She didn't want to hear the play-by-play or take sides.

Rescue arrived in the form of the doorbell—her pizza, finally. Grateful for the distraction, she leapt up from the couch.

She tipped the delivery guy and carried the pizza box into the kitchen. Without asking, she dished up two plates and carried them both into the living room. Jeremy still hadn't moved from the brooding stance he'd taken up on the couch.

"Here," she said, passing one of the plates over. "Hope you like pepperoni and mushroom."

He accepted it and sat up, balancing the plate on his knee. They ate their pizza in silence, staring straight ahead. When they were both done, she took his plate from him. "Want another slice?" she asked over her shoulder as she headed into the kitchen.

"No thanks." He stood, rubbing his hands on his thighs. "I appreciate it, but I should probably go."

She was tempted to try to convince him to stay, but he seemed to want to go, so she trailed him to the door and waited while he put on his sodden shoes. It had mostly stopped raining, at least, so he wouldn't get soaked all over again.

"Hey," she said when he pulled the door open. "Are you gonna be okay?"

He gave her a half-hearted nod. "It's not like it's the first time I've ever been dumped." He let out a shaky breath. "Thanks for letting me cry on your shoulder."

"You didn't actually do any crying," she said. "On my shoulder, or any other parts of me. Although, you can, if you need to. I've got a pretty good shoulder, right here. Two of 'em, actually. And they're both available."

He almost sort of smiled. "I'm good. Or I will be." His eyes focused on her, and he looked like he wanted to say something. His mouth opened, but all that came out was, "I'll see you later, Melody."

LACEY CALLED the next day and asked Melody to meet her for coffee. Melody was fairly certain she could guess what it was about, and agreed to meet her at the place near the yoga studio that afternoon. Melody arrived first and got in line. Lacey showed up a few minutes later in a T-shirt and the same cut-off shorts she'd worn to the picnic with her hair hidden under a baseball cap. "Sorry I'm late," she said.

"It's fine," Melody said. "I'll get the coffee, and you snag us that table over by the window."

When their order was ready, she carried it over to the table where Lacey was waiting, drumming her fingers on the Formica tabletop.

"I have to tell you something," Lacey said as soon as Melody was sitting down.

"I think I already know."

Lacey's face crumpled a little. "Jeremy told you, didn't he?"

"Yeah."

"I'm sorry for not telling you sooner. I feel bad about hiding it from you all this time."

Melody touched her arm. "You're not under any obligation to tell me anything until you're ready to talk about it. I'm just here if you need me, okay?"

"Thanks." Lacey picked at the cardboard sleeve on her coffee cup, frowning.

"So...are you okay?"

"Sure." Lacey gave a one-shouldered shrug. "I mean, I'm not the one who got dumped, right?" She made a noise that was probably meant to be a laugh, but it sounded more like a sob.

"It still must have been hard."

Lacey blew out a shaky breath. "It wasn't fun, that's for sure. It could have gone worse, I guess, but not much."

"He was just hurt. Whatever he said, he didn't mean it."

"Oh, I'm pretty sure he meant it." Lacey stared into her coffee, which she'd yet to touch. "It's not like it was anything I didn't have coming. I should have told him sooner. It wasn't fair to lie to him like that." She paused to suck in a long, measured breath, then looked up at Melody. "How is he?"

Melody didn't have any idea. She hadn't heard from Jeremy since he left her apartment yesterday. "I think it was a shock."

Lacey nodded, looking miserable. "He'll be okay." It sounded like she was trying to convince herself. "It's not like we were all that happy, you know? Even before I met Tessa, we were—" she faltered, "sometimes it was like I didn't even know why we were together."

"Why were you?" Melody couldn't help asking. She couldn't understand why anyone would stay with somebody when they were in love with someone else.

"You have to understand," Lacey said, shifting in her seat, "when Charlotte found out about us, it was ugly. She and Jeremy had been together for so long—even though they weren't *really* together for a lot of it, with him away at school on the other side of the country—everyone assumed they were going to get married."

"Didn't she know about the cheating?"

Lacey shrugged. "She said she didn't, but I think she did. She had to. It wasn't like he was subtle about it. I think she honestly believed he'd change. That he'd get it all out of his system in college, then come back to her and settle down."

"That seems kind of...naive," Melody said.

"Yeah, but that's Charlotte. She's always needed to be perfect: perfect grades, perfect clothes, perfect boyfriend. She and Jeremy were the perfect couple—or, at least, that's what she wanted everyone to think. She could turn a blind eye to his cheating for the sake of appearances as long as he was off at school—out of sight, out of mind, you know? But when she found out he'd been sleeping with me, on and off for years, that was too much. She completely lost it."

"How'd she find out?"

Lacey's eyes shifted away. "I sort of told her."

Melody's mouth fell open. "Why?"

"I wish I could say it was because I was trying to protect her, but…we were having a fight—about something stupid, I don't even remember now—and I got so pissed, I threw it in her face."

"Yikes," Melody said. "What happened?"

"She made a big scene. Broke up with Jeremy, and made sure everyone knew why. She didn't speak to me for almost a year. Things still aren't great between us, but she can tolerate being in the same room with me now, at least."

Melody wanted to feel sorry for Lacey, but she couldn't help thinking she sort of deserved it.

"It's okay," Lacey said, reading her expression. "You're allowed to think I'm shitty."

"I don't think you're shitty. I just think…you made some not great choices."

"I fucked up. No question."

"Okay, but how did you and Jeremy end up together after that?" She still didn't understand that part. It seemed like asking for more trouble.

Lacey sighed. "You have to understand, Jeremy and I were the bad guys, and everyone we knew kind of ganged up on us—our friends, our families. Everyone was pissed at us. Neither of us had anywhere else to turn, so we ended up turning to each other. It sort of pushed us together, you know?"

Melody nodded, and Lacey continued.

"It was never supposed to be serious. We were just goofing around. A couple of stupid kids screwing around behind my sister's back, thinking we could get away with it. But after it all came out, we sort of fell back into each other and it was like, what was the point of causing all that misery if it wasn't so we could be together? I don't think either of us ever stopped to think about whether it was what we actually wanted." She shook her head. "I'm not sure we were ever happy, to be honest."

"Are you happy now? With Tessa?"

"Yeah," Lacey said, breaking into a smile. "I am."

"Then that's all that matters," Melody said. "Tessa seems great."

Lacey's smile got wider. "She is. Better than I deserve, that's for damn sure."

"How long have you guys been..." Melody didn't know what to call it. Dating? Sleeping together behind Jeremy's back?

"Since May."

"Wow." So, before Melody had even met them. It explained a lot of things.

"Yeah, I know," Lacey said, pursing her lips. "I shouldn't have let it go on so long."

"Why did you? I mean, if you knew you wanted to be with Tessa, I guess I don't understand why you wouldn't just *be* with her?"

Lacey hunched forward, balling her hands into fists. "Because I was a fucking coward. I just kept hoping Jeremy would break up with me so I didn't have to be the one to do it. So I wouldn't have to tell him I was leaving him for a woman."

Melody had thought Lacey was utterly fearless. She was always so direct and self-confident, like she never had a single fuck to give. It was a shock—but also kind of heartening—to realize even someone like her could be paralyzed by fear.

"The thing is," Lacey said, "it wasn't even telling Jeremy that I was really afraid of. It was everything that came after. Telling him meant telling all our friends. And Charlotte. And our parents. It was just...it felt like a lot."

Melody nodded in sympathy. She'd watched her high school best friend come out to his parents. There'd been a lot of yelling, crying, and threats of military school and conversion therapy before they'd finally come around. "Have you told them yet?"

Lacey leaned back in her chair and smiled. "Yeah, I dropped the bomb at family brunch this morning. It turned out to be way easier than telling Jeremy. Go figure. Charlotte had to get in a few passive aggressive comments, since it wasn't all about her, but my dad barely even blinked. This macho Latino cop, and all he has to say is, 'Guess I don't need to worry about you getting pregnant anymore.'"

Melody laughed. "That's good, right?"

"Yeah. And my mom, she was actually thrilled. Couldn't wait to tell all her friends about her queer daughter, like it gave her more liberal academic cred or something. For, like, the first time, I'm not the black sheep of the family."

"Moms," Melody said, shaking her head.

Lacey snorted and reached for her coffee. "They're all fucking nuts, right?"

Chapter Twelve

It was a few days later when Melody saw Jeremy again. He was walking into the building as she stepped off the elevator in the lobby. "Hi," she said, heading toward him. "How are you?"

He gave her one of his work smiles. "I'm good."

"Really?" She studied him, trying to decide whether he was actually fine, or just pretending to be someone who was fine. He did look okay, though—almost perky, even.

"Really," he assured her, then glanced at his watch. "Sorry, I've got a meeting upstairs…"

"Sure, go ahead," Melody waved him off and watched him walk away. He was smiling, clean-shaven, with impeccably-styled hair and a freshly-pressed suit. No obvious signs of depression or wallowing. Maybe he was getting over the breakup okay. She hoped so.

He glanced back at her before he got on the elevator. Melody raised her hand, and he tipped his head in acknowledgement before stepping out of sight.

At the end of the week, Lacey called and invited Melody out for drinks at the bar where she worked.

"It's super low-key," she said. "It's just gonna be me, Tessa, and a few friends. Sort of a celebration type thing."

"What are we celebrating?"

"My coming out or whatever." Lacey sounded embarrassed. "It was Tessa's idea. It's really for both of us, to celebrate the fact that we're not sneaking around anymore. Lame, right?"

"It's not lame. It's sweet."

Lacey huffed out an irritable breath, and Melody could picture her rolling her eyes. "So, are you in or what?"

"Definitely in," Melody said, grinning.

"Cool," Lacey said. "Take an Uber. Parking's a nightmare at the bar—and that way you won't have to worry about driving yourself home. We're gonna get our drink on."

THE BAR where Lacey worked was in Studio City. It was one of those swank, speakeasy-style places that were all the rage at the moment. The drinks on the custom cocktail menu all had clever names like "Pig Ol' Bitties" and "French as Fuck," and they were made with ingredients Melody had never heard of, like Demerera and Chartreuse—which she'd thought was a color but was apparently also a liquor—or things she had heard of, but never would have thought to put in a drink, like fig jam or beets. Fortunately, she was saved the trouble of navigating the menu when the bartender—sorry, *alchemist*—brought over a bottle of champagne for their group.

Besides Melody, Lacey, and Tessa, there were two other women there: Devika and Kelsey. Devika had dark skin and thick copper braids pulled up into a twist on top her head—and the most perfect bone structure Melody had ever seen outside of a movie or magazine. Kelsey looked like a 1940s pin-up girl. She wore bright red lipstick in stark contrast with her pale skin, and her jet-black hair was pinned into retro victory rolls.

They made Melody feel like the Ugly Duckling, but that was a feeling she was getting used to since she'd moved to LA. People here were just better looking than the rest of the country. You expected it from the actors, but even people who didn't have anything to do with the entertainment industry were freakishly beautiful and stylish. It was a bit unsettling, honestly.

Lacey blew the bartender a kiss as he filled their glasses. "Thanks, Terrance." She was sitting between Melody and Tessa on one of the comfortable leather couches along the wall, with Devika and Kelsey in the two lounge chairs across from them.

"Anything for you, gorgeous," Terrance replied with a wink. He was beautiful, too. He looked like Luke Cage—bald and black with biceps as big as Melody's thigh—and was definitely probably gay. "Give me a wave when you're ready for something else."

"A toast!" Kelsey said, raising her champagne glass. "To this one…" she cast a significant look at Lacey, "finally getting her shit together."

"About damn time, too!" Devika chimed in.

"And to Tessa," Lacey added, gazing at her like she'd carried her out of a burning building. Which in a way, Melody supposed, she had. "For being patient and putting up with my sorry ass."

"I happen to love your ass," Tessa said, twining her fingers with Lacey's.

"Cheers!" Melody said as they all leaned forward and clinked glasses. She didn't know much about champagne, but this tasted like the good stuff. It felt nice going down.

"So, Melody, what do you do?" Kelsey asked, leaning back in her lounge chair and stretching her legs out in front of her. She was wearing wingtip Mary Janes with three-inch heels, like a femme fatale from a Raymond Chandler story.

"I…uh, work in IT," Melody said, tucking her black Converse out of sight under her seat.

"What kind of company?" Devika asked.

"Jeremy's company, as a matter of fact," Lacey said with a smirk.

"Oh, really?" Kelsey raised one perfectly plucked and penciled eyebrow. "Do tell."

"Um, there's not anything to tell." Melody wasn't sure what the others would think if they knew she'd hooked up with Jeremy back in college, but she didn't particularly want to find out. The fact that she and Lacey had both slept with him was weird enough —it would be even weirder to actually talk about it. Like, out loud. With all her friends.

"Don't worry. She's cool," Lacey said. "She went to MIT. She's like a genius or something."

"What do you do?" Melody asked Kelsey, changing the subject.

Kelsey shrugged. "Standard issue actress-slash-waitress. More of a waitress at the moment, but such is life."

"What about that audition you had last week?" Tessa asked. "It was for a movie, right?"

Kelsey rolled her eyes. "They wanted someone a little more anorexic. Too bad, too. Jon Hamm was in that movie."

"He came in here once," Lacey said. "I made him a martini. Extra dirty."

"Is he as good looking in person?" Melody asked. She'd binge-watched three seasons of *Mad Men* over a long weekend once. Don Draper might have been a disgusting, sexist man-child, but Jon Hamm was so yummy, she would definitely marry him and have a million of his babies if he asked.

"Better." Lacey grinned. "You know what they say about him, right?"

"You mean that he's got a foot-long schlong?" Kelsey said with a smirk.

Lacey nodded. "Terrance over there," she said with a head tilt in the direction of the bar, "decided he wanted to see for himself, so he followed him into the men's room."

"No, he did not!" Devika said, horrified.

"What was the verdict?" Melody asked. She wanted to know, okay? Sue her.

Lacey shrugged. "He used the stall."

"Probably just as well," Kelsey said, swirling her champagne around in her glass. "It's better to maintain the mystique."

"Do you get a lot of celebrities in here?" Melody asked, gazing around the bar. She hadn't had many celebrity sightings since she'd moved to LA, although she had spotted Jared Leto at a Trader Joe's once. He'd been wearing sweatpants and a torn T-shirt, and she nearly mistook him for a homeless man.

"A few. Mostly, it's commodities traders and bankers, to be honest. But we did get Emma Stone in here once. She was really sweet."

"Now you're talking," Devika said. "I like redheads."

"Is *that* why you keep trying to talk me into dying my hair red?" Kelsey asked.

"Maybe," Devika said, and leaned across the space between their chairs for a kiss.

So they were a couple, too, which made Melody both the Ugly Duckling *and* the fifth wheel. Fine. Whatever. She was used to it.

"Stop being so cute." Lacey stuck out her tongue. "It's disgusting."

"You know, you can be this cute now, too," Devika pointed out.

"Hey, you're right." Lacey turned her head and kissed Tessa—long and slow, taking her time about it. Lacey seemed so deliriously happy, Melody got a little teary thinking about how long it had taken them to get here, to a place where they were able to show affection in public.

"Okay. That's enough. Sheesh." Kelsey scrunched up her nose. "A little decorum if you please, ladies."

"We need more drinks." Lacey waved her empty champagne glass in the air and spun around to catch Terrance's eye. Her fingernails were freshly manicured and painted a pretty robin's egg blue. No more biting her nails, apparently.

"Hell yeah," Devika said, draining the last of her champagne.

Kelsey nodded. "*Lots* more drinks."

"Gin and tonics?" Lacey suggested. "I'm ordering us gin and tonics."

Terrance came and cleared away the champagne glasses, then left to get them a round of house-made gin and tonics. Melody had no idea how house-made gin and tonics were different from regular gin and tonics. Weren't all gin and tonics made in-house? That was the point of going to a bar, right—that they made the drinks on the spot?

"We need to fix Melody up," Tessa said, gazing at her with pursed lips.

Melody shook her head, alarmed. "We really don't."

"What's your type?" Devika asked.

"Men," Lacey supplied.

"Exclusively?" Kelsey asked.

"Um, yeah, pretty much," Melody said.

"Tragic." Devika made a face.

"Hey, men have their uses," Kelsey said, smirking. "Right, Lacey?"

Lacey snorted. "Some men more than others."

Melody squinted at her, trying to figure out if that was a reference to Jeremy, and Lacey lifted her eyebrows, smirking. Did that mean she *was* talking about Jeremy? And if so, was it an insult or a compliment?

Nope. Never mind. On second thought, she didn't want to know. The less she was privy to the sordid details of Lacey and Jeremy's relationship, the better.

"So, what do you do for a living?" Melody asked, turning to Devika.

"Pediatric nurse," Devika said.

"Oh, wow." Melody couldn't stand kids *or* the sight of blood, so she was in awe of anyone with the fortitude to work in children's healthcare.

Devika shrugged like it was nothing. "I work in a doctor's office, so I mostly just stab kids with needles."

"Don't change the subject," Kelsey said, narrowing her eyes at Melody. "How do you like 'em? Blond? Brunet? Skinny? Muscular?"

"Um," Melody said, trying not to picture Kiernan's floppy brown hair and soft smile. "I'm not sure."

"How about this: if you could bang any actor, who would you bang?"

Melody broke into a grin. Finally, a question she could answer without discomfort. She didn't even have to pause to think about it. "Chris Evans."

"Excellent choice," Tessa said.

"Shit, *I'd* even do Chris Evans if he was standing here," Devika agreed.

"I'm more of a Chris Hemsworth girl, myself," Kelsey said, flipping her hair.

"Yay, drinks!" Lacey shouted as Terrance returned with a tray of mason jars. They all cheered as he set them down, and he tipped an imaginary hat.

The house-made gin and tonic was delicious. And very strong. Melody could already feel it going to her head after a couple sips.

The four of them traded opinions back and forth about which celebrities they'd like to sleep with, until Kelsey and Tessa got into a heated argument over Kate Winslet versus Cate Blanchett—Melody came down firmly in the Kate Winslet camp, but elected not to publicly take sides—which devolved into a game of Fuck, Marry, Kill.

"Han Solo, Princess Leia, or Chewbacca," Tessa asked Devika after Terrance brought out their second round of gin and tonics.

"New movies or old movies?" Kelsey asked.

Tessa waved her hand. "Whichever."

"It matters," Kelsey insisted. "Right?" She looked to Melody for support.

Melody nodded in agreement. "Definitely."

"Old movies, then," Tessa said.

"Um…" Devika frowned, thinking it over. "Okay, marry Leia—I mean, *obviously*."

Tessa nodded. "Obviously."

"And kill Han Solo, which means I'd have to fuck Chewbacca, I guess."

"You'd *kill* Han Solo?" Melody said, aghast. Han Solo was the first man she'd ever wanted to marry. Her heterosexual mind couldn't comprehend such sacrilege.

Kelsey raised her hand. "I'd like to talk about the fact that my girlfriend just said she would *fuck a Wookiee*."

"I have a question," Lacey said, tilting her head. "Do you think he has, like, a man-dong under all that fur, or is it a red rocket like a dog?"

"He doesn't wear pants." Tessa's brow furrowed like she was considering the matter very seriously. "So, it'd have to be a dog penis, right?"

"Would you like to change your answer?" Kelsey asked Devika.

"Nah, I'm good," Devika said, smirking.

They all dissolved into giggles like it was the funniest thing they'd ever heard."

These drinks are really strong," Melody observed to her third gin and tonic. She felt like she was holding her own pretty well, considering, but the world was definitely going a little wonky around the edges.

Kelsey leaned forward and poked her in the knee with a shiny red fingernail. "Why don't you want to be fixed up?"

Melody shrugged, flopping back on the couch. "I'm just not interested in being in a relationship right now."

"Everyone's interested in being in a relationship," Devika said, shaking her head. "Anyone who says different is lying. Or fooling themselves."

"I was in a relationship," Melody admitted, swirling the ice around in her mason jar. "A serious one. I'm not ready to go there again yet."

Devika squinted at her like she wanted to ask something and was trying to decide whether to do it. "How old are you?" she asked finally.

"Twenty-two. Nearly twenty-three."

Tessa leaned across Lacey. "When's your birthday?"

"Next Wednesday, actually."

Melody had been trying not to think about it. She didn't have anyone to celebrate with, so it was just going to be another day. It was no big deal. There wasn't much point to birthdays after you turned twenty-one anyway.

"Shit, we have to take you out!" Lacey said, turning to Tessa. "Right?"

"Definitely," Tessa said.

"No, really," Melody said, shaking her head. "You don't have to do that."

"We're doing it," Lacey said, brooking no argument. "Dinner Wednesday night after you get off work. Okay?"

Melody couldn't help smiling. "Okay."

"I LIKE YOUR HAIR," Melody said to Kelsey when they were on their fourth round of gin and tonics—or maybe it was the fifth. Who could keep track? "And your makeup. And your..." she waved her hand in the air, "everything. How'd you learn to do that?"

"YouTube," Kelsey said. "No shit."

Melody felt all soft and fuzzy. Like she was wearing her favorite comfy fleece pajama pants, only around her brain. Alcohol was great—she couldn't remember why she didn't have it more often.

"Lacey, your girl is drunk," Devika observed.

Lacey squinted at Tessa.

"Not your *girl* girl. Your other girl." Devika tilted her head toward Melody.

"I resemble that remark," Melody said, sending herself into a giggling fit.

She was definitely going to have a hangover tomorrow. And she didn't even care.

"It's cool," Lacey said, patting her fondly on the arm. "We'll get her home."

Melody rested her head on Lacey's shoulder, snuggling up against her. "You guys are the best."

IT WAS a rude awakening when her phone rang the next morning. Her head felt like the inside of a snare drum.

"How's that hangover?" Lacey asked when Melody finally managed to locate her phone and answer it.

"Cataclysmic."

"Make yourself a Bloody Mary. It'll do the trick."

Melody did not happen to have the ingredients for a Bloody Mary lying around her apartment. And even if she had, the thought of more alcohol made her stomach want to jump out of her mouth and run around the room screaming.

"I'll keep that in mind," she mumbled, choking back the urge to vomit.

"Thought I should make sure you were still alive after last night. You were pretty drunk."

"Yeah." Melody rubbed her forehead with the heel of her hand. "Thanks for getting me home."

She didn't actually remember getting home. She remembered leaving the bar with Tessa's arm around her for support. And falling into bed. And Lacey taking off her shoes. Everything else was a hazy blur.

"Yeah, okay, I'll let you get back to feeling like shit," Lacey said. "But we're still on for Wednesday, right?"

Wednesday?

Oh, right. Her birthday.

"You really don't have to—"

"Don't be stupid," Lacey said. "It's your birthday."

ASIDE FROM THE enthusiastic birthday call from her mother first thing in the morning—complete with singing—Melody's birthday passed like any other day. And she was fine with that. Totally fine.

She'd been assigned to a software development project finally, though as a tester rather than a developer. It was a step in the right direction, at least. It meant she was on a project team now, working more closely with other people. But it was still brand new, and no one else on the team knew it was her birthday. Not that they necessarily would have cared, but maybe someone would have gotten her a card or a cake or something.

It was possible some small part of her had hoped Jeremy would stop by to wish her a happy birthday, but that was dumb. How would he even know? It wasn't like they were really friends. She didn't know what they were, but they weren't friends.

He wasn't friend material. He was too gorgeous, too rich, too unattainable. Even setting aside the awkwardness of trying to be friends with someone you'd had a one-night stand with, *and* the fact that he was Lacey's ex, there was that whole thing where his family owned the company Melody worked for. It was all a bridge too far.

She hadn't seen much of him lately, anyway. She'd only laid eyes on him twice since the breakup, and both times, he'd barely spared her a few seconds before rushing off. The two of them were casual acquaintances—nothing more. Now that he and Lacey and broken up, Melody was just a friend of his ex, which wasn't anything at all, was it?

It was fine, though. She didn't need Jeremy or anyone else at work to wish her a happy birthday, because she had Lacey and Tessa for that. Melody had her own friends now, and they were taking her to dinner for her birthday.

They'd suggested a Cuban place on La Cienega, which was perfect, because Cuban food reminded Melody of home. She went straight from work to meet them there. The food was great—not Florida great, obviously, but the garlic chicken was legit. The pitcher of sangria Lacey ordered for the table was also legit, but Melody only indulged in one glass, since it was a weeknight—and since she was still feeling gun shy after Saturday night's revelries.

In addition to being a yoga instructor, Tessa worked as a massage therapist, and she entertained them over dinner with stories about some of her weirdest clients.

"There was this one guy, super straight-and-narrow, like a banker or something—middle-aged, suit and tie, gray hair. Anyway, I left the room so he could strip down to his underwear, and when I came back, he was standing there in this sparkly red thong."

"Ugh!" Melody said, scrunching up her nose.

"Just goes to show," Lacey said around a mouthful of lechon asado, "you never know what kind of freaky shit people are hiding under the surface."

Melody tried to imagine any of the men at work wearing a sparkly thong under their business casual khakis. It was a genuinely disturbing thought.

"And he was really hairy, too," Tessa said. "Like Robin Williams hairy."

"Bear," Lacey said knowingly.

Tessa shook her head, causing a wisp of blonde hair to escape her ponytail and fall across her forehead. "I'm pretty sure he was straight."

"Straight guys don't wear thongs," Lacey said. "Except strippers."

"I'm telling you," Tessa said, pouring herself another glass of sangria, "this one did." She topped off Lacey's glass, then gestured to Melody's, eyebrows raised.

Melody shook her head. "How do you do it? Touching strangers like that—and mostly-naked strangers at that." She could barely stomach the thought of *getting* a massage from a stranger, much less giving one.

Tessa smiled and tucked her hair behind her ear. "It's not so bad. Bodies are just bodies. We've all got one."

"See, the thing that separates Tessa from normal people like you and me," Lacey said to Melody, leaning in conspiratorially, "is that she actually *likes* people."

"People are interesting," Tessa said. "Everyone has a story."

"Yeah, like that douche at the bar last night who told me I had wolverine tits." Lacey rolled her eyes. "He was a real Garrison Keillor."

"What does that even mean?" Melody asked, laughing. "What kind of tits does a wolverine have?"

"Who the fuck knows? People are disgusting." Lacey speared a fried plantain off Melody's plate and grinned. "Present company excluded, of course."

"Did you tell her about the Krav Maga?" Tessa asked Lacey.

"I signed up for Krav Maga classes," Lacey said, shrugging.

"Tell her why."

"I'm going to apply to the next LAPD academy training class. I figured Krav Maga would give me a leg up on the physical abilities test."

"That's great!" Melody reached out to squeeze Lacey's arm. Even without the Krav Maga, she couldn't imagine Lacey would have any trouble passing the physical test. "Have you told your parents?"

Lacey shook her head. "I'm gonna wait until I'm actually accepted. *If* I'm actually accepted."

"You'll totally get accepted," Melody said.

Lacey pushed her food around on her plate. "We'll see, I guess."

When the waiter came back to clear away their plates, Lacey said something to him in Spanish, and a few minutes later, he brought out a piece of tres leches cake with a candle in it and set it in front of Melody.

"Feliz cumpleaños," Lacey said. "They offered to sing to you, but I figured you'd probably get embarrassed."

"Thank you," Melody said, looking down at the table before her watery eyes betrayed her. "For saving me from the singing and for the cake. And dinner. For the whole night, basically."

"Make a wish," Tessa told her.

I want more nights like this, Melody thought, and blew out the candle.

Chapter Thirteen

*M*elody was baking scones for her book club.

Yes, fine, she had joined a book club. But it was *not* because of anything her mother had said. It was only because she liked books. And she liked talking about books. And she wanted to meet other people who liked talking about books.

Her social life had been on an upswing lately, but going out with Lacey and Tessa had given her a taste for more. It was possible she also missed being in school a little. Not that she hadn't been glad to put MIT and all associated memories in the rearview mirror, but her whole life until this point had basically been devoted to school. Now that she was done with it, there was an empty space she didn't know how to fill.

Work was ramping up, but it still wasn't challenging enough to keep her busy. If she managed to stay at Sauer Hewson for two years, they would pay for her to go back to school for her Masters of Engineering, but in the meantime…

In the meantime, she was in a book club, which was why she was baking scones on a Friday night when Lacey called.

"I need a favor."

Melody switched her cell to her other ear and pulled open the oven. "Okay." She peered at the tray of cranberry scones inside. She wasn't much of a baker, but she was trying something new. Because trying new things was supposed to be good, right?

"It's kind of a big one," Lacey said apologetically. The sound of a heavy bass line thrummed in the background, which meant she was calling from work.

"You want me to kill someone for you?" Melody frowned at the scones, trying to decide if they needed a few more minutes.

"Not quite that big. I'm at work and Jeremy's here—drunk. I need you to come get him."

Melody set the tray of scones on the counter and yanked off her oven mitt. "Now?"

"Yes. I'm sorry. I'll explain when you get here."

"I've got book club tonight, Lacey. I'm bringing scones."

"God, you're such a nerd."

"Hey! Who's asking who for a favor right now?"

"I'm sorry, but it's Friday night. You really need to get a social life."

"This *is* me having social life!"

"Please, Melody."

"How did Jeremy Sauer get to be my problem?" He'd barely talked to her in weeks, and now she was supposed to drop everything to haul his drunk ass home?

"He needs a friend tonight," Lacey said. "And I need someone to take him home or I'm going to get fired."

Melody gazed sadly at her cranberry scones and sighed. "I'll be there in twenty minutes."

THERE WAS a stalled car on the Ventura Freeway, so it was closer to thirty minutes before Melody made it to Studio City, and then she had to drive around for another five before she found a parking space.

She dodged around a pack of *Wolf of Wall Street* wannabes congregating inside the door and headed toward the back of the bar where Lacey was pouring something that looked like orange Kool-Aid out of a shaker into a sugared martini glass. When Melody caught her eye, Lacey nodded at her and said something to one of the other bartenders before making her way over.

"Where's the emergency?" Melody shouted over the peppy music blaring from the speakers.

"Down there." Lacey nodded toward the far end of the banquette.

Melody peered through the crowd and spotted Jeremy perched on a bar stool with his head propped in his hands. "That doesn't look like a very big emergency, Lacey."

"Yeah, well, when I called you, he was ranting and yelling and trying to get into a fight with some of my customers. Fortunately, he seems to have graduated from asshole drunk to mopey drunk."

"Why is he like this?" Melody asked. "What happened?"

The few times she'd seen him at work recently, he'd seemed fine. Granted, it was at the office, where he had appearances to maintain, but she had assumed he was at least past the ill-advised drunken antics stage of the breakup by now.

"Drew and Charlotte got engaged," Lacey said.

Charlotte and Drew? How long had that been going on? "I didn't even know they were dating," Melody said.

"Neither did Jeremy. They've been keeping it a secret for months and lying to him about it. I guess he and Drew had some kind of fight when he finally found out." She shrugged. "There's a lot of history. It's messy."

"I guess so." All these attractive people with their complicated romantic entanglements—it was like an episode of *Grey's Anatomy*, only with fewer gross medical procedures.

"Yeah, and coming right on the heels of getting dumped by me..."

"Yeeeaaah." The people closest to Jeremy had been doing an

awful lot of lying to him lately. Melody could understand why he
was upset, although she wished he hadn't chosen her book club
night to get sloppy drunk and need rescuing.

"I know we're not together anymore, but I still care what
happens to him, you know?" Lacey gazed across the room, frowning. "I just want to make sure he's got someone to get him
home safe."

Melody looked at Jeremy. He made a pitiful sight, slumped
over the bar, morosely swirling the ice around in his glass. "You
owe me," she told Lacey. "Big time."

Lacey gave her a lopsided grin. "You can put it on my tab." She
pointed out a hallway next to the bar. "Take him out the back,
okay? There might be paparazzi out front."

Melody followed her through the crowd of customers to the
banquette where Jeremy was sitting.

"Hey, Jeremy," Lacey said, tapping him on the arm.

"Huh?" He peered up at her with heavy-lidded eyes.

"Melody's gonna drive you home now, okay?" She nodded at
Melody, who was standing on his other side.

Jeremy's gaze swung to Melody and registered her presence
before returning to his drink. "I'm good where I am, thanks."

"Come on. Get up," Lacey said.

"I don't need a goddamn babysitter, Lacey, and I don't have to
do what you want anymore." His vehemence was undercut by his
slurred delivery.

"Jesus, really?" The crowd at the bar waiting to order drinks
was getting hairy, and one of the other bartenders was making
desperate, get-your-ass-back-over-here motions at Lacey. "Shit,"
she said, throwing her hands in the air. "I've gotta get back
to work."

"I've got this," Melody said. "Go on."

"Thank you," Lacey mouthed before rushing off.

"Jeremy, come on," Melody said, turning back to him. "Let me take you home." She took him by the arm and tried to urge him off the barstool, but he had at least sixty pounds and eight inches on her, and he didn't budge an inch. It was like Tweety Bird trying to move Hector the Bulldog.

He gave her a slow, dull-eyed blink. "What're you doing here, Melody?"

She gave up trying to pull him off the stool and let go of his arm. "Lacey asked me to drive you home."

"*Lacey,*" he echoed, dripping with resentment. "Of course she did. Because Lacey always gets everything she wants. She gets to cheat on me. She gets to fall in love with someone else. She gets *you.*"

"What are you talking about?"

"You two are only friends because I introduced you, but she's the one who gets to keep you after the breakup, and I get nothing —I get no one. I don't even have Drew anymore."

Ouch. But also? Not exactly fair. Maybe Melody hadn't reached out to him much since the breakup, but he hadn't done any reaching out either. If anything, he'd been keeping his distance. She'd thought that was what he wanted.

"Hey." Melody leaned over so she could look him in the eye. "No one gets to keep me. Lacey said you needed a friend tonight, so here I am, dropping all my Friday night plans *for you.*"

He looked away and didn't say anything. Because he was a big pouty baby.

"You know what?" she said, reaching her limit. "I'm missing my book club to be here right now. I read *Les Misérables*! Do you know how long that book is? Really long, Jeremy—it's *really* long! I baked scones, too. Cranberry ones!" she shouted, poking him in the arm for emphasis. "From scratch!" Another poke. "Which are now going to go to waste because you needed someone to take your drunk ass home. So you are going to get up off that barstool and let me drive you home, *do you understand?*"

For a moment, he looked taken aback by her tirade, but then he pushed himself to his feet, swaying a little. Melody fit herself under his arm and steered him toward the hallway Lacey had indicated, which led to the delivery entrance in the back.

Jeremy kept his arm around her the whole walk back to the car, leaning on her for support. He smelled like a distillery, and his steps were slow and lumbering, but he managed to keep himself upright and walk in a more-or-less straight line. Still, he was *heavy*. It was a relief when they finally made it to her car and she could deposit him in the passenger seat.

"Thank god," she breathed as she collapsed into the driver's seat. "It didn't seem like that long of a walk on the way to the bar."

Jeremy didn't say anything. He had slumped down in his seat with his head against the glass and his eyes closed.

"I'm sorry about Charlotte and Drew," Melody said, feeling guilty about yelling at him before. She probably should have checked on him more after the breakup. Maybe he'd been hoping she would reach out to him. "Do you want to talk about it?"

"No," he said without opening his eyes.

Alrighty, then, maybe not.

"You're not going to yack in my car, are you?" Skipping book club to drive him home was one thing, but vomit in her car was more than she was willing to put up with, no matter what he was going through.

He opened one eye wide enough to register his offense. "No."

"Good." She pulled up the GPS app on her phone and shoved it at him. "Put your address in there."

While he was doing that, Melody twisted around and dug a bottle of water out of her yoga bag in the back seat.

"Drink this," she told him, trading the water for her phone. She set the phone in the holder on the dash, buckled her seatbelt, and started the car.

"Melody?"

She glanced over at him, eyebrows raised.

"Thank you for coming to get me."

Her annoyance melted away, and she reached over to give his forearm a squeeze. "You're welcome."

HERE WAS a thing Melody had not known about Jeremy Sauer: he still lived with his mother.

In Professor Xavier's mansion from *X-Men*, apparently—or something that looked like the Hollywood Hills equivalent of it. Which—okay, if Melody's mom lived in a freaking *mansion*, she might still be living at home, too. Except, no, scratch that, not even in a mansion would she ever again live with her mother voluntarily.

"Wow." Melody goggled at the imposing architecture as she parked her car on the circular driveway in front of the massive front door. "What's it like, living in a castle?"

Jeremy gave an indifferent shrug. "It's just a house." He seemed to have sobered up a little on the drive, but his mood still left something to be desired.

"Really? 'Cause it looks exactly like the fairytale castles I used to imagine when I was a kid playing princess and the dragon. My dog Waffles was the dragon—he was a dachshund. Very ferocious." She held her hands up in the shape of claws and made a ferocious face.

The corner of Jeremy's mouth dimpled into something that might almost have been a smile. "Do you want to see the inside? Since you're here."

"Inside there? I don't think I'm dressed for it."

"You're dressed fine. It's not black tie. It's my house." He tilted his head. "Come on, I'll give you a tour," he said, pushing the car door open.

Melody turned off the engine and followed him, because how

often did you get an invitation to see *Lifestyles of the Rich and Famous* up close and personal?

He held the heavy wooden front door open and gestured her into a large entry hall. Inside, the house was as still and solemn as a museum after hours. Silvery light slanted in through a bank of cut-glass windows on the landing above, illuminating an enormous stone fireplace that looked like it belonged in a Viking earl's mead hall. A collection of stuffy formal furniture was arranged artfully around the room.

Between the somber furnishings, the dark paneling, and the gothic architectural elements, the effect was a lot more *Haunting of Hill House* than cozy family home. The only thing remotely warm or personal was a round table holding a collection of framed family photos.

"Is that you and Hannah?" she asked, pointing to a picture of a big-toothed boy with a cowlick holding a baby in his lap.

He smiled faintly. "Yeah, she spit up all over me two seconds after that picture was taken."

The photo beside it was of a gawky, teenaged Jeremy and a man who could only be his father standing on the deck of boat. "You look just like your dad."

"That's what everybody says." Jeremy gazed at the picture a moment before tilting his head. "Come on. You'll probably like the library."

"Library?" Melody said, brightening at the prospect. "Yes, please."

He ushered her down a hallway lined with oil paintings in heavy gilt frames and into the library. Wide-eyed, she drifted to the middle of the room and spun slowly, taking in the space around her.

It was everything she had ever imagined a library should be: dark and mysterious and ornate, with a marble fireplace and wood paneling and leather chaises and a huge wooden desk...and the books! Floor-to-ceiling bookcases covered every wall, and every single shelf was filled to bursting with books of every conceivable subject matter. There was even a library ladder! Her whole life, she had fantasized about having a library with a ladder.

She went straight to it and climbed up the first few rungs to caress the antique leather bindings on the top shelf.

"You like it?" Jeremy asked behind her. When she turned around, he was smiling.

"It's amazing!" She shook her head in wonder as she stepped down. "Did you spend hours in here when you were a kid? You must have."

He shoved his hands in his pockets, regarding the room blandly. "I wasn't really allowed in here when I was a kid."

Melody made a sympathetic moue. "Oh." It was possibly the saddest thing he'd ever told her. What was the point of living in this kind of splendor if you weren't allowed to enjoy it?

He shrugged. "I was never much of a reader anyway."

One of the paintings on the wall caught her eye and she drew in a breath. "Is that a Whistler? Like, a real Whistler? That he painted with his actual hands?"

He nodded. "My dad was a big art collector."

She moved across the room to study it up close. "It's incredible. I can't believe you have this hanging in your house!" The detail in the brushwork was extraordinary. It was a whole different experience than looking at a print or a photo on the internet. The urge to run her fingers over the texture of the paint was so strong, she clasped her hands behind her back to restrain them.

Jeremy came over to stand beside her. "I didn't know you were into art."

"Oh, I'm not, really. But I took an art history class for my humanities requirement and Whistler was one of my favorites. I love his nocturnes. They're sort of dreamlike, but still grounded in realism, you know? There's something soothing about them."

Jeremy cocked his head to the side, studying the painting like he was looking at it for the first time. After a moment, he said, "There's another one in the hall upstairs if you want to see it."

Melody bobbed her head, bouncing on her toes. "Yes, please!"

He led her back to the front hall and up one of the two grand staircases flanking the room. Past the landing with the cut glass, up another half-flight of stairs, then down a long gallery overlooking the entry. At the end, they turned into a short hallway where another Whistler was on display. Unlike the gray and gold cityscape in the library, this one was a seascape in cool blues and violets.

"This was always one of my dad's favorites," Jeremy said.

"It's beautiful." She could see why his father had liked it. It was a quiet scene: just a body of calm water stretching out forever with three small ships in the distance. Something about the sweeping horizontal brushstrokes and subtle interplay of color filled Melody with a feeling of peace.

While they were admiring it, a door at the end of the hall opened and Geoffrey Horvath stepped out wearing nothing but a ladies' pink silk bathrobe. "Jeremy!" he exclaimed, stopping short at the sight of them.

Melody's eyes widened. Beside her, she heard Jeremy suck in a sharp breath, which she assumed meant he was as surprised as she was to encounter the Sauer Hewson CFO wandering around in what she could only assume was the CEO's bathrobe. Yikes.

"Geoff?" Angelica Sauer appeared at Mr. Horvath's side in a silk peignoir that matched his pink robe. Her face froze when she saw her son. "Jeremy. I thought you were out for the night."

"Evidently." Jeremy's voice was as cold as she'd ever heard it.

Melody edged behind him, hoping maybe Mrs. Sauer and Mr. Horvath wouldn't recognize her. That would probably not be terrific for her future prospects at the company.

"There's no need to take a tone," Mrs. Sauer said.

"Really? My father's best friend is sleeping with my mother and you don't think that calls for a tone?"

Mr. Horvath cleared his throat. "Jeremy—"

"How long have you been sleeping with my mother?" Jeremy demanded.

"*Jeremy,*" his mother said sharply. "Obviously, this isn't how we wanted you to find out—"

"Does Hannah know?"

"No, of course she doesn't know. She's at a sleepover tonight."

"How long has this been going on?"

"I don't really see how that's any of your business."

"*How long?*" Jeremy shouted, loud enough to make Melody flinch.

His mother lowered her eyes. "Five years."

"Five years?" His voice sounded strangled. "You were sleeping with Geoffrey when Dad was still alive? When he was *dying?*"

Melody glued her eyes to the floor, trying to make herself invisible. She shouldn't be here for this—she shouldn't be hearing *any* of this. The situation was bad enough, but the fact that it was unfolding in front of a stranger made it all *so* much worse.

Jeremy's mother took a step toward him. "It's complicated. You don't understand. I was only trying to protect you."

"No, you were trying to protect yourself, Mom. Because that's the only person you've ever cared about."

Mrs. Sauer's cold mask cracked into pure anguish. She made another move toward Jeremy, but he spun on his heel and stalked off.

Leaving Melody on her own with Angelica Sauer and Geoffrey Horvath in their respective states of dishabille. So, basically her worst professional nightmare come to life, only in reverse, because in her nightmares, *she* was the one half-naked in front of the company's top officers.

She offered them a strained, apologetic smile and ran after Jeremy, who was halfway down the stairs already. By the time she caught up to him, he was sitting in the passenger seat of her car. She got in behind the wheel and twisted in her seat to face him.

He looked absolutely wrecked. Like a little kid who'd lost his parents. She'd thought his life was so perfect, but it was an illusion. Underneath the surface, everything was a mess.

"Will you get me out of here, please?" he said in a choked voice.

"Where do you want to go?" she asked, aching for him.

His jaw clenched. "Absolutely anywhere that's not here."

Chapter Fourteen

She took Jeremy back to her apartment, because she didn't know what else to do with him.

He didn't say a word in the car, or during the walk upstairs. As soon as she had the door open, he sank down on her couch and buried his head in his hands. "Fuck this whole month."

Melody set her purse down and sat on the couch beside him. After a moment's hesitation, she laid her hand on his back.

He sighed against her fingers, blowing out a long, shaky breath. "Lacey found someone else. Charlotte and Drew have each other. Even my mom has Geoffrey." He let out a bitter laugh. "And I've got nothing, because I screw up everything I touch."

There was that debilitating self-doubt again. Melody's hand moved up and down his back, following the lines of tension. "That's not true."

"All this time, I thought Geoffrey believed in me, but it turns out he just felt guilty about screwing my mother."

"You don't know that."

He scrubbed his hands over his face, head still bowed. "I was a complete ass to Drew, and now he's not talking to me. I treated

Charlotte like shit. And when I tried to be better, I still managed
to screw things up with Lacey."

Melody's fingers curled into his back. "I'm not sure what
happened with Lacey was entirely your fault."

He sat up, and Melody retracted her hand as he leaned back
against the couch. "I couldn't make her happy," he said, glaring at
the opposite wall. "If she'd been happy with me, she never would
have fallen in love with someone else."

Fair enough. On the other hand... "Maybe she just wasn't the
right person for you. You know, you might want to consider
widening your dating pool beyond the Lopez sisters. Just a
thought."

His glare swung her way and softened. "I'm sorry to drag you
into all my problems. You didn't ask for any of this."

She shook her head. "Do you not remember that whole thing
where you found me bawling my eyes out in my car? I owe you."
Which gave her an excellent idea. "Ice cream!" she said, leaping
up from the couch. "That's what you need!"

"You don't have to—"

"Shush," she said as she pulled open the freezer. All the ice
cream shops were closed, but she always kept a supply on hand
—for emergencies, of course, which this definitely was. She
carried the tub of ice cream and two spoons into the
living room.

"Extreme Maximum Chocolate Fudge Chunk," she said, dropping onto the couch and setting the ice cream between them. She
presented Jeremy with a spoon. "Pour vous, monsieur."

He accepted the spoon and arched an eyebrow as he peered
into the tub. "I don't know, are you sure it's chocolatey enough?"

"Mmmm, you're right," she said, excavating a chunk of frozen
fudge. "You'd think they could have found a way to squeeze a little
more chocolate in here."

"It's like they're not even trying," he agreed around a mouthful
of ice cream.

Between the two of them, they managed to polish off the whole container in the space of a few minutes.

"Feel better?" Melody leaned forward to set the empty tub on the coffee table.

"Actually, I kind of have a stomachache now," he said, rubbing his belly.

"Me too," she admitted, making a face. She pulled her legs up underneath her and rested her head against the back of the couch.

"So much for my miracle ice cream cure." Jeremy yawned and stretched his arms out in front of him. "Shit, it's late," he said, catching a glimpse of his watch. He sat up and reached into his pocket for his phone. "I'll call a cab and get out of your hair."

"And go where, exactly?"

"Back to my car," he said, swiping his thumb across the screen. Which wasn't an answer to her question.

"And then what? Back home to face your mother?"

The hand holding the phone stilled.

"That's what I thought." Melody took his phone out of his hand. "Stay here tonight. You can have the couch."

Jeremy bowed his head, then turned to look at her with an expression that was heartbreakingly vulnerable. "You don't have to do that."

"I know," she said. "I want to."

"Thank you." He exhaled a long breath. "I'm just—I'm so tired."

She got to her feet. "Stay here. I'll find you a pillow and a blanket."

By the time she came back with the linens, Jeremy had fallen asleep, curled up on his side with one hand tucked under his chin. He looked younger with all the tension in his face eased away—more like the carefree college boy she'd met in Boston three years ago. Only with a much better haircut, thank god.

He didn't even stir when she draped the blanket over him.

"Sweet dreams," she whispered before turning out the lights.

———

WHEN MELODY WOKE in the morning, Jeremy was gone. In his place was a note scrawled on the back of a grocery receipt:

Called a cab. Thanks for the ice cream and company. Next time's on me. —J

While she ate her breakfast of stale scones, Melody thought about the fact that Jeremy Sauer—billionaire bachelor and fixture of the Los Angeles social scene—didn't actually have that many friends. Not real friends, anyway. Not the kind of friends who were good for more than just drinking and partying. The kind you could confess your fears and weaknesses to. Friends who actually came through for you when you needed them.

Apparently, that was something they had in common. Which was why she called him later that day to see how he was doing.

He sounded happy to hear from her. In fact, he sounded pretty happy in general, which was a dramatic improvement.

"Did you work things out with your mom?" she asked.

"In a manner of speaking. In my family, we don't really talk things out so much as mutually agree to a détente."

"That sounds cathartic."

He made a grunting sound. "Catharsis isn't in my mother's playbook. Too messy and undignified. But she's agreed to come clean to Hannah, so that's something. She's telling her tonight. Should make for a fun family dinner."

Melody twisted the hem of her shirt around her finger. Even imagining it made her feel anxious for him. "How do you think Hannah will take it?"

"I don't know, honestly. She likes Geoffrey a lot. And she was younger than me when we lost Dad. She doesn't remember him as well as I do. Maybe she'll be fine with it." He sighed like he was trying to resign himself to it. "I probably overreacted. I always knew my parents' marriage wasn't exactly a storybook. And my father's been gone for three years. It's not fair to expect my mother to play the grieving widow forever."

Melody pressed the phone to her ear. "I think you're allowed to be upset that she hid it from you for so long." Her shirt was twisted so tight, her finger was going numb. "Although, I guess I can understand why she'd be afraid to tell you."

He let out an unsteady breath. "I feel like I've been handling a lot of things badly lately."

"In your defense, you've had a lot to handle." Melody doubted she'd be doing even half as well under the circumstances.

"I'm sorry I made you miss your book club last night. Thank you for coming to get me."

"That's what friends are for, right?" She tried to make the words sound breezy, like it was just an expression. Like it didn't mean anything.

"Is that what we are? Friends?" The way he said it didn't sound breezy at all. He sounded earnest. Like it meant something.

Melody squeezed the phone. "I mean, at this point, I don't think there's any way of avoiding it."

He laughed softly. "No, I guess not."

A FEW DAYS LATER, Jeremy came to Melody's office. He just appeared in the doorway and stood there, silently waiting for her to acknowledge him.

She nearly jumped out of her skin when she finally noticed him.

"Jesus," she muttered, pressing her hand to her chest. "I didn't see you lurking there."

"I'm not lurking. I'm standing here right in plain sight." His shirtsleeves were rolled up to his elbows, and there were veins running down his forearms. Melody was pretty sure that meant he worked out a lot. He definitely looked like someone who worked out a lot.

She realized she was staring and lowered her eyes, feeling her face grow warm. "You could have said hi or something to get my attention."

"I didn't want to startle you."

"That didn't work out so well, did it?"

He shifted his weight to lean against the doorframe, grinning. "No. Next time I'll say hi."

Next time? She wasn't even sure what this time was, and there was already going to be a next time?

"I had fifteen minutes to kill between meetings," he said, answering her unspoken question. "So, I thought I'd stop by and say hi."

"Hi." So, this was just a friendly visit? Because they were friends now?

"Hi." His tongue skated over his lower lip. "I'm not bothering you, am I? If you're busy—"

"Nope, not bothering me, not busy. Not that I'm not working, because I am. Totally." She waved at her computer. "Hard at work, that's me. No slacking off here, Mr. Sauer, sir."

He snorted. "I'm not your boss."

She narrowed her eyes at him. "You kind of are, though. Aren't you?"

He shook his head. "I'm really not. I'm just another worker bee in the same hive as you."

"The hive your mother owns a majority share of."

"Yeah, but that's my mother. That's not me." The smile slid off his face and his shoulders sagged. "Trust me, no one listens to what I say around here."

"Rough day in the trenches?"

He shrugged. "No more than usual." His eyes lit on the row of action figures lined up on the shelf behind her desk and he wandered over for a closer look. "You've got quite the collection here. It's like a little army." He poked her Ron Swanson bobble-head, setting it in motion.

Melody swiveled her chair around, watching him. "It's possible I might have an addiction. Don't tell upper management, though —oops, too late."

The corner of his mouth curled into an almost-smile. "Your secret's safe with me." He picked up her Black Widow Funko Pop! figure. It was one of her favorites, the GameStop exclusive from *Age of Ultron* with Captain America's shield. Jeremy frowned at it. "How do you decide which ones come to the office and which ones stay home?"

"Oh, well, it's a very complex system based on total randomness and whimsy."

He set Black Widow down—in the wrong place. Melody shoved her hands under her legs, resisting the urge to fix her position. It was fine. She could do it after he left.

He turned around and cocked his head at her. "I should probably let you get back to work."

She shrugged. "I can work with you here."

"Okay." His eyes flicked to her computer screen. "What are you doing?"

"You don't want to know. It's boring."

The project she'd been assigned to was an update to some of their existing software for airplane climate control systems. It wasn't sexy or exciting, like the cargo craft for the Space Station, but the commercial airplanes division generated 70 percent of the company's revenue, so it was where most of their bread was buttered. And people needed heating and air conditioning when they were trapped like sardines in a flying tin can, so here she was, writing scripts to test the functionality of the software the developers were writing.

Jeremy dropped into the extra chair and leaned back, making himself at home. "I do boring all day long. I'm great at boring. Try me."

"Okay," she said. "Well, right now I'm running a test to make sure our software doesn't break if a user decides to change the name of one of the sensors in the middle of a test. Like, if they name one of the air flow sensors 'air_flow_1,' but then on hour three of a six-hour test, they decide to change it to 'air_flow_alpha,' our software has to be able to handle that without barfing. Which is a technical term that means to stop working in an impressive and messy way."

The corner of his mouth twitched. "Sounds important."

"It is. I'm a very important person. That's why they've got me in the luxury office suite, as you can see." She gestured around the room in her best impression of a spokesmodel.

He nodded. "Lots of privacy."

"That's true. I do like the privacy. I mean, not that I mind company, either," she added, in case he thought she was trying to get rid of him. "I love company. It can get pretty lonely down here, so it's nice to have a visitor every once in a while." She felt herself flush and smiled to cover the extra color in her cheeks.

Jeremy smiled back, showing off all his dimples. "In that case, I'll have to visit again."

Chapter Fifteen

*H*e did visit again. And again. And again.

Now that they were officially friends, Jeremy started dropping by Melody's office regularly to chat or hang out for a few minutes. Since her job still wasn't presenting all that much in the way of a challenge, she was always glad to have a distraction. Especially today.

"Hey," Jeremy, said leaning his head into Melody's office.

She was on the phone, so she held up a finger. He started to back out, but she waved him inside. "Mom, I've gotta go, someone just came to my office... Okay... Okay. Love you. Bye."

"You didn't have to get off your call," he said apologetically.

"Trust me, I was grateful for the excuse."

Sometimes she wondered whether she'd be just as welcome if she tried to stop by his office up on the executive floor for an impromptu chat. Not that she was planning to find out and risk running into Geoffrey Horvath or Angelica Sauer—both of whom she'd successfully managed to avoid making eye contact with since the infamous peignoir incident. No thank you.

She didn't even know where Jeremy's office was, exactly, or

what it looked like. She could have just asked him, but since she had no intention of ever going there, what was the point?

No, she was content to stay in her cave on the fifth floor, entertaining the occasional visit from Jeremy whenever he deigned to drop by. He'd complain about all the backstabbing that went on in the upper levels of management, and she'd complain about the devs who were always trying to insist the bugs she'd found were her fault and not theirs. It was so nice to have someone to share all her petty office annoyances with, she'd almost stopped being weirded out that he was the CEO's son.

"I was thinking of walking over to the Coffee Bean," he said, lounging against the doorway. "You in?"

"Oh my god, yes." She grabbed her purse and stood up. "I need all the coffee today."

He raised an eyebrow. "Everything okay?"

"Fine," she said with a false, bright smile. "Just hankering for a caffeine fix."

On the walk over, Jeremy talked about the Cyber Genome project the Advanced R&D group had been awarded by DARPA. Ordinarily, Melody would have been super interested in something like that, but she was preoccupied by the conversation with her mother, so she ended up nodding along without really listening.

"Okay," he said when they were sitting down with their coffee, "you usually get way more excited about this nerdy science stuff. Talk to me, Melody."

She blinked at him. "What?"

"Your head's somewhere else today. What's going on?"

"It's nothing," she said, reaching up to adjust her glasses. "It's just—my mother's coming to town next week."

He leaned back in his chair, eyebrows raised. "From the face you're making, I take it that's a bad thing?"

"No, it's not bad, exactly. It's just..." She cast around for the right words and came up empty. "It's my mother," she said, like that explained everything.

Jeremy nodded knowingly.

"Don't get me wrong, I'm excited for her to finally see my apartment and to show her around LA. Really, I am." She didn't want him thinking her mother was awful, because she wasn't—she just had a special talent for driving Melody crazy.

"But..." he prompted.

"But she's going to pester me about my love life—or complete lack thereof—the whole time she's here, and it's going to be exhausting." She shook her head, grimacing. "And pretty insulting, frankly."

"So, make something up. Tell her you're seeing someone."

Melody scrunched her nose. "You mean like a fake boyfriend?"

He shrugged. "If it'll get her off your back."

"It's not that simple. She's not going to just drop it if I say I'm seeing someone. That will only pique her interest more. She'll have a million questions. And she'll want to meet him." She rubbed her temples. It was a terrible idea in so many ways, it made her head hurt just thinking about it.

"I could pretend to be your boyfriend," he said, like it was no big deal.

"Yeah, right." This wasn't a Lifetime movie. She wasn't going to hire a fake boyfriend to fool her mom.

"Why not?"

"Because it would be a lie. And a completely ridiculous lie at that."

"It's not *that* ridiculous. And if it would make your mother happy to think you've got a boyfriend, what's the harm? It's not like we have to get fake married and spend the rest of our fake lives together raising fake children. In a few weeks, you can tell her it didn't work out. No harm done."

"It's still lying." Melody wasn't sure he had a firm grasp on the whole lying-is-wrong concept. "Although..." she smiled to herself, "the look on her face when I told her I was dating a billionaire would be priceless."

"I'm game if you are." He raised his eyebrows expectantly.

Melody tried to picture her mother, with her bedazzled denim jackets and press-on nails, meeting Jeremy Sauer, upper-crust Ivy League dropout and heir to a corporate empire. It was too embarrassing to contemplate.

"Yeah, no," she said, shaking her head. "I appreciate the offer, but I'm just gonna stick with the truth."

HER RESOLUTION TO stick with the truth lasted all of twenty minutes after her mother stepped off the plane at LAX.

"You look pale," her mom said while they were waiting for her checked luggage, fruitlessly watching the empty baggage carousel spin. "How do you live in Los Angeles and not have a tan?"

Melody's mother was very into tanning. Her skin had been irradiated to a deep, freckled brown that contrasted sharply with her hair, which was bleached a yellowish straw color.

"I work in a windowless office all day," Melody said. "And I don't tan anyway. I just burn, then end up exactly as pale as before."

Her mom made a sour face. "That's your father's genes."

Every undesirable genetic trait Melody possessed came from her father's side—according to her mother.

"Oh! That reminds me. You know Sandy, at work?"

Melody did not know Sandy. Her mom had been working as a receptionist at a car dealership for the last year, and Melody had never met any of her coworkers there.

"Well, she met a chiropractor on Christian Mingle and they're getting married in Hawaii at Christmas! How about that? I told you internet dating wasn't just for losers."

"I'm not particularly Christian," Melody said, gritting her

teeth. "And I don't want to date a chiropractor. They practice junk science."

Her mom waved her hand dismissively. "My *point* is, there's lots of options out there for young women these days. You don't want to waste your youth—believe me, baby, it doesn't last forever." She squinted at Melody with a faint look of distaste. "You're such a pretty girl, you know. If only you made more of an effort with your appearance."

Melody rubbed her temple. "You know that's insulting, right?" They hadn't even made it out of baggage claim and her sanity was already slipping.

"I'm just saying, it wouldn't kill you to show a little more of your feminine side. You can't expect to attract a man if you're dressed like one."

Melody could not believe she was being lectured on her fashion sense by a woman wearing a turquoise velour tracksuit and platform flip-flops.

"Unless you decide to go gay," her mother continued. "Which is fine with me, if that's what you want. My friend Maryellen went to a lesbian wedding last month, and she said it was very tasteful."

"I have a boyfriend," Melody heard herself say before she realized she was doing it.

Pamela Gage, no fool, raised a single stenciled eyebrow at her daughter. "Since when?"

"Not long. Just a couple weeks. That's why I didn't say anything before. I didn't want to jinx it." It was shameful how easily the lies came to her—but she wasn't ashamed enough to take them back. Desperate times, etcetera, etcetera.

"What's his name? What's he do? How'd you two meet?"

"His name is Jeremy, and we met at work."

Her mom rifled around inside her purse. "Jeremy's a nice name. Does he do the computer whatsit stuff, too?"

"For, like, the millionth time, it's called IT, Mom. It stands for Information Technology. And no, he's a management trainee."

"Well la-dee-da." Her mom unwrapped a stick of gum and shoved it into her mouth. "You got a picture of Mr. Manager-in-Training?"

Melody shook her head. "I told you, we haven't been dating very long. We haven't gotten around to taking any pictures yet." She had an answer for everything. Who knew she was so good at this fake boyfriend stuff?

"Am I gonna get to meet this executive stud?" her mom asked, popping her gum.

"I don't know." Melody bit her lip. "It's kind of soon to be introducing him to my mother, don't you think?"

Her mother reached over and squeezed her cheeks like she was a toddler. "Honey, there's no such thing as too soon to introduce a boy to your mother."

Dear lord, what had she done?

MELODY CALLED Jeremy that evening while her mom was in the bathroom "putting on her face" to go out for dinner.

She was taking her to Jerry's Deli. Her mother didn't like spicy food, which, by her definition, encompassed everything from Chipotle to P.F. Chang's. It made it hard to find a decent restaurant her mother wouldn't complain about being "too ethnic." An old-school New York-style deli seemed like a safe bet, though, and her mom would probably get a kick out of all the celebrity photos on the wall.

"What are you doing tomorrow night?" Melody asked Jeremy when he answered. "Please say nothing."

"Nothing that can't be changed."

"Will you come to dinner with me and my mother?"

There was a pause before he answered, long enough that

Melody had time to regret asking. "As your friend or your boyfriend?"

She cast a wary look at the bathroom door. Her mother was tunelessly singing a Billy Joel song as she put on her makeup. "The second one."

"Okay," he said gamely. "I'll make reservations. Seven o'clock?"

"Nothing too trendy. Or too exotic. She likes really boring food."

"Boring. Got it."

Melody exhaled a long breath. "Thank you."

"Melody?"

"Hmmm?"

"Don't worry. It's going to be fine."

Easy for him to say. He didn't know her mother.

Chapter Sixteen

"*W*ow," Melody said when she opened the door the next night. Jeremy had shown up with two bouquets of roses. He was wearing a suit like he usually did at work, but without a tie, and the glimpse his open collar afforded of the dent above his collarbone was oddly distracting, like she'd turned into a heroine in a Regency romance. "You really did not have to go to this much trouble," she said, tearing her eyes from his unnervingly attractive throat.

"It's not every day you meet your girlfriend's mother," he said with a wink, beaming his super-powered smile at her.

Oh no. This was a terrible, horrible, no good, very bad idea. What had she been thinking? He was way too perfect. Her mother was going to want to eat him with a spoon, and Melody was going to die of mortification. Not to mention, she was never going to hear the end of it when she eventually told her mother they'd broken up.

Jeremy tilted his head at her. "Melody?"

"Yeah?"

"Are you going to let me in?"

"Right! Sorry!" She stepped back, and he leaned over to brush a kiss on her cheek as he moved past her. It surprised her more than it should have. He'd always been a cheek kisser. She'd forgotten, since it had been so long since they'd had any social interactions outside of work.

"Relax," he whispered in her ear. "It's going to go great."

She knew he meant well, but the suggestion had the opposite effect on her.

"Ohmygawd, is this him?" Melody's mother screeched, coming into the room. She was wearing platform sandals and a bright floral wrap dress which would have been almost tasteful, if not for the truly stupendous amount of cleavage it showed off.

"Hi," Jeremy said, beaming The Smile at her and holding out his hand. "It's an honor to meet you, Mrs. Gage."

Melody's mom glowed as she took his hand in both of hers and shook it enthusiastically. "Oh no, honey, you should call me Pam. And believe me, the pleasure's all mine." She grinned at him, clutching his hand way past the point where it started to get weird—because of course she did.

When she finally released him, Jeremy presented her with one of the bouquets. "These are for you, Pam." He held out the other one to Melody with a smile. "And these are for you."

As he passed them to her, he kissed her again. On the lips this time.

Melody's eyes fluttered closed and she leaned into him without consciously choosing to do it. The kiss was light and chaste, but his mouth lingered on hers almost tenderly before he pulled away.

Her eyes flew open again, and Jeremy's forehead creased, his expression drawn in a silent question: *Was that okay?*

She forced herself to smile back at him, like kissing was something they did all the time. The whole situation was giving her major flashbacks to the night they first met, which was just...not something she needed to be thinking about right now.

Oh, shit. Lacey. She'd just kissed Lacey's ex-boyfriend.

After Melody had gotten off the phone with Jeremy yesterday, she'd called Lacey and told her what she'd asked him to do, just to make sure she was okay with it. Lacey had laughed it off and said it was fine, but she might not have been so fine with it if she had known there would be kissing involved.

"Aren't you two just the cutest!" Melody's mom squealed, delighted. "Oh, baby, where's your phone? Let's get some pictures of you lovebirds together."

"Mom, no!"

"I think that's a great idea," Jeremy said, smirking at her. The next thing Melody knew, they were posing like a couple high school kids heading out to prom while her mother snapped approximately a million pictures.

"A little closer," her mom ordered. "Jeremy, honey, put your arm around her waist. That's right, just like that. Now, smile!"

Jeremy wrapped his arms around Melody, pulled her close, and planted his lips on her cheek.

"Perfect!" Pam said. "Hold it just like that!"

Melody gave her mom to the count of three before pulling out of Jeremy's grasp. "Okay, enough pictures. We're going to miss our reservation."

JEREMY'S CAR WAS A SLEEK, pearl gray Jaguar. Melody was surprised—she'd assumed his tastes ran a little flashier and less…mature.

It was more than fancy enough to impress her mother, though. She spent the first five minutes of the drive exclaiming over it and fiddling with the backseat climate controls, to Melody's chagrin.

After she'd gotten tired of playing with the car, her mother leaned forward between the two front seats. "So, Jeremy, Melody tells me you two met at work."

Jeremy's eyes slid over to Melody and he smirked at the lie. "That's right."

Melody felt herself blush, and turned her face the passenger-side window.

"And you're some kind of management trainee? How'd you swing that?"

"Well, actually—"

"Business degree," Melody supplied for him. "They've got a whole management program at Sauer Hewson for business school graduates."

She'd elected not to tell her mom about Jeremy's family or his net worth. Imagining how much more her mother would be sucking up to him if she knew how rich he was made Melody want to die. Not to mention how much harder she'd take it when Melody eventually told her they weren't dating anymore.

Jeremy cut another glance at Melody, eyebrows slightly raised. She gave him a pleading look.

"Yeah, I started right out of Cal State," he told her mother.

"Well, good for you, honey. It's nice to see a young man who's not afraid to work hard in order to make something of himself."

Before her mom could say anything else, Melody reached for the radio and cranked up the volume.

THE RESTAURANT JEREMY had picked was absolutely perfect: nice enough to make her mom feel special, but not so nice that she seemed out of place.

"Is that Dustin Hoffman?" her mother stage-whispered as the hostess showed them to their table.

"Don't stare, Mom."

Their table was in the far corner, thank god. Nowhere near the guy who may or may not have been Dustin Hoffman. Melody's mother exclaimed over the menu for a while before settling on the chicken cordon bleu. Melody got the crab cakes and a gin and tonic. And then a second gin and tonic, because dinner with her mother and Jeremy was one mortification after another.

It started with her mom telling Jeremy about the night she went into labor, because sure, who didn't want to hear about amniotic fluid and placentas over a nice dinner? When Melody tried to gently shut her down, her mother retaliated with a story about the time Melody was four and tried to pee standing up like a boy. Then there was the way her mother always laughed too long and too loud at everything Jeremy said, and how she kept touching his arm when she did it. Not light touching either, but, like, caressing his biceps. *Ew.*

Jeremy bore it all with a patience that bordered on saintly, but it made Melody want to crawl under the table and die.

"I'm so sorry," she said as soon as her mom excused herself to go to the ladies' room.

"For what?"

"For my mother. She's awful, I know. I'm sorry you're having to deal with it."

"Melody," he said, looking at her like she was the one who was crazy, "your mother's great. I really like her, and I'm having a good time. Why aren't you?"

"Because she's just so...her. Everything she says and does is expertly calculated to embarrass me."

He shook his head, smiling. "She adores you. And...okay, she's a little enthusiastic, and she's definitely her own person, but do you have any idea how lucky you are? To have a mother who's proud of you and doesn't mind showing it?"

Melody thought about Angelica Sauer, with her rigid smile and proud manners, and felt a flush of shame. "Oh, crap, Jeremy, I didn't mean—"

He held up a hand, still smiling. "I'm not trying to make you feel bad. Believe me, I know how family can drive you crazy like no one else on earth. I'm just saying...I like your mother. She reminds me of you."

"Oh." Melody looked down at her lap, uncertain whether she was more horrified or flattered.

"You know they play music in the bathrooms in this joint?" her mother announced when she came back to the table. "So classy." She hummed a few bars of some unrecognizable tune, smiling as she swayed her head along with whatever song was playing in her head. "You know, when you kids get married—"

"Mom!" Melody said, but her tone was less sharp than it had been.

"What?"

"We've been dating for all of two weeks, maybe just—cool it with the marriage talk."

"All right, baby. I'm sorry." Her mother leaned over to pat her hand. "I can't help if I'm a long-range planner."

Melody's eyes found Jeremy's across the table, and the way he smiled at her made her embarrassment melt away.

HER MOTHER KEPT up a light patter in the car on the way home. Somehow, Melody managed not to mind so much, even when her mother told Jeremy about the time she'd stuck Red Hots up her nose and had to go to the emergency room to have them removed.

"And that's why I used to call her my little Red Hot," her mother concluded proudly, as if she'd just told the story of Melody's first-place state science fair project—which wasn't a story she'd bothered to trot out this evening, by the way. Probably because it wasn't embarrassing enough.

Jeremy's hand settled over Melody's, squeezing gently. The warmth of his skin traveled all the way up her arm before settling in her chest. She swallowed and looked away, but she didn't move her hand. They were supposed to be dating; this was just part of the act.

When they got to her apartment, he walked them up to her front door, but begged off her mom's offer of a nightcap—apparently, her mom was living in a 1980s soap opera where people actually used the word nightcap—with the excuse that he had an early breakfast date with his mother.

"Do you hear that? What a good boy he is!" her mom said. "You better hang onto this one."

Melody clamped her lips together and cast her eyes to the heavens while her mother gave Jeremy a hug that fell squarely in the valley between overly-familiar and downright creepy.

"It was lovely to meet you, Jeremy. You take good care of my girl, you hear?"

"Don't you worry, Pam. I plan to do exactly that," he said with a wink, laying on the charm.

"I'm just gonna go on inside and leave you two alone to say your goodnights," her mom announced with the least subtle wink in the entire history of facial expressions.

"Thank you," Melody said to Jeremy once her mother was safely inside. "Seriously. Thank you so much."

"It was my pleasure," he said, smiling down at her. He'd been smiling almost the whole evening, and she felt warm and toasty from being in close proximity to it for so long. "You've saved my ass enough times by now, I'm just happy I could return the favor."

His eyes flicked over to the window, and he pressed his lips together to stifle a smile. "She's watching us through the blinds."

Melody sighed, her head falling forward in embarrassment. "Of course she is."

"We better put on a good show."

Melody shook her head. "You don't have to—"

But he was already tilting her head up, and then he was kissing her. Like, *really* kissing her. It was gentle and a little tentative at first, but it was definitely not chaste like the last one.

And it just went on. And on. The way you'd kiss someone you really, really liked. And the longer it went on, the less tentative it got, until his tongue was exploring her mouth, and she was kissing him back as much as she was being kissed.

It wasn't real—the rational part of her brain understood it was all for show. But the part of her brain that wasn't rational couldn't manage to focus on anything other than the fact that *she was kissing Jeremy*—and it felt amazing.

He was an outstanding kisser. She still had that data filed away from three years ago, but now she was getting a firsthand refresher course, and *holy shit*.

The thing was, it didn't feel fake. It felt like they were back on the sidewalk outside the Cask 'n Flagon and she was losing herself in him all over again.

She gasped against his mouth, breathless and entirely too swept up, and he broke away. For a long moment, he gazed down at her with eyes that were dark and unreadable. His arms were still wrapped around her, holding her tight, and she was clinging to him, and—oh, hey, one of his hands was on her ass. When had that happened?

She swallowed—hard. "Jeremy."

He let go abruptly and stepped back. She wavered at the sudden loss of contact, and his hand shot out to steady her. As soon as he was sure she wasn't going to fall—and wouldn't that be the perfect capper to this night, if she literally swooned at his feet—he released her again.

"You think she bought it?" he asked, smirking at her.

Melody cleared her throat. "Definitely."

"Good. Okay. Well, goodnight," he said, like everything was perfectly normal. Like he hadn't just kissed the ever-loving shit out of her. Like her stomach wasn't still doing somersaults because of it.

He turned away and headed back to his car.

So—okay. What?

Melody watched him drive away, feeling like she'd been hit by a truck.

Get a grip, she told herself. It was just an act. It had to be. *Right?*

If it had been real, he wouldn't have just walked away like that, like nothing had happened. He wouldn't have *smirked* at her like that.

"Look at you. Your cheeks are all flushed!" her mother observed when she finally went inside. "I'll bet the sex is off the charts with that one."

"*Mom,*" Melody groaned, praying for the sweet release of death. "I'm begging you."

MELODY WAS asleep when her phone rang in the morning. She'd been up half the night replaying that goodnight kiss with Jeremy in her head, and slept in later than she'd meant to. Groaning, she rolled over and fumbled for her phone.

Shit. It was Lacey.

She'd kissed Lacey's ex-boyfriend last night. Like, *a lot.* Shit.

Melody put the phone to her ear and squeezed her eyes shut. "Hey."

"How was your date with Jeremy?"

"Uhhh..." She tried to think of something to say that didn't involve Jeremy's tongue being down her throat.

"Was your mom impressed? He gives great mom, doesn't he? I mean, *my* mom hated him, but most moms love him."

"Yeah...she, uh, really liked him." She should tell Lacey about the kiss, shouldn't she? Yes—no. Yes. She should definitely tell her.

"I knew she would."

"You were right." Although...Lacey was totally on board with the whole fake-date thing, so maybe she wouldn't care that they'd kissed? It wasn't like it was real. Maybe she'd expected it. Maybe Melody didn't *have* to tell her.

"You okay? You sound funny. Is your mom totally stressing you out?"

"No, um—I mean, a little, but no, I'm fine." She should probably tell her anyway. Just in case she did care. Come clean, put all her cards on the table, face the music...and a bunch of other clichés she couldn't think of right now.

"You want me to stage an intervention? I can come help you entertain her this afternoon."

"No!" Melody said. "I mean, thanks, but I've got it. I wouldn't want to put you through that. Enjoy your Sunday."

"Okay." She could practically hear Lacey's shrug over the phone. "You wanna get dinner this week? I'm off Thursday."

"Definitely. We should definitely do that."

"Cool," Lacey said. "I'll call you later in the week."

"Great! Bye!"

Melody groaned and buried her face in a pillow.

Today was her mom's last full day in Los Angeles, so after Melody dragged herself out of bed and showered, she took her to The Grove.

Melody hated shopping malls, but her mom loved them, so there they were, wandering around a mall that wasn't all that different from any other mall in America, except at this one there was a slightly increased chance of spotting a C-list teen pop star or supporting television actor.

Her mom was pawing through the sale rack at Tommy Bahama like a professional shopper when Jeremy's name lit up the screen of Melody's phone. Her heart stuttered to a stop.

"Is that Jeremy?" her mom asked in a singsong voice, leaning over for a peek at the screen. "I'll just give you two a little privacy, shall I? Catch up with me at the UGG store."

Melody waited until her mom was out of earshot before answering. "Hey," she said unsteadily. She was torn between feeling relieved he'd called and afraid of what he might be calling to say.

"Hey." The sound of his voice made her stomach twist into knots. "I was just calling to check on you."

Melody's brain was jumping up and down, waving its arms and

screaming, *What was that kiss? Please explain,* but all she said was, "Oh."

"How's it going with your mom today?"

Melody stepped away from a gaggle of noisy middle-aged ladies and ducked under a potted palm. "Pretty good, I guess. We're at The Grove."

"When's she fly back?"

"Tomorrow morning."

There was a pause. "She's not going to think it's weird that I'm not around today, is she?"

"I told her you had plans today. It's fine."

"Good. As long as you don't need me." She couldn't get a read on his tone at all. Was he relieved? Disappointed? Indifferent? Ambivalent? She didn't have a clue.

Melody chewed on her lower lip. "No, I don't need you."

There was another pause, longer this time. "Well, I better let you get back to your shopping. I just figured I should call, since that's what boyfriends do."

"Thank you for last night," she said. "Really."

"Don't worry about it. It was nothing."

That was her answer, then.

It was nothing.

She was right. It had all been fake.

When Melody caught up to her mom, she was trying on a pair of hideous fleece boots she'd only be able to wear three days out of the year in Tampa. "What do you think?" she asked, spinning in front of the mirror.

"I think they're ridiculous. You'll never be able to wear them back home."

Her mother looked up at her and frowned. "Everything okay with you and Jeremy, baby?"

"Yep," Melody replied with an over-wide smile. "Everything's great."

Chapter Seventeen

"*T*hat looks suspiciously like a bribe," Melody said, eying the coffee and blueberry muffin Jeremy had just deposited on her desk.

Nearly two weeks had passed since The Kissing Incident, and they were both doing an excellent job of not talking about it. They'd settled into an unspoken mutual agreement to act like it hadn't meant anything. Which, clearly, it hadn't.

Melody was absolutely fine with this. She 100 percent did not want to talk about their supposedly fake kiss that had felt a lot more real than fake—a kiss she had never managed to tell Lacey about, by the way. Not dealing with it was her preferred mode of dealing with it. If Jeremy was fine with pretending it never happened, then so was she.

So fine with it.

"That's hurtful," he deadpanned, dropping into the spare chair she'd started to think of as his since he was the only one who ever sat in it. "Why do you think I need an ulterior motive to bring you coffee?"

"And a muffin," she pointed out. "Which you have never brought before. Not once."

He gave her a challenging look over the top of his coffee. "Maybe I'm feeling extra nice today."

She responded with a raised eyebrow.

"All right, fine. I need a favor."

"What is it this time?" She gave the coffee an experimental sniff. It was a vanilla latte—her usual go to.

Leaning back, he stretched his legs out in front of him and rested his coffee cup on his thigh. "Remember when your mother came to town and you begged me to pretend to be your boyfriend?"

Melody felt herself stiffen and covered it by reaching for the muffin. "I seem to recall you volunteered for that assignment," she said in something approximating a breezy tone. "But do go on."

"I need a date for this party next weekend."

The piece of muffin she was holding crumbled to bits in her fingers, sending a shower of crumbs across her desk. "I find it hard to believe you're hurting for female companionship," she said, struggling to keep her voice steady as she swept the crumbs into the trashcan.

"It's Drew and Charlotte's engagement party," he said, lowering his eyes. "It's awkward enough I have to toast my best friend's future happiness with my ex-girlfriend, but Lacey's going to be there, too. With Tessa."

Melody pursed her lips in sympathy. "Oh."

"I just thought—it'll be easier to face it with a friend. Someone who'll keep me from doing anything stupid, you know?" He looked up at her with hopeful eyes. "So, what do you say? Want to be my date for what is absolutely guaranteed to be a miserable evening—and before you answer, please remember I brought you a muffin."

"I'd be happy to," she said, powerless in the face of his big doe eyes. Even if she hadn't been a sucker for those blue eyes of his, she owed him.

"Thank you." Jeremy exhaled in relief, his shoulders slumping forward. "I really appreciate it."

Melody focused on the remnants of her muffin and tried to keep her tone casual. "So...this isn't so much me pretending to be your girlfriend as just being a friend you happen to be bringing as your date, right?"

"I guess, yeah."

She kept her gaze locked on the muffin, concentrating on breaking the rest of it into bite-sized pieces like she was performing brain surgery. "Because it might be weird, otherwise. You know, with Lacey there. I wouldn't want to—"

"No, of course," he agreed. "That would be bad."

"Right." Melody nodded absently at her devastated muffin. "As long as we're on the same page."

MELODY'S APARTMENT didn't have a full-length mirror.

All the other apartments she'd lived in had always had one—usually tacked to the back of the bathroom or closet door by some long-lost tenant decades past.

But this apartment was newish, and no one who'd lived here had ever seen fit to hang a full-length mirror. Or maybe they'd all owned free-standing mirrors. That was what people with money and nice things had, right? Matching bedroom sets with a big mirror in a fancy wooden stand?

Melody didn't have one of those. She had a mattress and box springs on a plain metal frame and a pair of mismatched nightstands from Goodwill.

Which was why she was currently standing on top of her toilet, frowning at her reflection in the bathroom mirror.

This dress certainly made her boobs look fantastic, but did they look *too* good? The last thing she wanted was to look cheap or slutty. Or, god forbid, like she was trying too hard.

Drew and Charlotte's engagement party was being held at the

Marina Del Rey Yacht Club. Melody had never been to a yacht club before. She wondered if the men would all be wearing navy blue dinner jackets and white captain's hats like Mr. Howell on *Gilligan's Island.*

Maybe not.

Anyway, in honor of the occasion, she'd put her contacts in for the first time in months, and wrestled her hair into a fancy up-do she'd learned from a YouTube tutorial. She'd also splurged on an expensive designer dress and shoes, which had cost more than most of the furniture in her apartment. She figured it was an investment in her new, professional adult life. In theory, it would be the first of many occasions in her future that would require a fancy dress. She'd tried to pick a style that was versatile and classic, so it would last her a while.

Melody hopped down from the toilet and slipped into her new shoes. They were Louboutins, just like the stars wore on the red carpet. She'd assumed outrageously expensive designer heels would be more comfortable than the cheap ones. Not so much. She'd been wearing them around her apartment for the last week to break them in, but they still felt like instruments of torture. Outrageously expensive instruments of torture.

She'd hoped maybe she'd feel more confident tonight if she were armored in designer duds. But even with her expensive new accoutrements, she still felt hopelessly out of her league. More like a little kid playing dress-up than a grown woman prepared to spend an evening rubbing elbows with the upper crust.

When she'd told Lacey she was going as Jeremy's date—strictly as friends, of course—and confessed she was nervous about fitting in, Lacey had snorted and told her not to worry about it. *"Half of them are snobs who won't like you no matter what you do, and the other half are jumped-up trash so busy pretending to have class they won't even notice you. And you don't have to worry about my family. We're all a bunch of rubes who've never been to a yacht club either. I promise you'll look great standing next to my Aunt Flora."*

At the knock on her front door, Melody took a deep, bracing breath. That would be Jeremy—and only five minutes late. *Ready or not, here I go.*

His eyes went wide when he saw her, and his mouth fell open.

"What?" she asked anxiously. "Do I look okay? I'm not over-dressed, am I? Or am I underdressed? I wasn't sure how formal it would be."

"No, you look great." A slow smile spread across his face. "Better than great. You look stunning, actually."

"Oh." She felt her cheeks redden. "Thank you." It would have been more of a compliment if he hadn't seemed so surprised, but she would take what she could get.

Jeremy waited while she locked her front door, then offered an elbow for her to hold onto. He smelled especially good tonight. He looked good, too, but then, he always looked good, and it wasn't like she hadn't seen him in an impeccably tailored suit before—it was his standard workday uniform.

"You ready for this?" she asked as he escorted her to the car.

His smile faded into a grimace. "As ready as I'll ever be."

He was driving a sporty black BMW coupe tonight instead of the Jaguar sedan he'd used to drive her mother to dinner. Melody was dying to ask how many cars he actually owned, but one look at his taut expression made her think better of it.

"Is there anything in particular you need me to do tonight?" she asked instead as he pulled away from the curb. He'd helped her through that mega-awkward dinner with her mom like a champion, and she was determined to do the same for him.

His grip tightened on the steering wheel, turning his knuckles white. "Don't let me drink too much. Or say anything shitty to anyone. If I start to act like an asshole—I don't know, drag me away or tell me to shut up or something."

"You're going to be fine," Melody said. "It won't be that bad. You'll see."

She'd make sure of it.

———

JEREMY'S HAND glued itself to the small of her back as soon as he helped her out of the car, and it stayed there as he ushered her inside—directly to the bar.

Drew's father knew how to throw a fancy shindig, that was for sure. Or more likely, he knew how to hire a team of professional party planners to throw a fancy shindig for him.

The ballroom at the yacht club was lit by literally hundreds of candles tucked into mossy, woodland-themed floral arrangements covering nearly every surface in the room. Combined with the garland-bedecked chandeliers sparkling overhead, and the view through the large picture windows of the moonlight reflecting off the water, it was like stepping into a fairy realm.

Once they were properly armed with drinks, Jeremy surveyed the room like he was girding himself for battle. There were no captain's hats in evidence, Melody noted with some disappointment. There were, however, one or two celebrities she recognized. And probably a few more she didn't recognize. Given Drew's dad's job, it was safe to assume a lot of the people in the room were involved in the film industry to some extent or another. It was a little exciting.

For about five whole minutes.

Rich people, Melody quickly discovered, were insanely boring. Jeremy's attention was monopolized almost immediately by a series of people intent on treating Drew's engagement party like a networking opportunity. Everyone he talked to seemed to have something to sell or some agenda to promote beneath the veneer of small talk. If they weren't looking for investors to finance their latest movie project, they were pushing a political initiative or their pet charity project.

Jeremy dutifully turned on his patented charm and played the game right along with them. It was strange, watching him flip a switch and transform into this whole other person who was confident, flirtatious, and, to be honest, a bit smarmy. She didn't like this version of him as much, although she could respect the skill —and the need for it.

Melody did her best to follow suit, plastering a smile on her face and nodding along with the conversation, despite the fact that most of the people made no attempt to include her past the introduction stage. Since she wasn't the one with the big fat checkbook, they seemed to have no use for her. She tried to pay attention, but it was all so boring—and faintly nauseating— listening to the barefaced posturing, pandering, and maneuvering of the rich and powerful. Not a single one of them said anything that sounded the slightest bit sincere. After a while, it all faded into a monotonous buzz of white noise.

What made it even harder to concentrate on the conversation was the fact that Jeremy kept resting his hand on the small of her back, like he wanted to let her know he hadn't forgotten she was there. It was sweet. The thing was, though, her dress had a plunging back, which she'd thought nothing of in the store. But now, standing in a roomful of Hollywood movers and shakers with Jeremy Sauer's palm pressed against her bare skin and his thumb idly caressing little circles against her spine, it was...distracting. Like, tingly, goose-bumpy, all of her nerve endings jangling distracting.

"Looks like you're in need of a refill," Jeremy said to her when there was a pause in his conversation with a red-faced gentleman from the Los Angeles Business Council. "Excuse us, won't you, Charles?"

Melody exhaled as Jeremy led her over to the bar again.

"Sorry," he said, relieving her of her empty wine glass and signaling the bartender. "I know this must be boring for you." Now that it was just the two of them again, he'd switched off the reflexive charm, and she could see the signs of strain in his expression.

"It's fine," she said. "Don't worry about me." She had a better understanding now of the burdens he'd shouldered and how they weighed on him, and she was all about making tonight easier for him. She wasn't there to have fun; she was there to be a good friend and give him whatever he needed.

"If it's any consolation, it's just as boring for me."

Of that, she had no doubt, but before she could reply, Drew appeared behind Jeremy and clapped him on the shoulder. "I should have known I'd find you at the bar, man!"

"Hey, there's the guest of honor, finally!" Jeremy pulled him into one of those bro hugs that involved a lot of hearty backslaps. "I was beginning to think you'd skipped out on your own party."

"Don't think I didn't consider it. This bash is a major snooze-fest." Drew's eyes drifted to Melody, and he raised his eyebrows slightly.

"You remember Melody," Jeremy said, slipping his arm around her waist. Which, okay, felt like something you'd do with a date-date and not a friend-date, but Jeremy was the one driving the bus tonight, so she went with it.

"I sure do," Drew said, grinning like he'd just been let in on some private joke. "Nice to see you again."

Melody gave him the polite smile she'd been perfecting all evening. "Congratulations on your upcoming nuptials."

The bartender dropped off their drinks, and Jeremy passed Melody a fresh glass of wine.

"Speaking of, where's the soon-to-be ball and chain?" he asked Drew.

Drew snorted. "Oh, man, don't let Charlotte hear you saying something like that."

"Don't let Charlotte hear you saying something like what?" asked a gorgeous, dark-haired woman who'd come up behind him. The infamous Charlotte Lopez, Melody guessed from the way she wrapped her hands possessively around Drew's arm and directed a cold glare at Jeremy—and the fact that she looked like a taller, thinner, frownier version of her sister.

For a split second, Jeremy went rigid, but then he fixed his billion-dollar smile back in place and beamed it at Charlotte. "I was just trying to tell Drew I didn't think you'd appreciate being referred to as the old ball and chain," he said, blithely throwing his best friend under the bus.

Charlotte gave him a tight smile. "Nice try, Jeremy, but I think we all know which one of you has the commitment issues."

Jeremy's smile froze in place, and he reached for Melody's waist like he was grasping for life support—which she figured was her cue.

"You must be Charlotte," she said in the brightest voice she could muster, sticking out her hand. "Congratulations on your engagement."

"Charlotte, this is Jeremy's...uh..." Drew gestured in Melody's direction, "Melody," he concluded helpfully.

"Nice to meet you," Charlotte said, taking Melody's hand and flashing a mouthful of blinding white teeth. "You must be Jeremy's latest girlfriend."

Which was the point in the conversation when one of them should have explained that they were just there as friends. That would have been the reasonable, straightforward thing to do. But Jeremy's hand was clamped onto Melody's hip like a vise, and he seemed to have gone mute, abandoning the ball in her court.

"That's right," she heard herself say, for reasons she didn't entirely understand. "I am."

Well, crap.

Chapter Eighteen

*J*eremy's fingers curled gratefully into Melody's hip, and she leaned into him, her smile widening to match Charlotte's. "I understand you're in law school."

"Yes, I'm in my second year at UCLA," Charlotte said, cutting her eyes to Jeremy.

"Melody! There you are!" Lacey said, bounding up to them. Because things weren't already awkward enough, apparently. Yay.

Jeremy paled at Lacey's appearance, and Charlotte's smile grew thinner as she turned to look at her sister.

"Oh boy," Drew muttered into his drink.

"Lacey! Hi!" Melody said, determined to ignore all the tension simmering around her. "Where's Tessa?"

"With my mom," Lacey said, hooking a thumb over her shoulder. "Being shown off to all her friends."

"You two know each other?" Charlotte asked, looking from Lacey to Melody.

"Yeah, Jeremy introduced us." Lacey grinned. "Melody's my yoga buddy."

"How nice." Charlotte's smile was frosty enough to lower the temperature of the room a few degrees. "It's so great that all of Jeremy's lovers can be friends."

Lacey's gaze drifted down to Jeremy's hand, which was still stapled to Melody's waist. She gave Melody a questioning look.

"Hey, I wonder when that band's going to start playing?" Drew mused to no one in particular.

"Excuse me. I see someone over there I need to talk to," Charlotte said before making a beeline for the far side of the room.

"That went well," Jeremy muttered, grimacing into his scotch.

"Better than I expected, honestly," Drew said with a shrug.

"Can I talk to you for a second?" Melody asked Lacey, taking her by the arm and leading her away from Jeremy and Drew.

"*Are you and Jeremy dating?*" Lacey asked, gaping at her.

"No," Melody said. "Definitely not."

"Are you sure? Because it *looks* like you're dating."

Melody sighed and shook her head. "Charlotte asked if we were dating, and Jeremy was floundering, and I may have accidentally...led her to believe we were. But we're not, I swear. I would never do that to you."

"Oh." Lacey frowned. "That's too bad."

Melody blinked at her. "Say what now?"

"I think you guys would make a cute couple. I've been sort of rooting for you to get together."

"Since when?"

Lacey smirked. "Since that night I called you to pick him up from the bar."

"Wait, you *want* me to date your ex-boyfriend?" Melody couldn't wrap her brain around it. It was too crazy.

"Why not? It's not like I'm still hung up on him. I just want him to be happy, you know?" Lacey poked her in the arm. "I want both of you to be happy."

Melody shook her head hard enough to make herself dizzy. "That's not on the table, Lacey. Like, really, so much not on the table. It's on the floor in the next room, it's so much not on the table."

Lacey rolled her eyes. "Girl, please. I've seen the way you two look at each other. I've seen the way you *are* around each other. There's something there."

"It's not like that," Melody insisted. "There's nothing—we don't have anything in common. Like, at all."

"Sure you do."

Melody shook her head again. "No, really—"

"You like each other," Lacey said. "What else do you need to have in common other than that?"

Melody's mouth had gone dry. "Not—not like that. Not like you're thinking."

Lacey shrugged. "Whatever you say—oh shit, looks like Tessa's about to hit the panic button. I better go rescue her from my mom's work friends." She pulled Melody into a quick hug. "Don't count Jeremy out on my account is all I'm saying."

Melody watched her make her way back to Tessa, who was at the center of a group of crunchy-looking middle-aged women. When Melody turned around to look for Jeremy, he was already heading her way.

"Hey, I'm sorry about all that," he said. "That was pretty awkward."

She shrugged like it was nothing. "We knew it would be."

"Is Lacey—?"

"She's fine. I told her the truth." She left out the part where Lacey had totally given them her blessing, because that wasn't something she knew how to tell Jeremy. *Oh, hey, did you know your ex-girlfriend thinks we should date? What do you think we should do about that?*

Yeah. No.

Guilt clouded his expression. "If you want, I'll tell Charlotte the truth, too."

Melody shook her head a little too vigorously. "I'd rather not have her thinking I'm a compulsive liar, thanks all the same." A nervous laugh escaped her. "We can maintain the charade for the rest of the night, right?"

Jeremy laid a hand on her shoulder, and a feeling of calm washed over her at his touch. "Only if you're sure you're okay with it."

She breathed in through her nose and out through her mouth, then forced herself to nod. "I'm sure," she said with a lot more conviction than she felt.

"Thank you." His voice had gone soft and sincere. "I know you aren't wild about lying, and I appreciate that you did that for me." His fingers squeezed her shoulder before letting go.

She pasted on a smile and tried to make her words sound bright. "Hey, that's why I'm here tonight. To look out for you." His tie was crooked, so she reached up to straighten it for him. "How are you holding up?"

He gave her a weary but sincere smile. "Better with you here." Something over her shoulder caught his attention and his expression went flat. "Mom."

Oh, fuck.

Melody stiffened and jerked her hands away from him. It hadn't occurred to her that his mother would be there. Although, in retrospect, it probably should have. Jeremy and Drew had been friends since high school, and their families traveled in the same social circles. Of course Jeremy's mother would be invited to Drew's engagement party.

"Hello, darling." Angelica Sauer leaned forward to brush a kiss on her son's cheek before her cool, appraising gaze zeroed in on Melody.

"Mom, you remember Melody?" Jeremy's hand slipped around her waist, tugging her closer.

It was the first time she'd been face to face with Angelica Sauer since that night at her house. The urge to flee was screaming in her hindbrain, but the reassuring pressure of Jeremy's touch kept her anchored in place.

"Of course," his mother said, smiling like the last time they'd met was at a Junior League luncheon and not when she'd been caught in flagrante by her son. "So lovely to see you again, dear."

"Good evening, Mrs. Sauer," Melody managed to say without stammering hardly at all.

Angelica Sauer's eyes lingered on Melody, narrowing slightly before she turned to address Jeremy. "Have you seen Andrew, by any chance?"

"Last I saw he was out on the terrace, I think."

"Smoking those wretched cigars, I expect. I'd better go round up Geoffrey so we can pay our compliments to the host." She honed in on Melody again, her expression inscrutable. "Enjoy the rest of your evening."

As soon as Jeremy's mother was safely out of earshot, Melody exhaled a long, shaky breath. "That was terrifying."

"Believe it or not, I think she actually likes you."

Melody shuddered. "If that's how she is around someone she likes, I'd hate to see how she treats the people she hates."

His gaze wandered to the bandstand. "It looks like they're about to start the toasts." The waitstaff had begun circulating through the crowd with champagne, and he snagged a pair of glasses off a passing tray.

A few minutes later, Drew's father, Andrew Fulton II, stepped up to the mic and grandly welcomed his guests. He looked like a banker with a Hollywood makeover: Botox, spray tan, and what Melody was pretty sure were hair plugs. His manner was easy and engaging, and his speech was so adroitly peppered with jokes, she couldn't help wondering if it had been scripted by one of the screenwriters he had under contract.

A woman who appeared to be his wife stood beside him, teetering slightly in her seven-inch heels and smiling as wide as her collagen lips would allow.

"Is that Drew's mom?" Melody whispered to Jeremy. She looked too young to have a grown son, but with all the plastic surgery, it was hard to know for sure.

"Stepmom. His second stepmom, actually. His mom died when he was twelve."

Melody felt a twinge of sympathy. Nothing about Drew's family seemed real. His stepmother was straight out of Central Casting, and as polished as his father's speech was, there wasn't a hint of genuine affection or emotion.

When Mr. Fulton finished his toast, he passed the mic to Charlotte's father. Robert Lopez made a marked contrast to Andrew Fulton's oily charm. He was barrel-chested with a weather-beaten face and thick mustache reminiscent of Edward James Olmos. Evidently not a man of many words, he offered a gruff but heartfelt toast to his daughter's future happiness before ceding the mic to his wife.

Lacey and Charlotte's mother was the effusive one in the family. She rambled enthusiastically about Charlotte and Drew, telling a long-winded story about the first time Charlotte brought him home for dinner. Dr. Lopez looked every bit the stereotypical feminist academic, from her salt-and-pepper hair and chunky earrings, right down to her comfortable sandals.

The crowd's attention was wandering by the time she wrapped up her toast, but then Drew stepped up to the mic and won them over again with his effortless charisma. Halfway through his surprisingly earnest testament of his undying love for Charlotte, Melody slipped her hand into Jeremy's.

"You okay?" she murmured, leaning toward him.

He nodded and gave her hand an appreciative squeeze.

When Drew's toast to his bride-to-be was over, the band launched into "When I Fall in Love," and the happy couple opened the dancing. Jeremy watched them silently, his face devoid of expression.

"Dance with me," he said as soon as the first dance was over and the band switched to "It Had to Be You."

"Um, did I mention I'm not a super great dancer?" Melody protested as he pulled her toward the dance floor. "I can do a pretty mean middle school shuffle-and-sway, but that's about as far as these dancing feet will get me." She hadn't grown up going to debutante balls and country club parties like Jeremy probably had. She couldn't even do so much as a simple box step.

"All you have to do is follow my lead," he said, positioning her left hand on his shoulder and taking her right in his. "You feel my hand on your back?"

She bit her lip and nodded, because, *yeah,* she'd been feeling his hand on her bare skin all night long, and she was definitely aware of it. Hyper-freaking-aware.

"My hands are going to tell you exactly where to go. Feel that?" He exerted light pressure on her shoulder blade. "That means we're going to go this way. And when I do that," he pressed gently on her hand, "it means we're going that way. Got it?"

"Um..." *Not really.*

"You'll get the hang of it," he promised, and started to lead her through a few slow, exaggerated steps. "Don't look at my feet, look at my eyes."

"But—" Melody looked up, and for a moment, she forgot to breathe. She wasn't used to being this close to Jeremy. He was *right there,* gazing at her with those insanely blue eyes of his, and it was a little like staring into the sun. "But if I'm not looking at your feet...how will I know where they're going?" she said, struggling to keep her voice steady.

"You'll know. But you have to trust me. Do you trust me?"

"Yes." It surprised her to realize it was true.

He was right, because once she stopped trying to concentrate on his feet, she started to feel the way he was guiding her along with the music, and it got a lot easier.

"See?" he said. "Just like that."

"I'm doing it?" she asked, surprised.

He smiled down at her. "You're doing it."

She wasn't nearly as bad as she'd thought. There must be something to that saying about needing the right partner, because by the time the band had moved on to the next song, she and Jeremy were moving in perfect sync.

After the initial bout of self-consciousness passed, it got easier for Melody to keep her eyes locked on his. She ended up getting lost in them after a while. They weren't solid blue like she'd thought. They were gradated—darker around the outside and lightening to almost silver near the pupil. And she'd never noticed that his nose was slightly crooked. Yet, somehow, the imperfection only seemed to add character to his attractiveness, which was outrageously unfair.

He was gazing back at her as intently as she was gazing at him, and there was this charged sort of energy between them, like completing a circuit. It felt like their hands were magnetized—like she couldn't have let go even if she'd wanted to. Not that she wanted to. It felt good being this close to someone again—communicating through touch rather than words; putting herself completely in his hands and letting everything go except the music and motion.

It was almost like sex, only without the sex part. Just the closeness, trust, and tactile communication. And okay, they were doing it in the middle of a room full of people, but it was easy to forget there was anyone else around when she was staring into Jeremy's beautiful blue eyes. Everything else fell away until it felt like they were in their own little world.

Which was another great thing about dancing: no one tried to talk to them while they were doing it. No more plasticky Hollywood types. No more pretending to be interested in conversations that didn't include her. It was just the two of them, completely wrapped up in each other. She could almost pretend they were the only two people in the room.

Until she felt him tense, his attention caught by something across the room.

"What's wrong?"

His eyes snapped back to her, and he shook his head. "Nothing. Nothing at all."

On their next turn, Melody caught sight of Lacey and Tessa swaying along with the music in a corner of the dance floor. "Do you want to go somewhere else?" she asked Jeremy.

He frowned. "Why would I want to go somewhere else?"

"If it's hard for you to see Lacey—"

"It's not," he said. "I thought it would be, but it's not."

Melody cocked her head, trying to decide whether he was telling the truth.

"Really. I'm happy right here, as long as you are. Okay?"

She nodded, not entirely satisfied. "Okay."

"I'm going to dip you now," he announced with a smirk. "You ready?"

"No!" she squeaked, but he was already tucking her under his arm and sweeping her into a sudden turn. As they came out of it, he stepped to the side, and his hand moved up to cradle the back of her neck as he lowered her. She fought the urge to tense up and tried to relax, trusting him to support her. When he pulled her back upright, she couldn't help but cling to him and giggle with the thrill of accomplishment. His arms tightened around her and he pulled her close, pressing his face into the top of her head before shifting her back into position.

They danced through the next three songs, managing to execute a couple impressive spins and another dip along the way, before Jeremy asked if she wanted to take a break. She didn't, but now that he'd mentioned it, she realized her feet were kind of hurting, and she needed to pee, like, a lot.

He went to procure them drinks and a couple seats while Melody headed for the ladies' room.

As she was touching up her lipstick in the bathroom mirror, she couldn't help noticing how flushed her cheeks were. It was probably from the wine and the exertion of the dancing. It definitely had nothing to do with Jeremy Sauer, or her prolonged proximity to him, or the way he'd been looking at her. Definitely nothing at all.

"You and my son cut quite a figure on the dance floor," Angelica Sauer said behind her.

Melody spun around, swallowing the urge to yelp in surprise. "Mrs. Sauer," she said in a small voice.

Jeremy's mother looked her up and down, and Melody felt herself grow smaller under the weight of her appraisal.

"Are you enjoying yourself?" Mrs. Sauer asked.

"Yes," Melody replied, forcing herself to stand up straight. "It's a very nice party."

"I wanted to thank you for your discretion about that unpleasant incident several months ago," Mrs. Sauer said, stepping closer. They had the restroom all to themselves, so there was no one to overhear them.

Melody's eyes flicked to the door, desperately hoping someone would come in and interrupt. "It wasn't my business to talk about," she said with more confidence than she felt. "In fact, I barely even remember it happened. What incident, right?" She let out a nervous laugh that made her sound like a little kid, and clamped her mouth shut before she could say anything *really* stupid.

Mrs. Sauer nodded slowly. "I looked into you, you know, Ms. Gage. That's an impressive resume you've built for yourself at such a young age. You've clearly worked hard to get where you are."

Melody couldn't figure out whether she was being complimented or threatened. Everything that came out of the woman's mouth seemed to carry an undertone of menace.

"My son doesn't exactly have the best track record when it comes to affairs of the heart," Mrs. Sauer continued without waiting for a response. "But you—you're a different breed from the other women he's been involved with. You're intelligent, focused, self-sufficient. Ambitious." She paused, long enough for a ball of dread to form in the pit of Melody's stomach. "I wanted you to know you have my approval."

Wait—*what?*

"You—your approval?" Melody stammered.

"I think you make a good match for Jeremy. And I wish you two every happiness together."

"Oh." Now would probably be an excellent time to tell Jeremy's mother she was not, in fact, dating her son, but Melody hadn't even had the nerve to correct Charlotte, so there was no way she was going to correct Angelica Sauer. "Um...thank you?"

"Well," Mrs. Sauer said with a dismissive nod, clearly considering the conversation closed. "I'm sure Jeremy's waiting for you."

"Right. Yeah. Good talk," Melody mumbled before making her escape.

Jeremy was waiting for her at a table on the far side of the dance floor. She sank down onto the chair next to his and snatched the wineglass he slid her way.

"Something happen?" he asked, eyebrows raising as she downed a large gulp of rosé.

She swallowed and shook her head. "Nothing, just—your mother..."

His jaw clenched preemptively. "What did she do?"

"She gave us her blessing." Which officially brought the tally of people who had offered her and Jeremy their blessing to two. *What was even going on?*

Jeremy burst out laughing.

Melody smacked him on the arm. "It's not funny! She thinks

we're dating, and I was too scared to tell her we weren't. She said we make a nice couple!"

He rubbed his hand over his jaw, still chuckling. "You're right. I'm sorry. It's not funny."

"Then why are you still laughing?"

"It's just..." he shook his head, his expression turning wry, "you're the first girlfriend she's ever approved of."

"But I'm not your girlfriend."

He took a swig of his scotch. "That's why it's funny."

Melody didn't find it amusing. She looked away, fixing her gaze on the dance floor. The band was playing "Embraceable You," and Drew and Charlotte were clinging to one another like they were the only two people in the whole world. Something about the sight of them made Melody unaccountably sad.

Jeremy bumped his shoulder against hers. "I told you my mother liked you."

Her head was spinning, and it wasn't from the wine. She swallowed around the sudden lump in her throat and nodded, her eyes still fixed on Drew and Charlotte.

"You okay?"

"Yeah, fine." She forced herself to smile.

"You know, we've probably been here long enough. We can go anytime you want."

"Whatever you want to do. I'm here for you tonight."

His eyes wandered to the dance floor, to Drew and Charlotte wrapped in each other's arms. "I think I'm ready to get out of here."

They were both quiet on the ride home. Jeremy spent a lot of time flipping through the satellite radio channels, and Melody turned away from him and stared out the window.

The Dodgers must have won tonight, because there were fireworks in the distance, little bursts of colored lights peeking out from beyond the downtown skyline. It reminded her of the fireworks the night of the company picnic, and how happy she'd felt.

She didn't feel happy tonight. She felt...empty.

When they got to her apartment building, Jeremy walked her to her door and pulled her into a warm hug. "Thank you for tonight."

"You're welcome," she said into his shoulder.

He didn't seem to be in any hurry to let go, and neither was she. His arms felt comfortably solid around her, and she let her eyes drift shut as she relaxed into him, resting her cheek against the rough fabric of his jacket.

When he let go, the night air hit her like a splash of cold water. He took a half-step back, then halted, gazing at her.

His bottom lip was slightly chapped, and she couldn't stop staring at it—couldn't stop thinking about what it would feel like if he kissed her right now.

She *wanted* him to kiss her.

The realization hit her like a whack in the forehead from a low-hanging tree-limb. It had been right there in front of her, plain as day, yet still managed to take her by surprise.

The hollowness she'd been feeling in the pit of her stomach all night was because she wanted what Drew and Charlotte had—and what Lacey and Tessa had. That closeness. That connection with another person. That knowledge that there was someone in the world who was on your side no matter what.

And she wanted it with Jeremy.

The sudden intensity of her feelings terrified her. She'd spent so long telling herself she'd rather be alone—that she absolutely, positively did not want to be in a relationship—the sudden sea change was disorienting. It was like the ground had shifted 180 degrees beneath her feet when she wasn't looking.

Melody stared into Jeremy's stupidly gorgeous face, frozen. If there was ever going to be an opportunity to say something—to do something—it was now. But she was far too shaken to move, much less form coherent words.

He reached for her shoulder, and his hand skimmed down her arm. Her eyes fluttered closed as she suppressed a shiver.

He bent down and brushed a light kiss against her forehead. "Goodnight," he said in a voice so soft, it was almost a whisper. Then he headed back to his car.

As soon as she was safely inside her apartment, Melody sank back against the door and squeezed her eyes shut.

Well, shit, she thought miserably, *I'm in love with Jeremy Sauer.*

Chapter Nineteen

It's not love, Melody told herself, over and over again. She was not in love with Jeremy Sauer.

It was a crush. A temporary infatuation. A passing fancy. Key word: passing. Meaning she'd get over it. Sooner rather than later, she hoped.

When she was thirteen, Melody had been obsessed with Adam Brody from *The O.C.* She'd bought every single magazine he appeared in, cut the pictures out, and pinned them into a giant collage on the wall next to her bed. Every night, she'd lay in bed listening to Fall Out Boy, stare at fifty different versions of Adam Brody's face, and pine.

Her crush on Jeremy was kind of like that, only instead of making a creepy murder collage, she sat in front of her computer and stared at old paparazzi photos of him. Yes, okay, fine, she had a Google Alert set for his name. But she would deny all knowledge if asked about the custom-coded spidering software she had running on one of her servers at home, extracting every photo he was tagged in on the internet.

But, hey, she didn't listen to Fall Out Boy anymore, so she'd grown as a person, all right?

The biggest difference between her crush on Adam Brody and her crush on Jeremy Sauer was Adam Brody had not routinely made flesh-and-blood appearances in her life. Unlike Jeremy, who continued his habit of dropping by her office whenever he was bored at work—which seemed to occur with increasing regularity. Like, seriously, did he not have any actual work to do?

Every minute at the office was spent in a perpetual state of dread and anticipation, wondering when she was going to see him again. Her stomach did flip-flops every time she heard footsteps in the hall outside her office, because she never knew when it was going to be Jeremy stopping by for a chat. She walked around the building with nervous butterflies, hoping she'd run into him at the coffee cart in the lobby, or on her way to the parking garage at the end of the day.

When she didn't, she'd swipe through the pictures on her phone her mom had taken of the two of them together and try to imagine what it would be like to be his girlfriend for real. Going out to dinner with him, just the two of them, or snuggling up on her couch watching Netflix—or, better yet, *not* watching Netflix.

She couldn't stop thinking about how it had felt to kiss him, and how much she wanted to do it again. How much she wanted to be around him, doing pretty much anything, even just talking. She really liked talking to him, almost as much as she liked kissing him.

So, yeah. It was nerve-racking and exhausting, spending her days on a dopamine roller coaster and trying to act normal whenever she did see him.

God, she hoped she was acting normal around him. There was this latent energy buzzing in the back of her mind whenever she was around him that made it hard to focus. Sometimes she'd catch herself staring at his mouth when he was talking, watching his lips move—his beautiful, perfectly-formed lips—and thinking about how they'd feel on hers. Then she'd realize she hadn't been listening to a word he'd said.

He didn't seem to treat her any differently than before, so she guessed maybe she was pulling it off? This was probably the one time her social awkwardness worked in her favor, since he was already used to her spaciness and nervous babbling.

But the thing that made it especially difficult to act normal, something she'd never noticed until recently, was how much casual touching Jeremy did. He bumped his shoulder against hers to punctuate a joke when they were walking side by side, squeezed her arm or shoulder to say hello and goodbye, and rested his hand at the small of her back whenever she preceded him through a doorway.

That goddamn hand at the small of her back was the worst of all. It was going to be the death of her.

Then there was that thing he did with his eyes. The way he looked at you when he was listening to you. Like he genuinely cared. Like you were important to him. Like he liked you better than anyone else.

And even though Melody knew it wasn't true, that it was how he was with everyone, it still made her all warm and squishy inside.

She felt like she'd lost control of her life. She couldn't control when or how often she saw him around the office, and she couldn't control how she felt when she *was* with him. How her eyes watered and her knees went wobbly. How much she thought about kissing him—and doing other things with him. How, when he touched her, it left a tingly spot on her skin she still felt hours later.

She couldn't make herself stop obsessing over him. But even worse, she couldn't make herself *do* anything about it.

She had considered telling Jeremy how she felt. She'd considered it a lot, but couldn't figure out how to start a conversation like that. She certainly couldn't do it at the office, or even on one of their occasional treks to the Coffee Bean in the middle of the workday. It wasn't the right time or place. Sure, she could theoretically ask him out for drinks one night after work, or suggest they hang out on the weekend, but the thought of it made her break out in hives.

Not metaphorical hives, either. Real, actual hives that made her chest red and itchy and didn't go away for a week.

The problem was, if she admitted how she felt about him and he didn't feel the same, it would all be over. No more popping into her office, no more inviting her to go for coffee, no more talking.

No more being friends.

The only thing that scared her more than the prospect of telling him how she felt was the prospect of losing his friendship.

So, Melody did nothing.

Her feelings for Jeremy were like Schrodinger's Crush. As long as she didn't open the box, their relationship existed in a state of quantum superposition: both possible and impossible at the same time. She was too much of a wimp to find out whether the cat was alive or dead.

Days passed. Weeks. Her crush didn't fade, and her courage didn't miraculously manifest. She started to resign herself to the idea that things would go on like this forever.

Then the day came when her web crawler turned up a paparazzi shot of Jeremy ducking into a restaurant, hand-in-hand with a former *America's Next Top Model* contestant. And the very next weekend, there were a bunch of Facebook photos of the two of them cozying up to each other at a club in West Hollywood.

So, that was that.

She'd probably had a better chance with Adam Brody.

"HOW ARE THINGS WITH JEREMY?" her mother asked the next time she called.

Melody was officially a terrible person. She had let her mom go on thinking she and Jeremy were still dating. She wasn't proud, but she'd done it out of self-preservation. As long as her mom thought she was happily coupled up, she wasn't nagging Melody about being single. Yes, it had required lying to her mom every time she asked about Jeremy, but Melody had gotten good at being vague and drawing from the truth to embellish the lies.

Yeah, no, there was no defending herself. It was wrong, and it was time to put a stop to it. Past time.

"Um, about that," Melody said.

Her mom made a concerned noise. "That sounds like bad news. Is it bad news?"

"Kind of."

"Are you pregnant?" As far as her mother was concerned, the only thing worse than being single was accidentally getting pregnant. Melody had had to listen to a lecture on safe sex every single time she went out with a boy in high school. Every. Single. Time.

She sighed. "No, Mom."

Her mother exhaled loudly. "Thank god."

"Jeremy and I broke up."

"What? No!"

"Yeah."

"What happened?"

"It's complicated."

"Did he cheat on you?"

Melody grimaced. "No, nothing like that."

"Did you cheat on him?"

"No! There was no cheating of any kind." She rubbed her forehead with the heel of her hand.

"Well, then I don't understand what could have happened. You two seemed so happy." She could practically hear her mom shaking her head sadly.

"It just wasn't working. We weren't right for each other."

"What does that mean?"

"It means we're too different. We come from different worlds."

Her mother was quiet for a moment. "You mean because he's rich?"

Sometimes her mom could be too perceptive. "Yeah."

"Oh, honey."

Melody closed her eyes. Even though it was a fake breakup of a fake relationship, the conversation was cutting too close to the bone. "It wasn't just that. There was other stuff, too." Her voice broke on the last word.

"Are you okay, baby?"

"Uh huh." Melody reached under her glasses and wiped her eyes. "I'm fine." She didn't want to worry her mom. It was just a stupid crush. She'd get over it eventually.

Her mother clucked in sympathy. "You know you're just as good him, right? You're better. *He* didn't get a scholarship to MIT, did he? Or build a computer from scratch when he was fifteen? Or win first place in the Academic Decathlon? You're the one who did all those things, and you never needed money to help you get there. You did it all on your own."

Melody sniffled. "Thanks, Mom."

"Here's what you need to do," her mother said. "First, give yourself a week to wallow. I know it hurts right now, and it's important to give yourself time to honor that pain. Then you dust yourself off, you go out and get a new haircut and fresh manicure, and you put yourself out there again, straightaway. A little hair of the dog is always the best cure for what ails you."

"I just—I don't think I'm very good at this dating thing," Melody admitted.

"Don't be silly, baby. It's not like it's rocket surgery."

Melody took her glasses off and rubbed her eyes. "Rocket *science*, Mom. And if it were, I'd be better at it."

"You've just had a little setback. You'll shake it off."

Melody had never been as optimistic as her mother. No matter how many boyfriends she went through, or how many jobs she lost, her mother always believed with unshakable certainty the next one was going to be The One—despite all prior evidence to the contrary.

"You don't need him," her mother said. "There's plenty of other fish in the sea."

Melody didn't want any of the other fish in the sea. She wanted Jeremy.

"CAN I CLOSE THIS?" Jeremy said the next time he showed up at Melody's office.

She exited out of the browser window with his *Town & Country* photoshoot before looking up at him. "Uh—what?"

He tilted his head. "The door. Can I close it?"

"Um...sure?" He'd never wanted to talk to her with the door closed before. So...that was new. And a little daunting.

"I'm going to tell you something, but you have to promise not to tell another soul." He looked dead serious, and now she was even more daunted.

"Okay." Her mind raced ahead to imagine the worst. A re-org, some kind of merger, layoffs—oh god, what if they were offshoring the IT department?

Jeremy sat down, leaning forward with his forearms resting on his knees. The creases in his forehead were deep enough to hold a pencil. "My mother and Geoffrey are getting married."

"Oh." Melody let out a huge breath. The relief over not losing her job was quickly supplanted by concern. "Are you okay?"

He shrugged. "I guess? I don't think it's really sunk in yet."

"When did you find out?"

"Last night. They told us over dinner. 'Pass the salt, dear—oh, and by the way, Geoffrey and I are getting married.'" Jeremy's impression of his mother was spot on. Melody had no doubt that was more or less exactly how it had gone.

"How did Hannah take it?"

"She's overjoyed. She adores Geoffrey. So..." He shrugged again.

"That's good, right?"

His expression was distant as he nodded. "Yeah." He looked like he could use a hug, and she really wanted to give him one, but there was a desk between them, and they were at the office. Even with the door closed, it was a dicey proposition.

"Do you want to get out of here?" Melody asked. "Go get some coffee or something?"

He shook his head. "I can't. I've got to get back upstairs. I'm in meetings all day." He pushed himself to his feet. "They're not making the official announcement for a few weeks, so don't say anything. I just wanted to tell you."

"Hey," she said as he pulled the door open. He paused in the doorway and looked back at her. "Let me know if you want to talk. I'm here, okay?"

The corners of his mouth curved upward. "Thanks. Maybe I'll call you later."

Melody waited by her phone all evening for him to call.

He never did.

He'd probably called the model. He was probably at her place, spilling his heart out while she comforted him.

At midnight, Melody gave up and went to bed.

Chapter Twenty

---

*F*or the first time since she'd started at Sauer Hewson, work was actually busy. There was a big deadline looming on the project she was on, which meant the developers were pushing out a lot of code, all of which had to be tested six ways from Sunday.

Tonight, Melody had been stuck at the office until nearly ten because the devs hadn't checked in their code until well after five. She'd had to wait around for them to finish it before she could write her test script, then she had to stay long enough to make sure there weren't any show-stoppers when she started running it.

By the time she made it out of the office, she was ravenous, so she decided to stop for a late-night cheeseburger and chili-cheese fries at her favorite burger place.

She despised drive-thrus, so she always parked and went up to the counter. She'd rather walk a few extra feet than have an unintelligible conversation over a crappy intercom that usually resulted in her order being bungled.

She was so exhausted, she didn't notice the man in the parking lot until he was right behind her. Which was stupid. She usually paid more attention to her surroundings, but one second she was writing code in her head, and the next, there was something that felt like the barrel of a gun pressed into her back and a man's voice telling her not to move.

Melody froze, a cold ball of fear uncoiling in the pit of her stomach. There was no one else around, and the security light in the parking lot was burned out, so even if someone in the restaurant happened to look out the window, they wouldn't be able to see anything in the darkness out back.

"Pretty thing like you shouldn't be out all alone this time of night," the man behind her said, close enough that she could feel the heat of his breath on the back of her neck. His voice was deep and cigarette-roughened, and he smelled like stale sweat and alcohol.

His hand tangled in her hair, pulling her head back as it slid through her ponytail. She choked back a sob as his fingers crept down the back of her neck and over the top of her shoulder.

He lifted her purse off her shoulder and yanked it down her arm. She let him take it, because that was what they always told you to do. *Don't put up a fight. It's only money. It's not worth your life.*

Just please, *please* let her purse be all he wanted from her. Her fingers clenched around the car keys in her hand, her thumb poised over the panic button.

"Don't turn around," the man said, then she heard the scuff of his shoes on the asphalt as he backed away. "Count to fifty before you move, you hear?"

Melody waited for a count of ten, her eyes burning with angry tears, then bolted for the restaurant.

HOURS LATER, Melody looked up as yet another police officer hurried past the bench where she was sitting without giving her a second glance. One of them was supposed to be driving her home at some point, but they all seemed determined to ignore her.

She couldn't drive herself home because her car was at the

burger place. The LAPD officer who had responded to the 911 call insisted on bringing her to the precinct in his cruiser to give a statement and look at mugshots, even though she'd told him she hadn't gotten a look at the mugger's face. And she couldn't even call a cab, because she didn't have any money or credit cards. She was stuck there, waiting. And probably forgotten.

It had to have been at least an hour—maybe two—since she'd finished giving her statement and they'd told her to wait on this stupid uncomfortable bench until someone could drive her back to her car. But she couldn't tell for sure how much time had passed, because the creep who mugged her had taken her phone. She was helpless.

At least she'd had her keys in her hand when he took her purse, or else she wouldn't even be able to get into her apartment. If she ever got home again, that was. She was starting to think she was going to grow old and die on this stupid bench.

She was about thirty seconds away from getting up and crying all over the desk sergeant when someone said her name—finally. Melody looked up, expecting a police officer, but it was Charlotte standing in front of her in jeans and a ratty old sweatshirt.

"Charlotte," she said, blinking in surprise. "What are you doing here?"

"My dad works here. He's on overnights this month and I was up pulling an all-nighter, so I brought him some dinner. What are *you* doing here?"

"I got mugged," Melody said. "Someone's supposed to drive me back to my car, but I think they might have forgotten about me."

Charlotte sat down on the bench beside her. "Are you okay?"

Melody nodded. "He just took my bag. And my wallet. And my phone. God, I really loved that bag," she said, blinking back tears. "I got it on sale."

"How long have you been here?"

"I don't know. I don't have my phone, so I can't tell what time it is anymore. I don't know what to do with myself without my phone."

"Stay here," Charlotte said. "I'll be right back, okay? You just wait here."

Melody had heard that one before. She was going to spend the rest of her life on this bench. Maybe she'd actually been killed in that mugging and this was purgatory, she just hadn't realized it yet. Oh god, she was living the last season of *Lost*.

Charlotte was only gone a few minutes before she came back with her dad. "I'm Detective Lopez," he said, thrusting a chipped coffee mug at her. "Here. Drink this."

The coffee was tarry, bitter, and tasted vaguely like fish, but it was blissfully warm, so Melody cupped her hands around it gratefully.

"You two know each other, huh?"

"Melody was at my engagement party," Charlotte told her dad. "She's Jeremy's girlfriend."

Melody wasn't sure whether lying to the police was actually illegal, but it was definitely bad, even if it wasn't against the law. So, she didn't say anything, because then she wasn't technically lying to Detective Lopez. She was just perpetuating a lie by choosing to remain silent, which was still pretty bad. Everything about tonight was the worst, basically.

"Guess it's a good thing I ran out of daughters for him to date," Detective Lopez muttered.

"Dad," Charlotte said sharply.

He sighed. "I'm sorry you've been stuck here so long. We get pretty busy this time of night, and we can't always spare a uniform."

"It's okay," Melody said. What was she going to do? Complain that the police were out protecting the city instead of playing chauffeur for her? "Thank you for the coffee."

"I called Jeremy." Charlotte sat down again and took Melody's hand. "He'll be here soon to drive you home."

Crap.

She hated the thought of Jeremy seeing her like this. On the other hand, she was desperate enough at this point, she'd probably get into a car with Ted Bundy if he offered her a ride home. Her dignity was a small price to pay.

"Yeah, okay," Detective Lopez said. "I'll be at my desk. Lemme know if you need anything."

Charlotte gave Melody's hand a reassuring squeeze as her dad shuffled away.

"You don't have to stay," Melody said. "Don't you need to get back to studying?"

"It's fine," Charlotte said with a tight smile. "I'm not leaving you here until I'm sure Jeremy's actually going to show up to take you home."

Melody clung to Charlotte's hand, unable to find the words to express how grateful she was. She felt awful for lying to her about being Jeremy's girlfriend, but that was nothing compared to how bad she felt about sleeping with Jeremy while he was dating Charlotte. Which was something Charlotte probably didn't know about. If she had, she definitely would *not* be holding Melody's hand right now.

Oh no—what if Charlotte had seen those pictures of Jeremy at the club with the model? Charlotte probably thought he was cheating on Melody, and that was why she was being so nice. Which only made Melody feel even worse.

"Melody?"

Jeremy stood in front of her in jeans and a wrinkled T-shirt, his hair all rumpled like he'd just climbed out of bed—which he probably had since it was the middle of the night.

Melody had never been so happy to see anyone in her whole life, especially when he knelt in front of her and wrapped her up in his big, warm arms. And yeah, she was maybe crying a little, but in her defense, it had been a long night and the tears had a mind of their own.

"I'm gonna go now," Charlotte said, standing up.

Melody extricated her face from Jeremy's neck. "Thank you so much."

"Yes. Thank you, Charlotte," Jeremy said with feeling, looking up at her.

She gave him a curt nod and left them alone.

"Are you okay?" he asked, turning back to Melody and taking both her hands in his.

"Yeah." She nodded weakly. "I just want to go home."

IN THE CAR, she rolled the window down and let the cold air blow on her face to chase away the smell of the police precinct and the memory of the mugger's breath on the back of her neck. Jeremy kept casting concerned glances in her direction, but he seemed reluctant to ask her too much about what had happened— which was good, because she did *not* want to talk about it.

"Thank you for coming to get me," she said after a while. "I didn't mean for Charlotte to call you."

"I'm glad she did. You know you could have called me yourself, right?"

"I lost my phone when I got mugged."

He looked over at her and frowned, but didn't say anything.

When they got to her apartment, he walked her to the door. Her hands were shaking so much, Jeremy had to take the keys from her and unlock it himself. He pushed the door open, but Melody stood rooted in place, staring into her pitch dark apartment.

"Do you want me to come in with you?"

She shook her head. "You don't have to do that. I'll be fine." She tried to sound strong, but the tremble in her voice gave her away.

"I know." Jeremy slipped his hand into hers. "But do you want me to?"

She bit her lip and nodded. "Yes."

Inside, Jeremy moved around the apartment, turning on all the lights without being asked. He just seemed to know it was what she needed.

When he was done, he came over and stood in front of her. She was still in the middle of the living room, because she didn't know what to do next. She was so exhausted, she couldn't think straight, but also, the thought of closing her eyes and trying to sleep terrified her, so she was stuck at an impasse.

He frowned at her. "Melody, are you okay?"

She nodded. The shock was wearing off, but what it left behind was mostly numbness.

Jeremy's frown deepened. "Did he hurt you?"

"No, he just..." She couldn't finish. She couldn't talk about how the man had run his fingers through her hair and over her skin, or how it had made her feel.

When Melody was a kid, someone had broken into the rental house she and her mom were living in. They'd taken their television, VCR—this was back when people still owned VCRs—and some of her mom's jewelry, but the worst part was, they'd trashed the place looking for valuables. Melody's bed had been overturned, and all her books and toys had been knocked off the shelves and strewn over the floor.

She had been traumatized. The thought that a complete stranger—a criminal—had been in her room and touched her things haunted her. Her pillows, her dolls, her favorite stuffed teddy bear she slept with every night—they'd all been contaminated by the touch of some invisible monster.

That was sort of how she felt now, only instead of a teddy bear, it was her own skin that had been contaminated.

"He scared you," Jeremy finished for her.

She nodded again, swallowing the bile in the back of her throat.

He enveloped her in a hug, and she managed not to cry this

time, but she did close her eyes and press her face into his chest. He smelled nice, and having his arms around her made her feel calm and safe. "I'm going to stay here tonight," he said, tucking her head under his chin. "I'll sleep on the couch, okay?"

She nodded against him, so relieved, she almost did start crying again. "Okay." Her voice was getting smaller and smaller, like she might disappear completely.

"What do you need?" he asked, still holding her. "Something to eat? I can make you something. Or do you just want to go to sleep?"

"I have to take a shower. I just want to wash off...everything."

He pulled away, skimming his hands down her arms. "You go do that, then. I'll be right here when you get out." Concern shadowed his eyes. She wanted to tell him she was fine, but it would have been too obviously a lie.

Ten minutes of standing under the hottest water she could stand, with the showerhead set to the most abrasive setting, helped Melody feel a little cleaner, at least. It also left her skin covered in angry red blotches, but she didn't care. After pulling on a sweatshirt and pajama pants, she wandered out to the living room with her damp hair tied up in a bun.

Jeremy was kicked back on the couch with the television on. "Feel any better?" he asked, looking up.

"Yeah, a lot." She dropped down beside him on the couch.

He gestured to the TV. "I can turn this off if you want to sleep." He was watching *Anchorman*.

"No, leave it on." It was one of her favorite movies. She settled back into the couch and pulled her legs up under her.

Jeremy had his arm stretched out along the back of the cushions, and when she leaned her head back, it was resting on him. If she were less tired, she might have been embarrassed for laying on his arm, but right now? She was not moving—not without a forklift.

Instead of pulling away, he dropped his hand onto her shoulder. "You want anything? I saw more Extreme Maximum Chocolate Fudge Chunk in the freezer."

The thought of eating anything right now made her feel ill, and anyway she didn't want him to get up, because she didn't want to lose the warm weight of his hand. She shook her head. "I'm okay."

He moved his hand anyway, took the throw draped over the back of the couch, and arranged it over her lap. It was nice, but not as nice as having his arm around her had been.

"Thanks," she mumbled.

He scooted closer and held his arms open. "C'mere."

Melody didn't need to be asked twice. She curled up against his side with her head resting on his chest, and he wrapped his arms around her, holding her tight.

"Better?" he asked.

"Mmmm," she agreed.

They watched the movie. Well, Jeremy watched it. Melody's eyes didn't even stay open for a full minute before drifting closed.

The last thing she remembered was the soft rumble of Jeremy's laughter in her ear.

SHE WAS ALONE on the couch when she woke in the morning, curled in a ball with her head where Jeremy's lap had been the night before. The apartment smelled like fresh coffee.

When she sat up, Jeremy smiled at her from the kitchen. "Sorry. I didn't mean to wake you." He pulled two coffee mugs out of the cabinet.

"It's okay." She stretched, wincing as her vertebrae cracked all the way up her spine. "What time is it?"

"Seven o'clock." He joined her on the couch and handed her a steaming cup of coffee. "You're taking the day off today, by the way."

"I can't," Melody said. "I've got to go in and check the log and write my bug reports."

"They'll survive one day without you. I already talked to the dev manager and explained what happened. No arguments. It's done."

"But—"

"Don't make me have security bar you from the building for twenty-four hours." He gave her his best scary eyebrow glare, which wasn't especially scary. "I'll do it if I have to."

"Fine," she conceded.

"Good. Unfortunately, I do have to go to work today, but I'm going to call Lacey and have her come hang out with you."

Melody shook her head. "Not necessary."

He frowned at her.

"I'm fine, honestly." And she was. In the light of a brand new day, she felt a thousand times better.

"Are you sure? Lacey won't mind."

"I'm fine. I promise. Anyway, I've got an exciting day of canceling my credit cards, replacing my driver's license, and shopping for a new phone ahead of me. I don't need a babysitter. Oh —" she said, frowning as she remembered something. "My car. It's still in the parking lot where..." The thought of going back there, even in broad daylight, made her feel less fine than she was a minute ago.

"No, it's not," Jeremy said. "It's parked out front."

"What?" She got up and looked out the window. Sure enough, her MINI was parked at the curb, right behind Jeremy's black BMW. "But how?" she asked, turning back to him.

"I've got a guy. I had him pick it up this morning and bring it over here." He shrugged like it was no big deal, like everyone had a guy they could call at six in the morning to pick up your car and drop it off somewhere.

"Thank you," she said, blinking away the prickling in her eyes. "You really didn't have to do that."

Jeremy pulled his wallet out of his back pocket and started

counting out twenty-dollar bills. "This is to get you by until you get your credit cards replaced."

"No! I can't accept that. You've done too much already."

He gave her the scary eyebrows again. "You don't have any credit cards, you can't get money out of an ATM, and you don't have your driver's license, so you can't even cash a check. Take the money."

He had a point. She couldn't even buy food. And she'd been so swamped at work, she hadn't made it to the store in two weeks. Her fridge was pretty much bare.

"I'm paying you back," she said, grudgingly accepting the bills he held out to her.

"Whatever," he said, shrugging.

She stepped into him and wrapped her arms around his torso. "Thank you. Seriously. I don't know what I would have done without you last night."

Jeremy's arms tightened around her. "I'm always here for you, Melody. If you need anything at all, I want you to call me. Promise?"

She nodded against his chest. "Promise."

THAT NIGHT, Melody called her mom to tell her what had happened. Predictably, she freaked out and threatened to fly to LA immediately.

"Mom, I'm fine, I promise. I don't need you to come here."

"I just can't stand to think of you going through something like this all alone, baby."

"I'm not alone. I've got friends. Lacey came over this afternoon..." she'd insisted on it, in fact, after Jeremy had called her and told her what had happened, "and Jeremy drove me home from the police station last night."

As soon as the words were out of her mouth, Melody winced, realizing her mistake.

"Jeremy, hmmm? I thought you two broke up."

"We did. We're just friends now."

"Is that so?"

"It doesn't mean anything," Melody said, trying to believe that was true.

"I still don't understand what happened. You two were perfect together."

Melody sighed and lay back on her bed, gazing at the ceiling. "We weren't perfect, believe me. It's just one of those things. We're much better as friends."

"Sweetie, I saw the way you and that boy looked at each other. The moment he walked into your apartment, I knew he was The One. Trust your mother on this."

Melody wished she could believe her. Desperately. But it was hard to trust the judgment of a woman with two failed marriages and a string of terrible boyfriends under her belt. Recognizing true love wasn't exactly her mother's gift.

If anything, her mother's blessing was confirmation of what Melody already knew: there was no future for her with Jeremy.

She needed to move on.

Chapter Twenty-One

*E*veryone went out of their way to be nice to Melody when she went back to work the next day. There was a card waiting on her desk signed by the whole project team, and her dev manager came by to ask how she was doing.

Jeremy checked in on her halfway through the morning, then again in the afternoon, and insisted on walking her to her car when she left that night. And the next night. And the night after that.

It was sweet of him to be so concerned, but she didn't need mother-henning. And she was getting tired of seeing that crease in his forehead every time he looked at her, like he was afraid she was something fragile in danger of breaking.

She wasn't. Okay, she'd had some nightmares, but nothing she couldn't survive. After a few days, she was even able to sleep through the night without the assistance of Xanax. It would probably be a while before she was ready to go back to that particular burger place, but she felt like she was doing an admirable job of moving past the whole unpleasant experience. She didn't need Jeremy constantly reminding her of it with all his concerned looks.

It took a full week before he seemed to believe her when she said she was fine and the crease in his forehead smoothed out. He stopped asking her if she was okay all the time, but he kept dropping by her office at least once day, even if it was just to say hi on his way to somewhere else.

Melody was always happy to see him—truly, she was—but it was painful, seeing so much of him and wanting so much more. He was so beautiful, it hurt to look at him, but she couldn't seem to make herself look away. Sometimes when he smiled at her, it felt like she was suffocating—like there was a weight sitting on her chest, crushing her, and she couldn't get out from under it.

She wished she could work up the courage to tell him how she felt. But realistically? That was never going to happen.

"SO, THERE'S THIS GUY," Lacey said one morning after yoga class.

Melody rolled her eyes. She knew exactly where this was going. Lacey had been trying to set her up on a date for weeks. What was it with people who were happily coupled wanting the rest of the world to be coupled too? She'd gotten almost as bad as Melody's mother with the nagging.

"There are lots of guys. The world is full of guys." Melody sipped her flat white, grimaced, and reached for a sugar packet. She was trying to break out of her vanilla latte rut. Try new things. So far, she wasn't impressed with the results.

"Yeah, but I think you'd hit it off with this one in particular."

"I told you, I'm not interested in going on any blind dates."

"Christ, what are you so afraid of?"

"That we won't like each other and I'll be stuck making small talk with someone I can't stand for two hours."

No way was she telling Lacey the real reason: that she had a stupid, life-consuming crush on Jeremy. Even though Lacey had said she didn't mind, it would be too weird. Jeremy was Lacey's ex, and he was always going to be her ex. It was awkward enough being friends with them both.

Also? She was pretty sure Lacey would push Melody to tell him how she felt if she knew. She might even decide—heaven forbid—to tell him herself. And that would be disastrous. It was easier if Lacey didn't know, so Melody could be miserable and obsessed and completely unhinged in private, without anyone bothering her about it.

"But what if you end up liking him?" Lacey persisted. "What if you actually had fun? Wouldn't it be worth taking a chance?"

Melody pretended to think about it. "No."

Lacey nudged her under the table with her foot. "I'm telling you, I've got a good feeling about this guy."

"That's what you always say."

"Yeah, but you've never gone out with any of them, so for all you know, I'm right every time."

"Why break your streak now?"

"Come on. One date, that's all I'm asking. Then I promise I'll never ask again."

"Never?" Melody lifted her eyebrows. Getting Lacey off her back was a persuasive case for doing it. "If I go out on this one stupid date, you promise you'll never ever try to fix me up again? Ever?"

Lacey crossed her heart with her finger. "You have to give him a real chance, though. No making up your mind in the first five minutes."

"Fine," Melody said. "One date."

Hey, there was always a chance—a slim chance, but a chance—Lacey was right. Maybe Melody and this guy would hit it off.

Maybe she could finally get past this fruitless fixation on Jeremy.

"It's gonna be great," Lacey said. "You'll see."

———

HE WAS CUTE, Melody had to give Lacey that much credit. Cute in a vintage-framed glasses and knit beanie kind of way, which happened to be one of Melody's favorite flavors of cute.

His name was Jonathan, and he was a screenwriter. Well, an aspiring screenwriter. He'd never actually sold a script, but that didn't stop him from constantly referring to himself as a screenwriter. It was impressive how often he managed to work it into the conversation.

They met for beers and burgers at a place in Santa Monica. It was decent, but overpriced, like most of LA. Jonathan said a lot of screenwriters ate there.

"What are you working on right now?" she asked him.

"It's called *American Dreamers*. It transcends genre, but I like to think of it as an anti-rom-com." He had nicotine stains on his fingers, and he kept tapping them on the table like he was itching for a cigarette.

"You mean like a drama about a couple breaking up? Or like a parody?"

"No, no, no, nothing like that." He shook his head, and his heavy black eyebrows drew together in a line. "See, on the surface, it's about this guy and girl who meet totally by chance at a train station. And over the course of this one night together, they have all these unexpected adventures that force them to confront their fears of intimacy. But on another level, it's really about the ways modern society and technology are making it harder for people to connect in a meaningful way, you know what I mean?"

"Mmmhmm," Melody said. "But...how's that anti-romance?"

"It's anti-conventional romance. Anti-cliché. Anti-everything in your typical, run-of-the-mill Hollywood rom-com. Like I said, it transcends genre."

"Right." Melody resisted the urge to tell him the whole thing sounded like one giant cliché. It was basically the exact same script every guy who ever went to film school seemed to write a variation of, like they all had to get it out of their system. It was

Before Sunrise and *Garden State* and *500 Days of Summer* all over again. Although, it still sounded better than that Ben Stiller action movie abomination Drew was trying to get made.

"See, the main character, he's a poet, right—a real sensitive, soulful type. He's making his money as a busker, playing guitar at the train station for money. Although, I'm thinking about changing it to the violin. Or maybe the accordion." He looked up at her. "What do you think is the more erotic instrument?"

"Um..."

"The violin, right? That's what I'm gonna change it to. Anyway, the girl, she's traveling home for her father's funeral, so she's, like, teeming with daddy issues, and her boyfriend just broke up with her, and she's in this really vulnerable place. But she's edgy and unconventional, you know? Like, she's got a pink streak in her hair and drives a vintage VW. That sort of thing."

So, basically, it was your standard thinly-veiled author-insert protagonist meets your typical Manic Pixie Dream Girl. Melody refrained from telling him that, though. Instead, she picked at her French fries while Jonathan rambled on about life, love, and people for the next hour.

He had a profound reverence for women, he said. All the most important people in his life had been women—his mother, his sisters, a string of female friends and girlfriends who littered his past. He didn't consider himself a feminist because he didn't believe people should limit themselves with labels. But he identified as a post-structuralist—whatever that meant. He loved David Foster Wallace, Jonathan Safran Foer, and the films of the Coen Brothers. He liked the platonic ideal of people more than he actually liked most people. Like, he loved that everyone had secrets hidden beneath the surface, but he hated the masks they all wore to hide their insecurities. Or something. Honestly, Melody wasn't paying much attention by that point.

Eventually, he got around to asking her what she did for a living. As soon as she started describing her job, his eyes glazed over. It wasn't his fault. Everyone always got the same look when she tried to explain IT, which was why she usually didn't bother.

He got more interested when she told him about some of the things the space division was working on. It turned out they both had an affinity for stories set in space, and they talked about their favorite sci-fi films until the check came.

He wasn't so bad, really. She could see why Lacey had thought they'd hit it off. It wasn't her fault they hadn't.

At the end of the night, he walked Melody to her car and told her she looked beautiful under the sodium lights in the parking lot, so she let him kiss her.

It was fine, and he was fine. But she felt nothing.

It wasn't anything like kissing Jeremy. Talking to Jonathan wasn't like talking to Jeremy, either. When she was with Jeremy, she felt really listened to. Appreciated. More alive.

She was never getting over him, was she?

"I DON'T EVEN KNOW why I'm surprised," Melody told Jeremy while they were waiting for their coffee in the lobby a week later. "They always do this. It's the thing with the Rey dolls all over again." She was ranting at him about the merchandising for the latest Marvel movie, and he was humoring her.

His brow wrinkled adorably. "The what dolls?"

She picked up her coffee and thanked the barista before turning back to Jeremy. "You know, Rey, from the new *Star Wars* movies?"

He nodded. "Right."

"When *The Force Awakens* came out, there was hardly any merchandise for her in the stores. She was the main character in the movie, and you could barely find a doll or action figure anywhere. I mean, can you even imagine if there hadn't been any Luke Skywalker toys when the original *Star Wars* came out?"

He frowned. "Um…"

"You can't, because it'd never happen. And they did the exact same thing with Black Widow after *Age of Ultron*. She has this big stunt where she drops out of the quinjet on her motorcycle, and when they released the motorcycle toy, it was Captain America riding it!"

Jeremy pressed his lips together like he was trying not to laugh.

"What?"

He shook his head. "Nothing."

"You think I'm crazy."

"I don't think you're crazy. I think you're passionate about things."

"Everyone's passionate about things," she said, feeling defensive.

The barista set Jeremy's coffee down, and he beamed his flirty smile at her the way he always did.

"Not like you," he said, turning back to Melody. "At least, I'm not. I can't think of a single thing I get half as worked up about as you with action figures."

They wandered away from the coffee cart and paused by one of the weird abstract sculptures decorating the lobby, neither of them in a particular hurry to get back to work.

"It's not about the action figures," Melody said. "It's about how the people making decisions at these companies view women, and it's about little girls who grow up thinking only boys can be heroes because that's all they ever see. People say, 'Oh, it's only movies,' or 'It's only TV, it doesn't matter,' but stories matter. They're our cultural mythology. They shape the lens through which we see the world."

Jeremy was smiling at her again. "See? You're passionate."

She felt her cheeks flush and looked down at her coffee.

"Hey." He nudged her with his elbow. "It's not a criticism. I think it's cool."

"There must be something you're passionate about. What about sports?"

He shrugged. "I like sports, sure, but I wouldn't say I'm passionate about it. Not like you are about...everything."

"Politics?" She didn't even know what his political affiliation was. She was afraid to ask, frankly. It was probably better she didn't know.

"Nooo," he said, shaking his head. "Hate talking about politics. Avoid at all costs."

"Okay," she said. "Work?"

He huffed out a laugh. "Right. Yeah, no."

She poked him in the arm. "You get excited about some of the stuff R&D's doing. I've heard you."

"Nah. I mean, yeah, I'm interested in some of the advanced technology projects we're developing because it's basically the only thing about this whole damn job that's not boring. But mostly, I like talking about it with you because I like how excited you get. Your cheeks get all rosy and your whole face lights up." He grinned at her. "Like right now."

Whenever he said something like that, Melody could almost convince herself he was flirting with her on purpose. It was easy to believe she was special to him when he was looking at her in that way he had—the way he was looking at her right now.

But then, someone else would come along, he'd beam his light at them, and Melody would remember she wasn't special after all —that was just the way he was with everyone. Which was exactly what happened.

"Jeremy," called out a tall blonde walking across the lobby toward them in high heels and a pencil skirt.

He looked over and his face lit up. "Chelsea! Hi!"

"Do you have a minute?" The woman's eyes narrowed as they flicked to Melody, evaluating how much of a threat she posed and quickly dismissing her as insignificant. She turned her attention back to Jeremy and smiled sweetly. "I wanted to talk to you about those operating metrics you sent out this morning."

"Yeah, of course." He glanced back at Melody. "You coming?" he asked, cocking his head toward the elevator.

The woman was scrutinizing Melody again. Probably wondering what Jeremy was even doing talking to a lowly IT girl.

Melody shook her head. "Go ahead. I'm going back for a cookie."

"Okay. See you later," he said over his shoulder, already walking away with Chelsea.

It was Friday afternoon, which meant Melody probably wouldn't see him later. She wouldn't see him again until Monday.

He'd go back upstairs with Chelsea and flirt with her over operating metrics for a while before leaving to go do whatever it was he did on the weekends. Hang out at some trendy club with a model, probably, and smile at her like she was the one who was special to him.

Jeremy was like the sun. It was warm when he was shining on you, but when he was shining somewhere else, he cast a cold shadow.

Melody went back to the coffee cart and bought herself *two* cookies as a consolation prize.

Chapter Twenty-Two

"*I*s that a bribery muffin I see in your hand?" Melody said when Jeremy showed up in her office a couple weeks later.

"Am I really that transparent?" he asked, scrunching his nose as he set a latte and blueberry muffin in front of her.

She smirked at him. "Kind of."

"Well, as it happens, I do need a favor," he said, dropping into the chair across from her.

"Anything."

His eyebrows lifted. "Don't you want to know what it is before you agree?"

"Nope." She couldn't think of anything she wouldn't do for him at this point. She'd probably take a bullet for him if he asked her to.

"So…you know how my mom's wedding is coming up?"

Melody nodded as she reached for her latte. Everyone at the company had been talking about it since they'd gone public with the announcement last month. Mrs. Sauer and Mr. Horvath were having a private ceremony at home with just the family, followed by a cocktail reception at the house later that evening. The guest list for the reception was relatively small, and there'd been a lot of gossip about who among the management had made the cut and who had gotten snubbed.

"Will you be my date?" Jeremy asked.

Melody nearly choked on her coffee. "Me?"

"Yes, you." He was looking at her like he was actually serious.

She cleared her throat. "Um...isn't there someone else you'd rather ask?"

"Like who?"

"I don't know." She shrugged. "Anyone."

She couldn't tell him she knew about the model because then she'd have to admit she'd been cyber-stalking him. Although, her searches hadn't turned up any new pictures recently, so maybe they weren't a thing anymore? Still, there had to be a line of women dying to be Jeremy Sauer's date to his mother's wedding.

"The thing is..." he ran his tongue over his lower lip, the way he always did when he was nervous, "my mother still thinks we're dating, which means Geoffrey and Hannah do, too."

Annnd there it was. Of course.

She rubbed her temples in frustration. "I can't believe you haven't fake broken up with me yet."

"I know, I know." He squeezed his eyes shut and pressed the heels of his hands to his forehead, like he was literally hanging his head in shame. "It's just...my mother actually likes you. And she's never liked anyone I've dated. So...she's been a lot nicer about... everything, basically."

Melody didn't have all that much room to judge, since she'd basically done the exact same thing with her mom. But at least she'd told her. Eventually.

"And it's not just her..." Jeremy looked up with a guilty expression. "Drew and Charlotte are coming."

"Oh my god! I can't keep lying to Charlotte after she was so nice to me. I can't do it."

"Just this one last time," he pleaded. "And then, I promise, I'll tell everyone we broke up. Just get me through this wedding first. Please, Melody."

She sighed. "Fine."

It wasn't in her power to say no to him. Not even about this. But she wished he'd asked her to take a bullet for him instead. It probably would have been a lot less painful.

"YOU LOOK BEAUTIFUL," Jeremy said when Melody opened the door for him.

He was wearing a tux because he'd been the best man at the wedding earlier, and, of course, he looked devastatingly handsome in it. Handsome enough to steal all the air from her lungs.

"Thank you," she said, ducking her head to hide the color flooding her cheeks.

She was wearing the same dress she'd worn to that first ill-fated dinner with Lacey and Drew, even though she'd had a fleeting thought that the dress might be jinxed. She wasn't a superstitious person, though, and she didn't believe a dress could be bad luck. That night had been awful for a whole host of reasons that had nothing to do with the dress, and tonight would be just fine no matter what she was wearing.

That was what she told herself, anyway.

Besides, she'd already bought two new outfits because of Jeremy, and there was no way she was laying out more money on a third. This dress was perfectly appropriate for the occasion: dressy without being *too* dressy, and conservative without being *too* conservative. There were going to be a lot of Sauer Hewson people there, so it was practically a work function, and even though Melody suspected a lot of them already thought she was trying to sleep her way to a promotion, she'd be damned if she was going to dress the part.

Most importantly, this dress fully covered her back. Because there was no way she'd be able to get through the night with Jeremy's hand on her bare skin.

He leaned in to kiss her cheek. "Thank you again for doing this."

God, he smelled fantastic. She didn't know what cologne he wore, but whatever it was, it was intoxicating. Everything about him was intoxicating. He'd been there all of thirty seconds and she already felt like she was losing her grip. Why did he have to be so wildly attractive? It made all of this so much harder.

She'd been working herself into an anxiety stomachache all day. It was one thing pretending to be his girlfriend when they were just friends. But now that she had actual feelings for him—feelings she was certain he didn't return—she had no idea how to do this. How was she going to get through a whole evening of having Jeremy so close to her—touching her, treating her like a girlfriend, maybe even kissing her—without giving away how she really felt? How was she supposed to survive something like that, knowing it was all phony?

Tonight was going to suck. In the biggest way.

"You've already thanked me a hundred times," Melody said, stepping away from him. "Let's just get this over with."

THE SAUER HOME looked slightly more cheerful than the last time Melody had seen it. Tonight, it was all decked out for the reception with swags of lavender ribbon and arrangements of candles and brightly-colored flowers on every table. It was also packed to the gills with uptight Sauer Hewson bigwigs, which dragged down the air of festivity a few degrees.

It turned out the house had an actual, honest-to-god ballroom, which Melody had missed on her prematurely aborted tour. And there was a real live string quartet in the corner playing chamber music, like something out of a Jane Austen novel. It was all extremely dignified and stuffy, which was exactly what she'd expect from Angelica Sauer.

There was a receiving line between Melody and the bar, so she fixed a smile on her face, grit her teeth, and got in line behind Jeremy to bestow her felicitations upon the newlyweds.

"There you are, darling!" Mrs. Sauer smiled regally as she presented her cheek to her son. In the press release announcing her engagement, she'd explained she would be keeping her late husband's name for professional reasons.

After Jeremy obliged her with a kiss, she turned to regard Melody. Her expression wasn't exactly warm, but it wasn't cold, either. "Melody, dear, I'm so delighted you could come." She clasped Melody's shoulders in a claw-like grip and kissed her cheek, enveloping her in a cloud of perfume.

"Congratulations, Mrs. Sauer. I wish you all the best."

"Jeremy told us what happened to you, you poor thing." She tutted in sympathy. "The crime in this city is absolutely out of hand. I hope you've recovered from your terrible ordeal."

"Yes, ma'am. Thank you," Melody replied, trying not to let her smile slip.

Jeremy's fingers trailed down Melody's arm, and even though she knew he was trying to be comforting, she couldn't help stiffening at the skin-to-skin contact.

He glanced at her, his brow knitting in concern, but then Mr. Horvath turned to greet them and Jeremy was forced to direct his attention to his new stepfather.

"Geoffrey, this is Melody Gage," Jeremy said, presenting her as if they'd never met before. Which, technically, they hadn't.

"Congratulations," Melody said, offering her hand like she had no memory of ever having seen Geoffrey Horvath in a silky pink robe.

"I'm delighted to meet you, Melody." He took her hand warmly in both of his. "We've heard a lot about you from Jeremy."

She refused to wonder what Jeremy had been saying about her

to his family. She couldn't afford to let herself dwell on something like that.

Hannah was standing beside Geoffrey, and she rolled her eyes when she saw her brother. "Can't believe you got out of this stupid receiving line by ducking out to pick up your girlfriend."

"Hannah, you remember Melody," Jeremy said, smirking at his sister.

"Yeah, hey," Hannah said with her usual enthusiasm.

"These things are the worst, aren't they?" Melody said.

"Worse than the worst," Hannah agreed.

Their initial obligations dispensed, Melody and Jeremy hit the open bar to arm themselves for the rest of the evening. Drinks firmly in hand, they plunged into the madding crowd—which was not so much madding as stuffy and deathly dull.

Jeremy powered up the charm machine and Melody politely smiled and nodded her way through the next half hour, pretending to be interested in Jeremy's conversations with various Sauer Hewson muckety mucks. To his credit, he kept trying to draw her into the conversations, but she couldn't muster the will to play the game with any enthusiasm. Every time Jeremy introduced her to someone new, it was all too clear what conclusions they were jumping to.

It was a truth universally acknowledged, that a single woman with a much wealthier and more successful boyfriend, must be an opportunist angling to marry into money. All the disdainful disregard and knowing sideways looks she received when people learned where she worked and what she did communicated what they thought of her.

So maybe she didn't do as good a job of pretending to be interested in talking to people as she could have. It wasn't like any of them actually cared about her anyway. They were all too busy sucking up to the boss's son to pay much notice to his gold-digging girlfriend.

Not that he actually introduced her to anyone as his girlfriend.

Jeremy only ever referred to her as his friend when he alluded to a relationship at all. Which Melody knew he was doing for her benefit, to try to avoid spreading the lie any further than they had to. But it didn't matter. People were going to make their own inferences no matter what he said.

So, screw 'em. Melody pasted a fake smile on her face, shook all the hands presented to her, and mentally checked out of the conversation while they talked budgets, earnings forecasts, and management plans like they were at the office instead of a wedding reception. Although, from what Melody knew about Angelica Sauer, she wouldn't have wanted it any other way.

It was a relief when a temporary reprieve from the tedium arrived in the form of Hannah, recently released from the hated receiving line.

"No one will give me any champagne," she whined to her brother.

Jeremy arched an eyebrow at her. "That's because Mom gave the staff specific instructions where you're concerned. Fool her once, and this is what you get."

Hannah turned to Melody with wide, hopeful eyes. "You want to be my friend, don't you?"

"Nice try," Melody said. "No way am I going to risk pissing off your mother. Sorry."

"Go ask the bartender to make you a Shirley Temple," Jeremy said.

Hannah scrunched her nose in distaste. "Do I look eight?"

"To me, Shorty, you will always be eight," Jeremy replied affectionately.

Hannah rolled her eyes and wandered off, probably in search of someone sucker enough to sneak her a glass of champagne.

There was yet another Sauer Hewson big cheese heading Jeremy's way, but Melody had spotted Charlotte standing alone on the other side of the room and excused herself before she could get trapped in another boring conversation.

"Charlotte, hi," Melody said, tapping her on the shoulder.

Charlotte turned and smiled at her. "You're looking much more cheerful than the last time I saw you."

"Yeah, it's amazing what a difference it makes not having been mugged in the last few hours. Thank you again, by the way, for being so nice to me that night."

"I'm just glad you're okay."

Melody glanced around. "Where's Drew?"

Charlotte nodded toward the other side of the room. "Networking with some people from the chamber of commerce. It's always business at these things."

"Yeah, I'm learning that," Melody said with a sigh.

Charlotte smiled in commiseration. "I thought I'd finally be done with events like these when Jeremy and I broke up, but now that I'm marrying Drew, I guess this is my life now."

Melody couldn't help glancing over at Jeremy glad-handing a gaggle of Sauer Hewson execs. "It's a small price to pay, though, right? For happiness, I mean."

Charlotte's gaze drifted to where Drew was standing beside his father and her smile softened. "Damn right."

Melody asked about the wedding plans, and Charlotte launched into a monologue on the tribulations of choosing flowers, cakes, and bridesmaid's dresses until the string quartet quieted and Jeremy moved to the center of the room to ask for everyone's attention.

By then, Drew had appeared at Charlotte's elbow, nodding a silent greeting to Melody. Something about the look he gave her felt oddly pointed, and she wondered Jeremy if had told him their "relationship" was fake. She hoped that didn't mean Charlotte knew, or else she'd really feel foolish.

Jeremy turned out to be a gifted speaker, which shouldn't have been a surprise considering his natural charm. He managed to be funny and warm without being overly sentimental. His toast was so perfectly calculated to please his mother, Melody couldn't help wondering if Angelica Sauer had written it herself. Which was an ungenerous thought, but she wasn't feeling especially generous tonight.

When Mr. Horvath stepped up to toast his new bride with a string of carefully chosen platitudes, Melody tuned out. She watched the bubbles rise in her champagne flute and tried to calculate how much longer they'd have to stay. There'd be cake, of course. Then dancing, presumably. But for how long? An hour? Two? A lot of the guests were old, so maybe it would wind down early. Maybe she was almost halfway through this miserable night, and then Jeremy could drive her home and she'd never have to do this ever again. Never have to pretend to be something she wanted so badly to be or feel this particular emptiness in the pit of her stomach.

Melody felt Charlotte nudge her and looked up. Angelica Sauer was speaking now, and Melody realized with a rising sense of panic that she was looking straight at her.

"It is my dearest wish," Mrs. Sauer said, "that my children find as much happiness with their chosen partners as I have with mine." She raised her glass to Melody before turning to Jeremy and leaning up to kiss his cheek.

"I'll be damned, the Ice Queen actually likes you," Charlotte whispered.

Drew saluted Melody with his champagne flute. "Pretty sure that's a first. I don't know how the hell you pulled it off, but kudos."

Melody tried to smile, but she had that same headachy, vomity feeling she got from trying to read in a moving car. This was all so wrong. Jeremy's friends and family shouldn't be treating her like she belonged here when it was all a lie.

She gulped down her champagne while they were cutting the cake and excused herself as soon as the jazz trio that had replaced the string quartet started up the first dance.

She'd thought she could handle all of this, but she was wrong.

It was too hard. It was flying too close to the sun, and any second now, her wings were going to melt and send her crashing back to earth.

She ducked into the powder room to hide for a few minutes until her heart had stopped racing. But she couldn't stay in the bathroom all night, so she touched up her lipstick, took a deep breath, and ventured once more unto the breach.

When she rejoined the party, Jeremy was dancing to "Unforgettable" with his mother while Hannah danced with Geoffrey. Melody watched from the ballroom doorway as they traded partners, and Jeremy twirled a giggling Hannah across the dance floor.

Drew and Charlotte were dancing by then, too. Charlotte reached up to smooth Drew's hair, and he kissed her, slowly and deeply, not caring who might be watching. Their love was so painful to watch, Melody had to turn away. She wanted what they had so badly, and she was never going to have it—not with Jeremy, at least.

She shouldn't be here. She wasn't a part of any of this. She was an imposter, standing on the outside looking in.

Turning on her heel, she slipped out of the ballroom and wandered down the hallway leading to the library. It was wonderfully quiet and deserted in that part of the house, so she lingered there, admiring the oil paintings lining the walls and avoiding the reception.

Until Jeremy came and found her ten minutes later.

"Hey," he said. "I've been looking for you." He ran his hand down her arm, raising goose bumps on her skin.

"Sorry," she muttered. "I just wanted a break from the party for a minute."

He frowned and squeezed her hand. "You okay?"

She forced a smile. "Yep. Fine."

"Come dance with me?" he asked, tugging on her hand.

Her shoulders hunched as she let him lead her away. She couldn't say no—it would look bad if they didn't dance—but she was petrified at the prospect of having his arms around her. How was she going to maintain eye contact while they were dancing without him seeing right through her?

The band was playing "Can't Help Falling in Love," like some kind of cruel joke. Jeremy guided her onto the dance floor, but instead of taking her hand the way he had the last time they'd danced, he slipped both his arms around her waist and pulled her close.

Melody stiffened for a second, taken off-guard, before she wound her arms around his neck. Jeremy held her and swayed to the music, their bodies pressed together in what felt more like an embrace than a dance.

It was torture.

Every breath filled her senses with his scent, making her light-headed. She tipped her head toward his chest so she wouldn't have to look at him. If she let herself look into those perfect blue eyes, she was afraid she might drown.

The unfairness of it all made the back of her throat burn. She was standing inside this perfect moment, with Jeremy's arms wrapped around her and his cheek warm and prickly against her temple, and it was a lie.

None of this was real. None of it belonged to her. She was just a placeholder until some better girl came along.

The second the song ended, Melody twisted out of his arms.

"Where are you going?" Jeremy asked.

"I just need some air," she said without looking back.

She headed for the French doors leading out to the garden, followed the gravel path away from the terrace, and didn't stop until she was standing in front of a tiered fountain at the edge of the lawn.

It was a cloudy night, so there were no stars reflected in the surface of the water, just the dull glimmer of a few tarnished coins in the murky depths. Long forgotten wishes, left there by Hannah maybe, or a younger Jeremy. The sight of them made Melody's chest ache.

She heard footsteps crunch on the gravel behind her and shut her eyes.

"Hey," Jeremy called out. "Melody?" His hand closed on her arm. "What's going on with you?"

She forced herself to look at him. "Nothing."

"Really? Because you've been acting annoyed with me all night. Did I do something to piss you off?"

She shook her head. "No, it's nothing like that."

"Then what? Because you've made it pretty clear you don't want to be here."

He was angry with her, and she couldn't blame him. She'd been a terrible date. But she *didn't* want to be here and couldn't tell him why.

"I'm just tired of pretending," she said, hugging herself against the chilly night air.

Something dark passed across his face. "Jesus. I'm really sorry, Melody. I swear, I will never again ask you to pretend you have feelings for me. I had no idea how hard it was for you."

Shit.

Now she'd hurt him, which was the last thing she ever wanted to do.

"That's not it," she said desperately. "You don't understand at all."

His jaw clenched. "Then explain it to me. Please."

"Jeremy, I..." She didn't know how to say it. She didn't know if she *could* say it. It was like she was standing on a narrow ledge with nothing but gaping darkness below. She was too afraid of falling to move.

"Well?"

Melody sucked in a shaky breath and stepped into the unknown. "I'm not tired of pretending I have feelings for you, I'm tired of pretending I *don't*."

Jeremy's mouth opened, then closed again. "What?" he said, barely above a whisper.

Now that she'd gone and opened her big mouth, there was no turning back. "I don't want to be on a fake date with you, Jeremy, because I want to be on a real date with you."

He looked stunned, like he didn't know what to say. Like he didn't know how to tell her he didn't feel the same way.

Humiliation trailed its icy fingers down her spine. She never should have said anything. She'd ruined *everything*. Now that he knew how she felt about him, they wouldn't be able to be friends anymore. Sure, he'd try to pretend otherwise, but she could see exactly where this was going. He'd start distancing himself. Pulling away from her. Pretty soon, they wouldn't talk at all.

She was going to lose him.

Chapter Twenty-Three

*I*t was the worst feeling in the world, standing there with her feelings laid bare, knowing Jeremy didn't feel the same way. If only she'd kept her mouth shut.

Melody fixed her eyes on the gravel path under her feet, wishing it would open up and swallow her. Why wasn't there ever a pool of quicksand around when you needed one? The cartoons she'd watched as a kid had given the impression life would have a lot more quicksand. Or any quicksand. But all she'd ever encountered was metaphorical quicksand.

"Melody." Jeremy's voice sounded strained, like he could barely even say her name.

She didn't want to hear this. She wanted to cover her ears and run away. Or burrow under the lawn like a gopher and hide. She would do anything not to have to stand there and listen to Jeremy try to explain how he liked her, but just as a friend. How he cared about her, but not *enough*. Not the way she wanted him to.

She didn't want to be let down easy, she wanted to fling herself into the sun.

"Why do you think I offered to be your pretend boyfriend in the first place?" he asked.

What does that even—why was he asking her that? Melody threw up her hands. "I don't know. Because you felt sorry for me?"

He blew out a breath. "I didn't feel sorry for you. I wanted to be close to you."

She looked up at him and blinked slowly, like an owl in a nature documentary. "You wanted to be close to me?" she repeated, stunned.

He huffed out an unsteady laugh, shaking his head. "Yes."

"Then why didn't you ask me on an actual date?" she shouted, not even caring if anyone could hear.

His tongue skimmed over his bottom lip. "I didn't think you'd say yes."

Her mouth fell open. "You're Jeremy Sauer, one of the country's most eligible bachelors! You've dated models and actresses! And you were afraid to ask *me* out?" It was utterly banana pants. She would have laughed if she hadn't felt so much like crying.

He ducked his head. "None of the things that impress other women ever work on you. You always see right through me."

"Well, that's true," she said, biting back a smile.

He took a step toward her. His eyes were wide and sparkling in the moonlight. "I honestly didn't think you liked me like that."

"I didn't," she said. "Until I did." It felt like she was falling. Like she had vertigo. Like the tectonic plates were shifting under her feet. She honestly wasn't sure how she was still upright.

Jeremy took another step closer and put his hands on her shoulders. "I'm going to kiss you," he said, quiet and very serious.

Melody swallowed around the lump in her throat and nodded. Vigorously.

He bent his head so his lips were barely an inch from hers, and paused, maddeningly out of reach. "Just so we're clear," he murmured, his breath a tantalizing tickle on her lips, "this isn't pretend. It's for real."

Her eyes fluttered closed as his lips finally met hers. His

mouth was warm as summer, and he tasted like coming home at the end of a long day.

It was a perfect kiss, like something from a fairy tale or the end of *The Princess Bride*. Tender, but with a sizzle of electricity that left her toes tingling. Except it was so much better than a fairy tale, because it was happening to her and it was *real*.

Before she could stop herself, she started giggling against his mouth, which brought their perfect kiss to a screeching halt.

He tipped his head back to look at her, forehead creased.

"I'm sorry," she gasped, curling her hands into his lapels to keep him close. "It's just...all this time, you know? We're so stupid."

He smiled and wrapped her up in his arms, pressing a kiss into her hair. "At least we got there eventually."

She nuzzled into his neck and just...breathed him in. "Thank god."

"Hang on." He let go of her and stepped back. "I have to do this right."

"Do what?"

"Melody," he said, taking both her hands in his, "will you be my date for my mother's wedding?"

She started laughing again. "I'm already your date for your mother's wedding!"

"I want it to be a real date. Officially. No more pretending, from this moment on."

"Yes." She was smiling so wide, her cheeks hurt. "I would love to be your real date."

Jeremy's gaze dropped to her mouth. Then he kissed her again, and there was absolutely nothing tender about this kiss. It was hungry and bruising and...*wow*.

Her hands roamed over his body of their own accord until— yes, as a matter of fact, she *was* squeezing that gorgeous ass of his that had been taunting her for months. He moaned against her mouth in response, and she seriously wanted to climb him like a tree, but that was so not happening in this dress—damn this stupid, narrow skirt!—and anyway, they were only a few yards away from his mother's wedding reception, so that would probably not be a super great idea.

Jeremy pulled back and rested his forehead against hers, breathing heavily.

"Any chance we can cut out of here early?" she asked, her hands still clutching his ass.

He squeezed his eyes shut. "I can't. I wish I could—god, you have no idea how much I wish I could. But I think my mother will actually put a hit on me if I duck out this early." He opened his eyes. "Unless...you wanted to feign sickness?"

"No way," she said. "No more lying. If we have to stay, then we'll stay."

His thumb caressed her jaw and he kissed her—just once, lightly, like he was afraid of getting too carried away. Which was probably wise. The way he was looking at her right now made her want to drag him into the bushes and jump his bones, wedding receptions be damned.

"Come dance with me again?" he asked.

She would have preferred to stay right where they were and make out some more, but dancing sounded good too—and a lot safer—so she nodded and let him lead her back to the party.

His arms wound around her waist as soon as they stepped onto the dance floor, and she sank into his chest, deliriously happy. The jazz trio was playing "Our Love is Here to Stay," and it felt like a sign, a promise of what was to come.

"Leave some room for the Holy Spirit, you two," Drew teased, dancing past with Charlotte.

Jeremy raised his middle finger and held Melody tighter.

"Do you want to take a break?" he asked after two more songs, nuzzling his nose against her hair.

"Nope," she sighed. "I'm good." But then she worried maybe he'd asked because *he* was tired of dancing. "I mean, unless you want to take a break? Because I can totally take a break if you want to. I'm not, like, opposed to breaks if—"

"Melody," he interrupted, smiling, "I don't want to take a break. I love having you in my arms."

"Okay, good," she said, snuggling back into him. "Because I happen to love being in your arms, so that works out pretty well." She could stay there like that forever. Except...well, except for the fact that as long as they were here it meant they weren't back at her place having sex, which was what she *really* wanted to be doing.

Whoa.

She was going to have sex with Jeremy tonight.

At least...she assumed they were going to have sex. Unless he had some chivalrous idea about waiting until they'd gone on an arbitrary number of dates first. In which case, she was going to have to talk him out of that scheme right away. Because it was stupid.

It wasn't like they hadn't totally had sex already. She just wanted to do it again. Soon. Like, really soon. There was a chance she was going to spontaneously combust if she didn't get him naked in the next few hours.

"Melody?" Jeremy said. "You okay?"

She looked up at him. "Yeah...why?"

"You're sort of trembling."

"Oh. Whoops." She definitely had not meant for that to happen. But that was what she got for thinking about Jeremy naked when he was holding her in his arms. "Um, maybe a drink would be good, on second thought."

He led her over to the bar, holding tight to her hand the whole way. "Scotch neat and a glass of the red," he told the bartender. "You sure you're okay?" he asked, turning back to Melody with a frown.

"I'm fine," she promised, and rose up on her tiptoes to kiss his cheek. How crazy was it that she got to do that? Like, whenever she wanted? And he actually seemed to like it? She shook her head, smiling up at him. "I was thinking about—" She clamped her mouth shut when the bartender pushed their drinks toward them.

"About?" Jeremy prompted, handing her her wine.

Melody waited for him to pick up his scotch before dragging him far enough away that they wouldn't be overheard. She leaned in close, rising up on her tiptoes again to whisper in his ear. "I was thinking about getting you naked."

His eyes went wide, and he grabbed the back of her neck with his free hand and kissed her—right there in the middle of the party, surrounded by his family, coworkers, and everyone. And not chastely, either.

"Whoa, cowboy," she said, smiling as she pushed him away. "Not here."

"You know," he murmured, low and intent, "we can't leave, but we could slip out for a few minutes and finish our tour of the house. I never got to show you my room last time." His eyebrows waggled suggestively.

It was too adorable, him asking her up to his room in his parents' house like a teenager. She couldn't help laughing. "Jeremy Sauer, are you trying to lure me up to your bedroom?"

"Maybe." He smirked. "Is it working?"

"Yes." She laughed again. "Yes, yes, yes."

Chapter Twenty-Four

*T*hey took a meandering route upstairs using one of the back staircases so no one would see them leaving the party. Jeremy led her through a maze of hallways before stopping in front of a closed door that looked exactly like all the other closed doors they'd passed.

Before Melody could ask if this was it, he pushed her up against the door and kissed her—hard. His hands were on her shoulders, pressing her back against the wood, and she had to grab onto him so her knees didn't give out beneath her. He reached down to turn the knob and they stumbled into the room, but his strong arms held her upright as he kicked the door closed with his foot.

When their mouths separated, she gasped for air, then looked around her and gasped again. Because his room? Was insane.

It had a fireplace. And a couch. And a chandelier. Also? It was ginormous.

"This is your bedroom?" she said, spinning around and gaping. "You realize this is bigger than most of the apartments I've lived in, right?"

Instead of answering, he kissed her again. She ran her fingers over his chest and down, until she found the button on his tuxedo jacket. When she had it undone, she pushed it off his shoulders, and he let go of her to shrug his way out of it and toss it onto a chair. He was wearing suspenders underneath, and she wasn't sure why, but it did something to her—the sight of him in his crisp white dress shirt and suspenders.

Melody closed the distance between them again, dragging his head down to her mouth. His hands moved around to her ass and pulled her flush against his hips. If it hadn't been for this damn narrow skirt, she would have jumped into his arms and wrapped her legs around his waist.

Instead, she settled for running her hands over his stomach, which was deliciously flat and firm. She tugged at his shirttails, desperate for skin-to-skin contact. The moan he let out when her fingers found his bare skin only made her want to touch him more.

But when she went for his belt buckle, he wrenched himself away, capturing her hands and moving them off his pants. "Melody, we can't. We have to go back to the party in a few minutes."

"I can be fast. Really, really fast."

"The thing is," he said, quietly solemn—and *oh*, the way he was looking at her was a lot, "I want to do this right. And this..." he gestured between them, "isn't right. You deserve so much more than a quickie, and I want to give it to you. Will you let me do that?"

"Fine," she said. "Even though it's really hard." He pressed his lips together, suppressing a laugh, and she groaned. "God, you're like a child. Go ahead, laugh."

Instead of laughing, he rested his forehead against hers, skimming his palm over her cheek.

"We can still make out though, right?" she asked.

He did laugh then, as he pulled her over to the bed—which was huge and looked like it had been built for kings to deflower maidens on—and sat her down beside him on the edge of the mattress.

He pulled her legs across his lap, and they proceeded to make out like teenagers. Good old-fashioned making out, the kind she hadn't done since high school. The kind of making out you tended to stop doing once you started having sex. She'd forgotten how nice it could be, just *kissing* and actually savoring it, because you weren't in a hurry to move on to the next step.

Eventually, Jeremy moved her out of his lap and gently laid her back on the bed so he could kiss his way down her neck. Melody curled her fingers into his hair, pleased to discover it actually did feel like velvet.

But now that her mouth wasn't busy, her brain started to wander off on its own. A lot had happened in a short span of time, and she hadn't had a chance to process it all yet. So while Jeremy was kissing her, her brain was working on its own thing. And the problem was when she was thinking about something, she couldn't help talking about it, because of her brain-to-mouth filter being defective.

"So, when you kissed me before..." she said as Jeremy licked his way into her cleavage.

"Hmmm?" he murmured from between her breasts.

"At my apartment, when my mom was watching."

He groaned. "Are you for real talking to me about your mom right now?"

"When you kissed me that night," she continued, undaunted, "was that real or fake?"

He stopped kissing her breasts and propped himself up on his elbow. "It was real," he said, frowning. "Obviously, it was real. How could you not know that?"

"I don't know! I thought—" She shook her head. "You did it, and then you just left. And you didn't say anything about it the next day, so I thought maybe you kissed all your fake girlfriends like that."

His mouth curved into a smile. "How many fake girlfriends do you think I have?"

"I don't even know how many real girlfriends you have."

He bent down to kiss her breastbone. "One."

She shoved him off her. "What?"

He laughed and tapped the end of her nose with his index finger. "You, Melody. It's you."

Her stomach did a double somersault with a twist on the end. "You want me to be your girlfriend?"

"Of course I do." He leaned forward to kiss her.

"Wait," she said, because she couldn't just let herself be happy.

He stopped kissing her.

"There aren't any other women?" she asked. "Really?"

He pushed himself upright on the bed, his expression turning serious. "Ask me what you really want to ask."

She sat up, tucking a wisp of hair behind her ear. "I just thought—assumed, I guess...you've been seeing other women. I mean, it's okay that you have, it's not like we were dating for real or anything. And you're...you know, *you*, so I'm guessing you haven't been celibate since you and Lacey broke up."

"I have, actually."

She scrunched her forehead in confusion. "You have been seeing other women or—"

"I've been celibate. I haven't been with another woman since Lacey."

"Really?" It came out more dubious than she'd meant it to.

He looked down at his lap. "Ouch."

"No—" She wrapped her fingers around his wrist and squeezed until he lifted his eyes to her again. "I didn't mean—I just...I saw the pictures online."

He stared at her, uncomprehending. "Pictures?"

"The *America's Next Top Model* runner-up?"

"Oh, her." He rolled his eyes. "That was nothing. Trust me."

"You looked pretty cozy to me."

He pressed his lips together and shook his head. "Yes, okay, I went on some dates because I thought I didn't have a chance with you and I was trying to move on. But none of those dates went anywhere because none of those women could compete with you. What you saw in those pictures is as far as it went."

Melody bit her lip. "Okay."

Jeremy's face fell. "You don't believe me."

She wanted to believe him. She hated that she couldn't just take him at his word. It wasn't that she cared if he'd been sleeping with other women since he and Lacey broke up—she only cared if he was lying to her about it. There was a small part of her that couldn't help being afraid he was still the same lying cheater he'd been three years ago.

"I'm trying," she told him honestly. "I'm really trying."

His mouth twisted. "I deserve that, I guess."

"I'm not sure you do," she said, taking both his hands in hers. "But the thing is, I don't really know. We've been—I don't even know. Work friends, I guess? And in some ways, I feel like I know you really well. But then there are these huge portions of your life I know nothing about. I don't know how often you go out or who you go out with. I don't know what you like to do in your spare time, or how you spend your weekends. I don't even know if you have any friends besides Drew."

"You're right." He brought one of her hands to his lips and kissed it. "I kept you at a distance," he said, stroking the back of her wrist with his thumb, "because I was afraid of what would happen if I let myself get close to you. The truth is, I haven't been able to stop thinking about you since you came back into my life. But I was with Lacey—"

Melody swallowed and lowered her eyes.

Jeremy gave her hand a squeeze. "And then I wasn't, and I was finally free to get closer to you, but I didn't know how to close the distance I'd put between us. And by then, the two of you were friends, so I wasn't even sure I should. I was afraid to tell you how

I really felt—afraid you didn't like me the way I liked you. So, I tried to play it cool, because I was a coward. But I couldn't stay away from you. That's why I always dropped by your office."

He paused, and Melody made herself look at him. His eyes were dark and earnest, and she wanted to kiss him again, but this was too important. There were things they needed to say to each other. They'd both been hiding their feelings for so long, they needed to throw open the doors and let the light in.

He swallowed and went on, his voice unsteady. "The few minutes I got to spend with you were always the best part of my day. You made me feel—" He stopped and looked down at his lap, avoiding her eyes. "I feel like I can be myself when I'm around you, like maybe who I am isn't so bad."

"Jeremy," she whispered, but he squeezed her hand again and kept going.

"I was afraid of wearing out my welcome, so I tried not to bother you too much, and I tried to be content with just being your friend and not allowing myself to hope for anything more. But when I kissed you that night—" His eyes found hers again, and he licked his lower lip. "I meant every bit of that kiss, Melody."

Hearing him say the words made her heart hammer against her ribcage, like it did when she was having a panic attack. But it wasn't panic she was feeling—it was euphoria.

"I want you in my life—all of it. Assuming you want to be in it."

"I do, Jeremy. I do." Her voice cracked on the last word.

He nodded slowly. "So, you can ask me anything. Anything at all you want to know, ask me and I'll tell you the truth. No more lies. No more secrets. You're it for me, Melody. There's no one else."

Her breath caught. Whatever doubts she might have had about his past, she was absolutely certain he was telling the truth now.

"Do you want to know how many women I've slept with?"

"Jeremy—"

"It's okay," he said. "You deserve to know who you're getting involved with before we get too far into this."

It sounded like he was trying to give her a way out—an exit strategy in case she wanted to change her mind.

Which she definitely did not want. No matter how many women were lurking in his past, she'd already made the decision to trust him with her heart. And she genuinely believed he was worth it, despite the anxious voices in her head. Now she needed to convince him of that.

Melody surged forward and kissed him before he could say anything else, letting her lips speak for her heart. It was everything, kissing him. Nothing had ever felt so right. She wanted to spend the rest of her life kissing him exactly like this.

"You're it for me, too," she whispered against his mouth, holding his face in her hands. "I don't care about your past or the other women. I mean, okay, I care," she corrected, "but I care more about this." She laid her hand over his heart.

His eyes were wide and shining, and she could feel his breath hitch in his chest, so she kissed him again. It nearly undid her, how vulnerable he was, and how easily she could break him with a few careless words.

Her hands slid around his neck, pulling him even closer. She wanted more of him than she could reach sitting like this on the bed. She *needed* more of him. "Remind me again why we're not having sex right now," she groaned as his mouth traveled down her throat.

He pulled back to look at her, his eyes dark with desire. "Because when I take you," he said, dragging the pad of his thumb over her lower lip, "I want to be able to take my time and savor every inch of your body." He moved his mouth to her ear, his breath heating her skin. "I want to make you scream my name. Is that okay with you?"

That was...*wow*. *So* okay with her. God. So. Okay. Nothing had ever been as okay as that was.

When his tongue started doing things to her ear, she forced herself to push him away.

"Jeremy," she gasped, holding him at arm's length.

"Melody." He actually growled her name, which was just so...incredibly hot.

"We need to get out of this room right now," she said hoarsely.

His forehead creased in bemusement. "Why?"

"Because if we don't go back to the party—and I mean right now—I'm going to tear all your clothes off, and there's not going to be anything you can do to stop me."

He grinned and planted a kiss on her forehead before standing up and tugging her off the bed. She took a minute to fix her hair in his bathroom mirror, reapply her lipstick, and generally make sure she didn't look like someone who'd been rolling around on a bed with the hostess's son.

When she was ready, he took her hand and led her through the same circuitous route back downstairs. The party was still in full swing, and they headed straight to the dance floor, sinking into each other's arms again.

The rest of the evening passed in a mad haze of excited anticipation. But eventually, an hour or so later, the guests started to depart. When there were only a few stragglers left, Jeremy dutifully asked his mom if she needed him to do anything before he took Melody home.

Angelica Sauer, bless her, gave her son a knowing smile and sent them on their merry way. Melody could have kissed her.

Jeremy grabbed Melody's hand and dragged her toward the door, ignoring several people trying to get his attention to make their goodbyes. He signaled one of the valets to bring his car, then wound his arms around Melody, tugging her close. "Have I told you how beautiful you look in that dress?" he murmured into her ear.

"Feel free to tell me again." It was chilly outside, but Jeremy's arms, wrapping her up tight, were all the warmth she needed.

"Almost as beautiful as you're going to look out of that dress," he said, low and growly.

Her knees went wobbly, but by then, the valet was pulling up with Jeremy's car. He walked her around to the passenger door and handed her inside.

As they were pulling away from the house, she reached over and rested her hand on Jeremy's thigh, exerting light pressure. He looked down at her hand, then over at her, eyebrows raised.

Melody smiled and slid her hand a few inches up his leg.

Jeremy swallowed—hard—and reached up to unknot his bowtie. Shifting the car into a higher gear, he pushed the speed limit the whole way back to her apartment.

Chapter Twenty-Five

$\mathcal{J}$eremy reached for her the instant they were out of his car, like they'd been separated by an insurmountable distance for an unbearable span of time, not a few inches for thirty minutes. He tucked her under his arm, holding her so close, there wasn't an inch of space between them.

Melody was more than happy to nestle into him and let him guide her up to her apartment. She felt dazed, almost like she was drunk. But she wasn't drunk on alcohol; she was drunk on Jeremy. On tonight. On what was happening between them. Her whole body was buzzing with potential energy, like a spring that had been pulled taut and was waiting to be sprung. If she held her hand out, she was certain it would be shaking. Instead, she slipped it under his tuxedo jacket and held on to his waist.

As soon as they'd crossed the threshold into her apartment, Jeremy spun her around and pushed her up against the door, slamming it shut as his mouth crashed against hers. Her neighbors were probably not happy about that, but Melody couldn't seem to care, because Jeremy's tongue was hot and slick against hers, and she could feel his arousal pressing against her hip.

"Melody," he whispered against her lips, and, *oh wow*, she only ever wanted to hear him say her name in that particular breathy murmur from now on. "Beautiful Melody," he said, kissing her again and again. "My Melody."

"Yours," she agreed, rising up on her tiptoes and sinking her fingers into his hair.

There was a part of her that couldn't believe this was actually happening. But at the same time, with Jeremy's tongue sliding against hers, she was intensely, keenly, *supernaturally* aware that yes, this was, in fact, happening. This remarkable, amazing thing she'd been dreaming about was finally happening *right now*. To her.

Jeremy's forehead dropped against hers, and this time, she wasn't the one trembling. He was.

"Are you sure about this?" he asked, his voice hoarse, his hands tightening around her waist. "Because I can wait...for as long as...I just want—"

"Hey." She took his face in her hands. "I'm sure. Do I look like I'm not sure?"

"I don't want to screw this up." His eyes were bright and wide open as he gazed at her. She loved his eyes, how expressive they were. And she loved the crinkles around his eyes. And his dimples. And his mouth—he had the best mouth. She wanted to kiss it right now.

So, she did.

"You're not screwing it up," she murmured between kisses. "I won't let you."

When he smiled at her, she felt something warm and wondrous unfurl in her chest. She always felt that way when he smiled at her, but this time, it was different. This time, she knew he was smiling just for her. She *was* special.

Her hands scrabbled at his clothes. He was wearing way too many layers, and she couldn't get at him, not the way she needed to. She pushed his jacket off his shoulders and took a second to appreciate the sight of his suspenders again before shoving them aside and tugging at his shirttail.

When she got her hands under his shirt, she sighed with plea-sure, her fingers roaming over his abs and around to the small of his back. By then, he'd dragged the zipper of her dress down, and she shimmied out of it, letting it fall to the floor at her feet.

Jeremy went still, taking in the sight of her, naked except her lacy black bra and thong. A smile pulled at the corner of his mouth. "I knew you'd look even better out of that dress."

Melody grinned and stepped out of the puddle of fabric at her feet, kicking off her heels. She laid her palms on his chest and pushed him in the direction of her bedroom.

His fingers dug into her hips, pulling her along with him as he stumbled backward. He bent down to kiss her again, but without her shoes, the difference between their height was too much, so he lifted her up off the floor to bring their mouths closer. She wrapped her legs around his waist, and he spun her around and carried her toward the bedroom.

It took them a while to get there, because they got distracted a couple times along the way. She nearly had her way with him up against the wall in the hallway. After that there was a minor colli-sion with a lamp, but she never liked that lamp anyway, so what-ever. Eventually, they made it to the bed, leaving a trail of discarded clothing in their wake.

His calloused hands caressed her fevered skin as he guided her back onto the mattress. Their mouths crashed together. Messy and desperate. Teeth scraping against lips and loud, panted breaths.

They couldn't get enough of each other. She arched beneath him, buzzing with desire as their bodies slid together. Slow. Then urgent. Then slow again. In perfect unison. Two halves of the same whole.

Together. They were together.

At last.

"Wow," Jeremy said later. "That was—"

"Yeah," Melody agreed. She was curled up on her side with Jeremy's body wrapped around hers, and she never, ever wanted to move from this spot.

"You need anything?" he asked, nuzzling the back of her neck. His hand slid up her leg, coming to rest on her hip.

She sighed a contented sigh. "Nope. I'm perfect right here."

His lips brushed the top of her shoulder. "Good."

She closed her eyes and nestled into the pillow, feeling satisfied and secure. Perfectly at peace. Enveloped in the satiny warmth of his skin.

She was right on the verge of drifting off to sleep when he said, "I like to watch basketball."

Her eyes opened again. "Okay?" She wasn't sure what she was supposed to do with that information at this particular moment.

"You said you didn't know how I spend my free time. I watch basketball on the weekends."

"Oh." She smiled and tugged his arm around her tighter. "Okay."

"Also football. And baseball. And hockey. Soccer, too, if there's nothing else on."

"So...I'm getting the sense you're maybe into sports a little?"

"I guess," he said, brushing her hair to the side. "What about you?"

"Me? Uh, no, I don't really watch sports."

"What do you like to do in your free time?"

"Um," she said. "Well...I like to watch TV, I guess."

"What kind of TV?"

"All kinds. I mean, not reality TV. Or cop shows. Or multi-camera comedies. But everything else."

He let out an amused breath. "What's your favorite show that's on right now?"

"I dunno. *Orphan Black*, maybe. Or *Doctor Who*."

"So, like, sci-fi stuff?"

"Yeah. I mean, I like other stuff too, but yeah."

"That's cool," he said, yawning. "There's a basketball game on tomorrow I was going to watch."

"Oh, okay." She bit back a twinge of disappointment. Just because they were dating now didn't mean they were always going to be joined at the hip. She was perfectly capable of doing her own thing tomorrow while he watched his basketball game.

"I was hoping I could talk you into watching it with me," he said.

Oh.

"And then afterward, maybe you could show me one of your favorite shows?"

Oh.

"That's—I'd really like that," she said, smiling.

"Yeah?"

She twined her fingers with his and tucked his hand under her cheek. "Yeah."

The wind was picking up outside, and she snuggled against him, listening to the sound of it blowing the wind chimes on her neighbor's balcony and the slowing of Jeremy's breath as he drifted off to sleep.

That thing where she'd tried to convince herself she wasn't in love with him? Yeah, that was dumb. She was definitely in love with him. Ass over teakettle in love. So in love, it felt like there wasn't enough room in her chest to hold it all.

She was going to tell him, too. Not right now, because of him being asleep. And also because she thought that might be rushing things. They'd only been together for a few hours, even if it felt like it had been forever in the making.

But she was going to tell him. Soon.

She wasn't going to wait to tell him how she felt anymore. She wasn't even afraid to be the first to say it. She wanted to be the first. He deserved that, and she was going to give it to him.

Right now, though, she was going to fall asleep in his arms. Because she was exhausted.

She had a big day of being in love with Jeremy to look forward to tomorrow. And every day after that.

She needed to rest up for all that happiness waiting for her.

Chapter Twenty-Six

A FEW MONTHS LATER

"*A*s much as you like sports, I can't believe you've never watched *Friday Night Lights*," Melody said as the credits rolled at the end of another episode. She'd only introduced Jeremy to it last weekend, and they'd already binged most of the first season together on her couch.

He yawned and stretched one of his arms overhead. His other arm was wrapped around her. "I was probably too busy getting wasted. That was pretty much all I did in high school."

She poked him in the ribs where she knew he was ticklish. "What a catch you were." He responded by grabbing her waist and burying his face in her neck, right where he knew *she* was ticklish.

Her phone chirped on the coffee table, and she wriggled out of his grasp to see who'd texted her. "Tessa wants to know if we're coming to Lacey's party Friday."

Lacey had been accepted into the Los Angeles Police Department's recruit training academy, and Devika and Kelsey were throwing her a party at their place to celebrate. Melody was looking forward to it, but she and Jeremy hadn't actually talked about it yet.

"Of course we are." He pushed himself to his feet and went to the fridge for more beers. "You know how long she's been talking about wanting to be a cop?"

"We don't have to go is all I'm saying. I mean, *you* don't have to. I could go alone. I really don't mind if you don't want to come."

It would be their first time socializing as a couple with Lacey and Tessa. Lacey had been incredibly cool about the whole situation, but Melody couldn't blame Jeremy if he didn't want to hang out with his ex-girlfriend and the woman she'd left him for, not to mention all their friends.

He peered at her over the top of the fridge door. "Are you trying to tell me you don't want me to come?"

"No! It's not that at all. I want you there, it's just—if you think it'll be uncomfortable, you don't *have* to come."

"Lacey and I get along fine now. And I can take whatever shit her friends want to give me, as long as they're nice to you." He popped the caps off two bottles of beer, then looked up at her again, frowning like he'd just thought of something. "Oh, wait, are her parents going to be there?"

"I don't think so."

"Good. Her parents *hate* me."

Melody snorted. "I can't imagine why."

"I never said I didn't deserve it." He set a fresh bottle of beer in front of her and sank back onto the couch, propping his bare feet up on the coffee table.

"I'm about to RSVP for us, so this is your last chance to back out."

"They're your friends," he told her simply. "I want them to be my friends, too."

"Okay," she said, beaming at him.

He took a swig of his beer. "Oh, hey, that reminds me, my mom wanted to know the dates your mom's going to be here."

"The twenty-fourth through the twenty-seventh," Melody said absently, typing out her reply to Tessa. She stopped and looked up at him. "Wait—why does your mom want to know when my mom's going to be in town?"

"Because she wants to meet her. I think she wants to have her over for dinner or something."

"No," Melody said, horrified. "No way. That can never, ever happen."

"Come on—"

"I'm serious! We can't let your mom and my mom meet. It would be like mixing bleach and ammonia—the chemical reaction will kill us all."

He laughed. "I think you might be exaggerating the danger a little."

She shook her head. "I'm really not."

His hand settled on her thigh. "We can't keep them apart forever, you know. At the very least, they'll have to meet at our wedding."

Melody's heart stuttered in her chest. She lowered her phone and looked at him. "Wedding?" she repeated to make sure she'd heard him right—that it hadn't been an accident.

"Well, yeah. I mean, eventually." A slow smile spread across his face. "Hopefully. One day."

Whenever he smiled at her like that, it made her stomach flutter like a kaleidoscope of butterflies. It was a different smile than the one he offered up so easily to hostesses, colleagues, and baristas. The smile he reserved for her was gentler and less brilliant. It wasn't cocky or flirtatious, it was open and a little uncertain—like a question hoping for an answer.

This time, the butterflies in her stomach felt more like a cyclone than a kaleidoscope. *He wants to marry me.* He was being super casual about it, too, like it was a given. Of course they would get married one day. Why wouldn't they?

She leaned over and kissed him, smiling against his lips. "We'll have to elope, then. Not to Vegas, though. Somewhere with a beach."

He tugged her back onto the couch so she was nestled up against him again. "One more episode?" he said, digging the remote out of the couch cushions next to him.

"The game just started," she pointed out.

"Yeah, but the Panthers are about to go to State. It's the season finale."

"The Dillon Panthers went to State ten years ago, but your favorite non-fictional team is playing right now. I wore my Lakers shirt today and everything."

He'd bought it for her when he took her to her first Lakers game. They'd had floor seats behind John Legend and Chrissy Teigen. Melody had never cared much about basketball before, but it was different watching it with Jeremy. She loved doing things he loved; it made her want to love them, too.

"One more episode. The game will still be waiting on the DVR when we're done."

"But we'll get spoiled if we don't watch live."

"Not if you stay off your phone," he said, taking it out of her hand and tossing it onto the other end of the couch.

"I could just tell you if the Panthers win State, you know."

"Don't you dare!" He held up a warning finger. "No spoilers!"

"Fine." She leaned her head back against his shoulder. "One more episode, then we watch the game."

Jeremy dismissed the "Are you still watching?" dialogue box, and the next episode of *Friday Night Lights* started playing.

"This show is so good," he said forty-three minutes later when the episode ended. He was crying a little, but he didn't try to hide it. She loved that about him—that he wasn't ashamed to cry over a television show.

"Yeah, it is." She reached under her glasses and wiped her eyes. Even though she'd seen the episode at least a dozen times, it still made her tear up, too. "Ready for the Lakers now?" she asked, reaching across Jeremy's lap for the remote.

"Wait." He took her face in his hands and kissed her. His

mouth was soft and prickly at the same time, and it tasted malty from the beer he'd been drinking.

"Okay," he said, smiling at her as he pulled back. "Now I'm ready."

Melody's stomach did that fluttering thing again. She dropped the remote and climbed into his lap, straddling his thighs with her legs.

"I thought you wanted to watch the game," he said, smirking at her.

"I do." She curled her hands around the back of his neck and slid her fingers into his hair. She loved his hair; she wanted to have her fingers in it always. "But I also want to kiss you some more."

He grinned and wrapped his arms around her. "Kissing is so much better than basketball."

"Definitely," she agreed, pulling his mouth to hers.

They didn't watch the game that night, after all. Whatever. It would still be there tomorrow. They had the rest of their lives to watch basketball.

Much later, after they'd moved to Melody's bed, Jeremy tugged her into his arms and said, "I never knew it was supposed to feel like this." Her purple Lakers shirt was still in the living room, where he'd tossed it after he'd undressed her.

"Hmmm?" she murmured sleepily. She was using his chest as a pillow, and his voice was all rumbly in her ear.

"Having a girlfriend," he said, laying his hand on the small of her back. "Being in love."

They'd been exchanging the L-word freely for over a month now, but Melody's heart still skipped a beat whenever he said it. She never wanted that feeling to go away.

"What did you think it was supposed to be like?" she asked.

"I thought it was all about pretending—pretending to want things you didn't want and like things you didn't like. Pretending to be someone you weren't. I thought that was what all relationships were like. But being with you isn't anything like that."

"What's it like?" she asked quietly.

"Like I found my best friend."

Melody lifted her head to look at him, but it was too dark to see anything more than the outline of his head against the pillow. "Come here," she said, reaching for him in the darkness. There were tears in her eyes when she kissed him.

Jeremy touched her face, his fingers spreading out over her cheek. "That wasn't supposed to make you cry."

"It's the good kind of crying," she told him. "Because I found my best friend, too."

Acknowledgments

FIRST AND FOREMOST, I need to thank my husband, Dave, and my daughter, Emma, for all their love and support. Also for putting up with my cranky ass while I was writing this.

Thank you to my extraordinary cheering squad of friends, who provided encouragement and/or feedback along the way: Mikaela Dufur, Lisa Lozano, Danielle Dupré, Lisa Ludvik, Joanna Cotter, Dena Miccolis, Tammy Kentner, Amy Morgan, and Sharon Cochran. Thank you also to my editor, Monica Black, who kept me on the straight and narrow.

Finally, I want to thank every single person who has ever commented on, recommended, or squeed over one of my fanfics. Your enthusiasm has given me the strength to keep on writing over the years, even when it felt like an insurmountable task. For that, you have my eternal gratitude and affection. <3

About the Author

SUSANNAH NIX lives in Texas with her husband, two ornery cats, and a flatulent pit bull. When she's not writing, she enjoys reading, cooking, knitting, watching stupid amounts of television, and getting distracted by Tumblr. She is also a powerlifter who can deadlift as much as Captain America weighs.

www.susannahnix.com